FORTUNATE
SON

FORTUNATE
SON

J.D.
RHOADES

The following is a work of fiction. Names, characters, places, events, and incidents are either the product of the author's imagination or used in an entirely fictitious manner. Any resemblance to actual persons, living or dead, is entirely coincidental.

ISBN: 978-1-947993-10-5
eISBN: 978-1-947993-11-2
Library of Congress Catalog Number: 2018949975

First hardcover publication: August 2018 by Polis Books LLC
1201 Hudson Street Hoboken, NJ 07030
www.PolisBooks.com

POLIS BOOKS

ALSO BY J.D. RHOADES

The Jack Keller Series
The Devil's Right Hand
Good Day in Hell
Safe and Sound
Devils and Dust
Hellhound On My Trail

Breaking Cover
Broken Shield
Ice Chest
Lawyers, Guns, and Money
Gallows Pole
Storm Surge

To my good and great friend, David Terrenoire. If you never give up, how the hell can I?

CHAPTER ONE

The day that Tyler Welch learned his real name, he was up before the dawn and on the road as the sun came up. Two-a-day football practices were scheduled to start in three weeks, and he'd been dismayed when he looked down and saw what he was sure was a roll of fat—a small one, to be sure, but still a roll—forming around his belly. A summer job at Quizno's wasn't something that promoted maximum fitness, and he suddenly felt guilty for every Peppercorn Steak sub he'd sucked down on one of his too-brief meal breaks instead of a healthier turkey sandwich, or even a salad. Football practices in late summer North Carolina heat and humidity were going to be unforgiving enough without carrying extra pounds, and Tyler wanted that starting quarterback slot in his senior year of high school more than he wanted oxygen.

He could hear his parents moving about in their bedroom as he slipped out of the house. The morning was still cool, but muggy, foreshadowing the oppressive blanket of heat and moisture that would descend as the sun rose. Tyler performed a few brief stretches, impatient to get on his way, before ascending the brief slope of shady driveway that led to the main road. He paused a moment, looking back at the modest brick house he shared with his parents and younger sister. He took no notice of the faded and dented black Firebird that passed by, slowed, then sped up and accelerated away down the long stretch of country road that ran by the house.

He started at a fast walk, ramping up quickly to a slow jog. He couldn't seem to find the rhythm, that coordination of stride and breath and effort that would eventually lift him up and carry him along as if of its own accord. Every step thudded on the hard-packed earth by the roadside, every breath rasped in his lungs. Gradually, though, he began to fall into the old familiar groove, and he smiled as he picked up the pace. He was so pleased to be back in the swing of things that he didn't notice the black Firebird as it passed him again, going the other way. It was good to be just turned eighteen and alive and rocking along in fine—if not perfect—shape under a hazy pale-blue Carolina morning sky, with nothing but possibilities ahead.

He'd almost completed his second mile by the time he finally noticed the black Firebird, and only then when it passed by, moving slowly. Tyler caught a glimpse of the driver's face, pale under a shock of thick black hair, before the vehicle was past him. It slowed, then pulled over to the side of the road, blocking his path. Tyler pulled up to a stop, his brow furrowed in annoyance. He'd just gotten going, and now this asshole was in his way.

The paint on the old Pontiac was peeling in spots and discolored in others. The golden outline of the mythical bird on the hood had faded to a pale yellow, the left rear quarter panel dented. The driver got out and stood in the open door for a moment, looking at Tyler. He looked to be in his early twenties, painfully thin, dressed in ragged blue jeans and a long-sleeved plaid shirt that was too heavy for summer. The eyes that looked out at him from under the thick fringe of his hair were a brilliant blue that looked disturbingly familiar to Tyler. He didn't know who this guy was, but he gave Tyler the creeps. He'd been well-raised by a good Southern family, however, and his default mode was courtesy.

"Hey," he said. "Do you need help?"

The driver didn't speak for a moment. Finally, he smiled. The lopsided smile looked familiar, too. "Get in the car, Keith," he said. He raised his right arm, and Tyler saw the gun for the first time.

"That…that's not my name," Tyler answered, his eyes fixed on the barrel of the weapon. Despite the rising sun's heat, he felt cold in the pit of his stomach.

"I know your name, Keith," the driver said. "I know it better than you do. Get in."

Tyler thought of running. He knew he was fast, but no one was really faster than a speeding bullet. He had a brief thought of charging the gunman, taking the gun away, beating his assailant into the ground. But the cold black circle of that gun barrel was enough to crush any illusions Tyler might have had about being a hero. This wasn't a movie. He knew he had to get into the car, but his legs didn't seem to want to work.

"Get in, little brother," the gunman said. "I'm not gonna tell you again."

Tyler felt a sudden stirring of long-repressed memory triggered by the word "brother." He knew where he'd seen those eyes, that smile before. "Mick?"

The gunman smiled. "That's me."

"Holy…where have you been, man?"

The smile slipped a little. "Here and there."

Tyler was having trouble believing it. Mick had dropped out of his life years ago. Tyler had thought about him for years. Until he'd stopped. He felt a twinge of guilt. "It…it's good to see you." He gestured toward the gun. "Except for that, I mean."

The man looked down at the gun, then back up. "Yeah. Sorry. Didn't know how you'd react. You bein' an upstanding citizen and all now." The gun never wavered.

Tyler swallowed. "Why don't you put it down?"

"My doctor told me I got trust issues. Now get in the car."

"Where…where are we going?" Tyler said.

"To find Mama. She needs us."

"I have a…" Tyler almost said "mother," but the way the gunman's eyes narrowed stopped him.

"Okay," he said. "Okay. I'll come with you. Just be cool, okay?"

The gunman gave him that lopsided grin again. "Oh, we're cool, Keith. We're way cool. Now come on. There's not much time."

"Jesus," the man with the headphones said. "He's really beating the shit out of her."

He glanced over at Chance, who'd put on her own headset. She gritted her teeth at the sound of another blow hitting flesh. "We need to do something," she said.

The woman inside the house was no longer crying out, no longer pleading or cajoling. They couldn't tell if she was unconscious or dead, or if she was just riding it out. The voice of the man administering the beating was raised, but they couldn't make out the words, he was shouting so angrily.

"We need to do something." Chance said again. She whipped off her headphones and started towards the door of the room where they'd set up their surveillance. It was the front parlor of an abandoned house across the street from their target, and Chance's boots echoed on the hardwood floorboards in the empty space.

"Hold it!" the DEA agent with the headphones barked. "We spent weeks getting authorization for this surveillance. I'm not blowing it for some minor domestic disturbance."

"Minor? He's going to kill her!"

"If he does, then we've got him. But right now, Deputy Cahill, you need to remember you are here as a courtesy to local law enforcement. This is a DEA operation, not some country barn dance gone wrong. You fuck this up and I'll charge you with interfering in a federal investigation. So you just *stand the fuck down*."

Chance stared for a moment, her hand on the front door. She let the hand fall away. "You really are a prick, Winslow," she said.

"Yeah, no shit," Winslow said. "Welcome to the big time, Deputy Cahill." He cocked his head, looking for all the world like a dog who'd just been asked if he wanted to go out. "It's over, anyway."

Chance could hear the bang of the screen door from across the street. She stole a glance through the ragged curtain and milky glass of the front door. Their target was striding down the walkway of the tiny wood-frame house, his face still clenched with anger. He got into an aging black Mercedes convertible with the top down. In this neighborhood of New Orleans, known as Arabi, the car, even old as it was, stuck out like an evening gown in a dive bar. The fact that it hadn't been stolen or stripped was evidence the owner was connected. Chance could see him grip the wheel, staring straight ahead. Slowly, he lowered his head to rest on the steering wheel. It was all Chance could do not to yank the door open, walk over to the Mercedes, pull the son of a bitch out of that fancy car, and cuff his sorry ass before hauling him off to jail. "Someday soon, Charleyboy," she whispered, "Someday real soon."

"That's the spirit," Winslow said. The man in the Mercedes straightened up, started the engine, and pulled away from the curb.

"We should at least check and see that she's not dead," Chance said. She didn't trust herself to look at Winslow.

"She's not." Winslow reached under the console and pulled out a small black cellphone. "But let me set your mind at ease." He punched speed dial.

Savannah heard the soft vibration of the cheap burner phone she'd stashed beneath the cushions of the faded couch. Slowly, grimacing with the pain in her ribs and stomach, she got on her hands and knees and pulled it out. "I'm okay," she said without preliminaries.

"You sure?" Winslow said.

She reached over and fished a Marlboro Light out of the crumpled pack on the coffee table. "I didn't use the safe word, did I?" She lit the cigarette. She didn't know if her hands were shaking from the fear or the hangover that made her head pound along with the throbbing in her ribs.

"No." He almost sounded proud of her. "You didn't. Hang in there, Savannah. This'll all be over soon."

She took a drag on the cigarette. The smoke, as always, calmed her nerves. "And we get our immunity when this is over. Both of us."

"You do. What happens to Charleyboy depends on how well he plays along."

"He'll play along," she said. "When he finds out what I've done, he'll have to."

"You're being really brave here, Savannah."

Jesus, he was really laying it on thick. She barked out a short, bitter laugh. "Yeah. Right." She took another drag on the cigarette. "You find out about the other thing? About my boys?"

"We're working on it. I promise."

She sat up. "You'd better come through on this, Winslow. Or you get nothin'. You hear me?"

There was a brief pause. Winslow's voice when he spoke had lost even the false warmth he'd shown earlier. "You don't want to be making threats, Savannah. You're not in a real strong position here."

Don't I know it, she thought. *That's why I'm doing my own search. My own way.* "Just remember what I said." It sounded weak and pitiful even to her. She broke the connection. She shoved the burner back beneath the couch, then sat there on the floor, her knees pulled up to her chest. She finished the cigarette, staring at the peeling wallpaper.

"**H**ome sweet home," Mick said as they pulled up in front of the house.

"How'd you know where I live?" Tyler said.

"I know a lot about you, lil' bro," Mick said. "Big football star, huh?"

"I do all right." He felt absurdly defensive about it. From the sound of it, Mick—if it was Mick, which he still had trouble believing—had had a harder life than him. He felt that twinge of guilt again.

"Oh, don't be so modest, Keith. You're supposed to be All-State this year." He got out. "Come on. You're going to need to get some things."

"What do you mean?" Tyler got out on his own side.

"We're going to need some cash," he said. "And I reckon you're going to want to at least pack a toothbrush and a change of underwear."

"Wait a minute," Tyler said. "I've got a little money, but—" "And I'm betting these nice folks with this nice house have a lot more."

Tyler stopped. "I'm not stealing from them!"

"Okay," Mick said. "Then I will."

Tyler set his jaw. "Like hell." He started for Mick.

Almost lazily, Mick raised the gun and pointed it at Tyler's face. "Now, now," he said. "Is that any way for a preacher's boy to talk?"

"They're my parents, Mick."

"No," Mick said, "they're not." He lowered the gun slightly.

"They raised me. They took care of me. A lot better than…" He stopped. He'd tried to forget about his biological mother, and his parents had provided scant information about her. All she knew was that she'd walked away from him. But he couldn't say that now. The gun was aimed straight at his face again, Mick's finger tight on the trigger. His eyes were full of fury. That was a look Tyler remembered. He was beginning to believe.

"You want to watch what you say, little brother," Mick said, his voice tight. "Mama's in trouble. She needs us. And we're going to help her."

"What are you talking about?"

"I'll explain later," Mick said. "Now get a move on."

Tyler's hand trembled as he opened the door. He imagined he could feel exactly where the gun was pointed at his back, could almost feel where the bullet would go in. He went inside, Mick close behind him.

"Nice place," Mick said as they entered the living room.

"Thanks," Tyler replied, then immediately felt foolish, not knowing if Mick was being sarcastic.

"Must be good money in this preachin' game." Mick walked over to the mantel above the fireplace. He scanned the photos there: Tyler in his football uniform. A much younger Tyler under a Christmas tree covered with uneven lumps of tinsel. A picture of Tyler between his mother and father, proudly holding up a newly caught fish. Mick took that one off the mantel and looked down at it.

"Don't," Tyler blurted out.

Mick looked up. "Don't what?" he said. "Don't even look? Your mommy and daddy," he almost spat the words, "too good for me to even look at?" Tyler didn't answer, just looked at him helplessly. "Or you think I'm going to break it? That what you think of me?" He put the picture back on the mantelpiece with exaggerated care. "They must have made me out to be some kind of evil motherfucker, lil' bro."

Actually, Tyler thought, *nobody's even mentioned you for years.* He kept silent.

"Come on," Mick said impatiently. "Get your shit. And the money." He followed Tyler into his room. His eyes were expressionless as he surveyed the football posters on the wall, the shelves of trophies, the cases of ribbons, but Tyler felt he was being judged nonetheless.

"Well, don't just stand there," Mick said.

"Look," Tyler said, "There's money in my dresser. I saved it up. It's almost five hundred bucks. Just take it and go."

"Now where'd you get that kind of cash?"

"Working. Working at Quizno's."

"And how long it take you to save up almost five hundred?"

"I don't know. A few months."

Mick smiled. "And in just a few minutes, it's going to be all mine," he said. "All that work seems kinda pointless now, don't it?" He walked over and patted Tyler on the shoulder. "I can tell I got a lot to teach you about how the world works." It was the closest that Mick had approached so far. Tyler seized the opportunity. He swung at Mick's chin as hard as he could. The blow connected solidly, knocking Mick's head to one side. Just as quickly, however, Mick whirled back, his right hand whipping the gun across Tyler's face. Before he knew what was happening, Tyler was on his knees, his head reverberating from an explosion of pain. He tasted the coppery tang of blood in his mouth and felt a slow, warm trickle of blood down his cheek. He felt the barrel of the gun against his temple.

"You're family, Keith," Mick said softly. "My own flesh and blood. Which is why your brains aren't all over that wall right now. But don't. Push. Me."

"That's...not my name," Tyler whispered. He felt tears mingling with the blood on his face.

There was a long pause. At that moment, Tyler knew he'd gone too far. He knew he was going to die. He began to pray softly. "Our father, who art in heaven..."

Mick interrupted him. "It's a good thing I'm here," he said. "Else you might have forgotten who you are."

The gun barrel was suddenly gone. Tyler didn't look up. "Hallowed be thy name..." he whispered.

Then Mick was back, kneeling beside him. Tyler turned to look, his eyes bleak and hopeless. Mick held a towel in his left hand. He pressed it against Tyler's cheek almost tenderly. "Here," he said, "let me look." Tyler was numb with shock at the sudden display of concern. He winced slightly as Mick wiped away the blood. "You got any Band-Aids?"

"In the bathroom. Cabinet above the sink." Tyler slowly got to his feet as he heard Mick rummaging in the medicine cabinet. He thought of trying to run. Later he would wonder if it was fear or guilt that stopped him.

Mick came out of the bathroom with the box in one hand. He put the gun down on the dresser by the bathroom door. "You can't hit no harder'n that," he grinned, "guess I got nothin' to worry about." He shook some bandages out of the box and began taking them out of their wrappers. "Don't look so shocked, Keith," he said as he began applying them to the wound on his cheekbone. "Who do you think used to patch you up when you were little?"

"I don't know. I don't remember."

"That was me, little brother," Mick said. "I took care of you. And now I need your help." He put the last of the bandages in place and took Tyler's shoulder. He looked into his brother's face earnestly. "Mama needs your help, too."

"Why?" Tyler said. "Tell me why either of us should do anything for her."

Mick straightened up. "What do you mean?"

Tyler got to his feet. "She left us, Mick. She walked out. And she never looked back."

Mick grabbed Tyler by the shoulders. "No!" he yelled. "That's *bullshit*! That's the *lie* they told you to cover up what they did to us." The sudden return of Mick's fury stunned Tyler back into silence. That ferocity was something Tyler remembered all too well. Mick turned him toward the door and picked the gun up off the dresser. "Get your stuff," he said, his face now expressionless. "And don't forget the money."

"**S**o," Chance said. "*She's* our asset."

"*Our* asset?" She wanted to smack that condescending smirk off the man's fat face, but she didn't take the bait. Finally, Winslow nodded. "She thinks she can turn Charleyboy. And when Charleyboy turns, he can help us bring Luther down."

"In exchange for his safety."

"Among other things. Or so she thinks. "

She narrowed her eyes. "She mentioned her boys. What's that all about?"

Winslow turned back to the recording console set up on a collapsible table in the empty room. He began logging the last recording on a laptop computer perched on the table. "A few years ago, she lost her kids. Two boys. They got adopted out. She wants to know where they are. How they're doing."

Chance shook her head. "You didn't promise her that, did you? Those records would be sealed."

He shrugged, not looking at her. "I said we'd try."

She looked out the front window. *Asshole*, she thought to herself.

After she'd smoked the cigarette nearly down to the filter, Savannah unfolded herself from her position on the floor and got to her feet. She looked in the dulled mirror over the fireplace and ran a finger lightly over the cut on her cheek. The bruise around it was rapidly swelling into something she couldn't easily cover with makeup. She winced and took her finger away. She sighed, then winced again as the intake of breath sent stabs of pain through her ribs. Normally, she could see the blow coming and cover up. This time, however, it had come from out of nowhere. She couldn't even remember what she had said to set him off.

She knew Charleyboy was under a lot of pressure. She had walked on eggshells for the past month as he brooded and drank at the kitchen table, smoking cigarette after cigarette, the last one of every evening slowly burning down between his fingers as he nodded off. The immobility, the passivity, was the surest sign that something was drastically wrong. From the moment she'd met Charleyboy, she'd been drawn to his vitality, his energy. He'd seemed to be perpetually in motion, and she had been caught up and drawn along in the wake of it, laughing along with him in delight at the great ride they were sharing. There was money and whiskey and smoke and pills and powder to go around. It was good times for everyone. And if sometimes the good times went a little too far—well, there wasn't really any such thing as too far, was there? She was a party girl, always had been, since she'd found out at fourteen that a pretty face and blossoming figure could get her into the places where the fun was, places a hell of a lot more interesting than the single-wide trailer she'd shared with an alcoholic mother and an aunt who'd checked out of reality years ago.

As she checked her face and body in the mirror, Savannah had to notice, not for the first time, the deeper, more permanent damage that time was doing. Her body was still reasonably firm, even if the curve of hips and ass had grown a little more pronounced. Charleyboy had always said he liked her curves better than the rail-thin model look, anyway. But the face was beginning to show the years and the mileage, the laugh lines deepening inevitably towards crow's feet. It took a little longer these days to put a face on. Even when she did, Charleyboy was too preoccupied most of the time to notice. He had always been quick with a compliment or an endearment. It was one of the things she loved about him. But now, he seemed so wrapped up in whatever was bothering him, it was as if she wasn't even there. Until she said something to make him mad. Then she was there, but as a focus for his anger.

But it would be okay, she told herself. He'd be back. He always came back. And he'd be tender and sweet to her, tell her he loved her and always would. There'd be gifts. Their relationship in the times after he hit her was always like falling in love all over again. And the sex…well, there was nothing quite as hot as make-up sex. She smiled to herself. It was going to be all right. But then she looked back into the mirror, hugged herself, and shivered. *Someone's walking over your grave*, her mother's slurred voice said in her mind.

She had always known, in the back of her mind, that the good times couldn't last forever. She always knew the party would end. Someday. Now, the day was rushing toward her like a black hurricane, and she only hoped she'd found a way to ride it out.

CHAPTER
TWO

He was still in the grip of the sick, shaky feeling he always had after he'd lost it like that. Charleyboy hated losing control. But he seemed to be doing it more and more these days. He knew the trouble he was in was what was making him so stressed. Actually, being in trouble with Mr. Luther created something somewhere beyond stress and in the neighborhood of mortal terror. But that wasn't Savannah's fault. He'd always been able to charm his way out of whatever scrapes they'd been in before. This one, however, was something he might not be able to get them out of, and Savannah's constant presence served as an infuriating reminder of how badly he'd failed both of them. It wasn't logical to take that out on her, he knew. But he couldn't seem to control it. And since hitting her was just another form of failure for her to remind him of, he hit her again.

He took a deep breath. He needed to focus. Mr. Luther could sense when someone was feeling weak or unsure. And he would exploit it without mercy, working that raspy, insinuating voice into the tiniest cracks in his victim's confidence, widening them until he levered them open like an oyster and devoured whatever was inside.

He pulled the Mercedes up to the iron gate. A voice came from a speaker box by the driveway. "Yeah?"

It was one of the seemingly endless parade of cousins that served as Mr. Luther's inner circle. This one had sworn up and down that his name was Zig. He and his twin brother, who stated with equal solemnity that his given name was Zag, were Luther's favored bodyguards.

"It's Charleyboy," he said. "Mr. Luther's expecting me."

There was a brief silence on the other end, then the black iron gate ponderously swung wide.

"C'mon up to the house, *Angus*," the speaker said. Charleyboy could hear the malice beneath the words. Ever since Zig had learned his given name—Angus Charlebois—he and his dimwitted brother had used it to mock him and his Cajun heritage. Charleyboy took a deep breath and tried to steady himself.

He drove down the long dirt driveway, past the paddocks and barns of the horse farming operation that served as a cover for Mr. Luther's other interests. A few thoroughbreds raised their heads and looked at him incuriously before going back to cropping grass.

The house was a sprawling one-story glass and wood structure that seemed to be assembled mostly of afterthoughts. There was no obvious coherent plan; wings and rooms had been added on apparently whenever space was needed and money could be found. A pair of gleaming, jacked-up 4X4 pickups sat at the end of the driveway, next to a vintage Mustang convertible with the top down. Zig leaned against the fender of the Mustang, six foot three inches of country bumpkin that time and his uncle's employment had whittled down to bone, gristle, and pure meanness.

"Unc's 'round back," Zig grunted. He levered himself up off the fender like it was a major imposition, turning and trudging sullenly towards the back of the house. He didn't look back to see if Charleyboy was following. That was about par for the course; Zig rarely spoke except to make fun of Charleyboy's given name or make some crude remark about Savannah. Charleyboy pondered just how nice it would feel to put a bullet in the back of the redneck's head right then. He toyed with the thought lovingly for a moment, then put it away as they rounded the house.

Mr. Luther sat on a rickety camp stool in the shade of an ancient oak tree. He was dressed in frayed khaki pants, a wife-beater T-shirt stained with sweat, and a battered old porkpie hat. He fanned himself slowly with a tattered magazine, the limp flesh of his skinny old arms wobbling with the motion. His attention was fixated on the dog that hung a few yards away.

The dog was a young pit bull, already bearing battle scars across his shoulders and head, his muscles bulging and grotesquely knotted. His jaws were locked on a leather bag that hung from a rope slung over a nearby branch. Zig's brother Zag held the other end of the rope, pulling the bag off the ground high enough that the dog's hind legs jerked and twisted in the air. He could have released his locked jaws at any time and returned to earth, but he hung on as if for dear life. A low, terrifying snarl came from the dog's throat as he whipped his head back and forth. Something inside the bag screamed in pain and fear.

Charleyboy took a step back. The sound of agony seemed to whip the dog into a greater frenzy. He tightened his jaw lock and worried the bag even more viciously. There was the sound of crunching bone and the screaming stopped.

Mr. Luther cackled. "Tole you he was badass," he said to Zag. "Din't I tell you? Let 'im down, boy, and let 'im get his ree-ward." Slowly, Zag let the dog down, still grinding his teeth against the tough leather bag. Zag approached the dog carefully, then quickly moved to seize him by the collar. He led the animal away, the leather bag still in his teeth. Blood dripped from the bag onto the carefully manicured grass.

Mr. Luther turned to Charleyboy, his eyes bright in his lined and wrinkled face. He had a weak chin and prominent nose that gave him the look of a turkey buzzard. "That there's Ajax," he said, gesturing towards where Zag and the dog were disappearing into a long, low building that housed the kennels. "Some nigger calls himself a rap star thinks he's got a dog that can beat 'im."

Charleyboy tried to keep his voice level. "Looks like he's got his work cut out for him."

"Hah," Mr. Luther said. "Damn niggers done took over football, basketball...they even thought they's gonna take over golf. I aim to see they don't take this sport over, too. We gotta have something that's ours." He wiped his hands on his pant legs. "Now, boy," he said, his voice sharpening. "You got my money?"

Charleyboy took a deep breath. *Here we go*, he thought. "Not yet," he said, "But—"

"Then tell me why I shouldn't string your skinny Cajun ass up in that there tree and let Ajax work on you."

"Because I have a way you can make more."

"Oh, you do, do you?" Mr. Luther's laugh was somewhere between a wheeze and a choke. "You think you got a way to make money I ain't thought of yet? This I gotta hear."

"Caspar Gutierrez is bringing a package in from down South," Charleyboy said, keeping his voice level. "A hundred kilos. Maybe more."

Luther's eyes narrowed. "I'm listenin'," he said.

"I know when. And I know where."

That laugh again. "An' if I write off the money you owe me, you'll tell me, right?"

"Cheap at the price, wouldn't you say? A load that big, and Gutierrez along with it."

"Wait a damn minute," Luther said. "Gutierrez is going to be there hisself?"

"It's a new distributor. He wants to meet the big man personally. And he's bringing cash." Luther was silent, his eyes on the ground, thinking it through. Charleyboy took enough encouragement from the silence to plunge ahead. "You've been scrapping with Gutierrez for five years now. I'm putting him, a major package, and a pile of cash in your hands. Take him, the money, and the drugs, that'll give you a monopoly in this end of the state. That ought to be worth the forty K I owe you."

Luther rubbed his chin. "Yeah. If it's true." He looked sharply at Charleyboy. "If it ain't..." he gestured towards the tree, "...you'll be hangin' by your thumbs from that limb. An' while Ajax is tearin' your balls off, Zig an' Zag'll pay a visit to that lil' redhaired gal o'yours." He grinned nastily. "They always did like that gal."

Charleyboy tried not to clench his fists. "There's no need to bring her into this."

"Sure there is." Luther chuckled. "She's your weakness, boy. An' since you were dumbass enough to let me know it, I own you. That's the way of the world." He chuckled again, the laugh turning into a rasping, phlegmy cough. "Now," he said when the spasm was over. "Tell me. When and where. And how strong he's comin'."

Charleyboy hesitated.

"You think I can't get it out of you anyway?" Luther demanded.

"Just tell me the debt's canceled, and I'll give you all the information I have."

"I'll tell you the debt's canceled when I have the package, the money, and Gutierrez's head in a bag. Now start talkin', before I get impatient."

"Okay. Okay. There's an airstrip, out in the country. Just a long concrete runway with a couple of hangars. The guy who owns it does crop dusting, but he's going broke at it. He's got a cousin in Florida who's big in real estate or something. The market's down, so the cousin's trying to, I guess you could say, diversify. He's fronting the cash."

Luther frowned. "The crop duster's going into distribution?"

"No. He's just providing the place to meet and to store the package while it's being cut. The cousin's flying in. Gutierrez is meeting him with a van."

"What kind of security?"

"He doesn't think anyone else knows. You might catch him by surprise."

"When?"

"Two days from now. Midnight."

Luther mulled it over. "Huh," he said finally. He looked at Charleyboy.

"You're wondering how I know all this," Charleyboy said.

"Yeah," Luther said. "I am."

"The crop duster drinks. When he drinks, he talks too much. He wanted to know if I wanted to come in on it."

"Uh-huh," Luther said. He didn't sound convinced. Finally, he stood up. "I'll think about it," he said. "Somethin' about it I still don't like, though." He looked at Charleyboy appraisingly. "Maybe I'll have Zig or Zag stay with that gal of yours, just for insurance."

Charleyboy felt the sweat running into his collar. "Gutierrez might come heavy. You're going to need every gun. Just in case."

"Well then," Luther said, "maybe the two of you can come with us. I'll let you know." He turned away in obvious dismissal.

Charleyboy desperately tried to think of something else to say, some comment that would clinch the deal, but nothing came. It was all in Luther's hands now. As he watched Luther's retreating back, Zig appeared at his elbow.

"I can see myself out," Charleyboy said.

"No, you can't," Zig said. He followed Charleyboy out to the parking lot and watched him get in the car. Charleyboy glanced in the mirror as he bumped down the driveway. Zig stood and watched for a moment, then turned and walked back towards the house. When Charleyboy saw that, he reached down and picked up the cell phone. He glanced down as he dialed the number he knew now by heart.

"Speak," a voice said on the other end.

"It's me," Charleyboy said.

"Of course it is." There was a pause. "Are the fish biting?"

"A couple of nibbles. But I feel pretty good about it."

"Okay." There was another pause. "You've backed the right team," the voice said finally.

I hope so, Charleyboy thought. "Yeah," was all he said. "I know." He snapped the phone shut.

I sure hope so, he thought again. *For both our sakes. Mine and Savannah's. Because I can feel it in my bones. This is our last chance.*

CHAPTER THREE

Carl Welch heard the sound of the ax as he came up the front walk, a grunt followed swiftly by the sharp crack as metal met and prevailed over wood. The sound echoed in the trees that surrounded and loomed over the isolated house.

The door opened before he reached it. Glenda stood there, a smile on her lined face. As he approached, she opened her arms and swept him into a warm hug. "It's good to see you, Carl."

"You too."

"How's Marian?"

He shrugged. "Well, you know how it is. She has her good days and her bad days."

"You tell her I asked after her, you hear? I hope she feels better."

"I'll do that." There was a brief uncomfortable silence, the type that would normally be filled by small talk. The news he brought, and the favor he meant to ask, had filled his mind and squeezed out the usual easy pleasantries. "Wyatt's out back," she finally said.

"I heard."

She looked at him and sighed. "Took the ax from the mud room right after you called and walked out without sayin' a word. Been chopping away like a beaver ever since. And it ain't like we didn't already have plenty of firewood."

"He knows I'm not bringing good news."

"No one ever does," she said. "Not any more. Or bad news, either." She scowled. "Guess we found out who our friends are. At least you stood by him."

"It was no trouble," he said softly.

"I know it was. Don't lie to me," she said, then smiled. "It ain't right for a preacher to lie. Now get out there before he runs out of logs to split and starts in on my rosebushes."

Tall trees ringed the yard, looking down on the man in the center who stood before a thick oak stump used as a chopping block. He was a big man, over six feet, and broad. He still had the build that had made him a high school football star, long ago. The dark hair had thinned now and receded from the top of the large, square-jawed head. Sweat ran down his ruddy face and darkened the already stained t-shirt he wore. As he approached, Carl noticed the red and white Budweiser can sitting on the ground a few feet away. He frowned at that, but decided to let it go for the moment. "Morning, Sheriff."

Wyatt McGee stopped and leaned the ax against the block without looking up. He took a large faded bandanna from his back pocket and mopped the sweat from his brow. He stuffed the rag in his pocket, picked up the beer can, and took a long pull. Only then did he look the other man in the eye.

"Don't call me that. I ain't sheriff anymore."

Carl shrugged it off. "Way I see it, Wyatt, it's like any other title you earned, like Colonel or Congressman or whatnot. You earned it, you don't ever lose it."

McGee looked away again. "I did." He picked up the ax again, but he didn't pick up another log. He just hefted it in his hands, turning it this way and that.

"My boy's gone," Carl said.

McGee stopped his examination and looked up. "Tyler?"

Carl just nodded.

McGee sat the log on the block and swung the ax again in a long arc over his head that split the log in two as if it was passing through air. "Call the sheriff's department."

"I did," Carl said. "They said he most likely run off. He's eighteen, they said, and he can do what he likes."

"That's true."

"Tyler wouldn't do that. Not without telling me or his mama."

McGee leaned on the axe. He took the bandanna out and mopped his face again. "You speak to Henry?" Henry was the chief deputy who'd replaced McGee as acting sheriff after he'd resigned. After a few months, the County Commissioners made it official, and Henry had coasted to easy electoral victories ever since in a county where challenging a sitting sheriff was a quick route to permanent unemployment if you lost.

"Yeah. Took me a while, but I finally got to him. Times have changed over there, Wyatt."

McGee picked up the beer can, drained the last drops, then crushed it and tossed it back to the ground. "Good. So what did Henry say?"

"He said the same thing. Tyler took the money he'd saved and he run off."

Wyatt shrugged. "You never can tell what someone'll do."

"I can. I raised that boy like he was my own. No. He *was* my own. Something's happened."

McGee picked up another log, sighed, set it back down. "I can't be of any use to you, Carl. Not without my badge."

"I reckon you're the same man you always were. Badge or no

badge. And you got a stake in this, too. You're the one who got him out of that place. Away from that woman. And brought him to me."

The big man looked away. "That wasn't me," he said. "It was the Social Services people."

"On your say-so."

"Well, that was back when my say-so meant something."

"It still does."

McGee shook his head. "It shouldn't."

There was a pause. "You know," Carl said, "The Chinese believe when you save someone's life, you're responsible for that person ever after."

McGee snorted. "I met a couple of Chinese fellas when I was in the Marines. We got drunk in Manila. They told me that's a load of crap."

"Well, it ought to be so."

"Damn it, Carl…" McGee stopped. "Sorry. Need to watch my language."

"It's okay. Put a quarter in Glenda's swear jar. But I still need your help."

McGee leaned the ax on the chopping block and sat down on the block. "I wouldn't be no good to you, Carl," he said again.

"You don't trust yourself."

"No."

"'Cause you were wrong. One time."

"He could have died. I could've sent an innocent man to the death house."

Carl shrugged. "Like I said—"

"Right. He *confessed*." Wyatt McGee spat the word like a curse. He stood and picked up the ax again.

"Wyatt," Carl said, "You think splitting every log in the county's gonna get you to forgive yourself?" McGee put another log on the block. Carl felt his frustration rising. "You need to do something good again, Wyatt. This hiding away is poisoning you. It's turned you old before your time." He walked over and picked up the empty can. "Look at you. Drinking in the middle of the day."

Wyatt's face darkened. "You need to mind your business, Carl."

Carl shook his head, fighting his own anger down. "I thought my boy was my business."

McGee hefted the ax. "Well, he ain't mine." He raised the blade and brought it down so hard that it not only split the log, it wedged itself deep into the oak of the block. He was still trying to work it loose as Carl walked away.

CHAPTER FOUR

Chance pulled her compact Chevy pickup into the packed-earth driveway next to the single-wide trailer where she lived. Neither truck nor trailer was new, and they both showed their years on the outside, but both were solid and well maintained on the inside, and most importantly, they were hers outright. She'd inherited her father's aversion to debt, and she'd scraped together every dime for the vehicle and the home on her own. She got out and looked around at the wooded lot the trailer sat on, knowing that someday, that tiny piece of land in St. Charles Parish that her father had saved for would pass to her. She was in no hurry for that day, however, and she wished he'd gotten to enjoy it as much as she had. In the meantime, it made the long drive to work worthwhile. Which reminded her, it was time she called her dad. First, however, she had to deal with the frantically yapping dog who was throwing himself against the wire of his pen that sat beneath a small copse of trees in back. "Dang it, Jonas," she called out in good-natured irritation, "I'm comin'!" When she opened the gate, the black-and-white springer spaniel shot out, circled her a few times in wriggling ecstasy while she bent down and tried to pet him, then tore off into the woods to relieve himself. She climbed the wooden stairs, let herself in, and got a Diet Coke from the trailer's wheezy fridge. By the time she'd taken it back outside and plopped down in the canvas camp chair that sat by the steps, the dog had returned, carrying a ragged tennis ball in his jaws. Chance ruffled the dog's ears as he dropped the ball at her feet. When she picked it up and threw it, the dog bounded off. She took a long pull off her soda, pulled out her cell phone, and hit the speed dial.

Her father picked up on the first ring. "Hey, Lil' Bit."

She hadn't realized until she heard her father's voice how roiled she still was inside, how much she needed to hear that calm, measured tone. She could see him in his tattered easy chair by the phone, his white cane leaning against the side table. "Hey, Dad. How's it going?"

"Oh, you know," he said. "This getting old shit isn't for sissies. But there's only one way to stop it, I guess."

She laughed. "You're not old, Dad."

"Yeah, I am. So what's going on with you? How's my grand-dog?"

The dog in question had brought the ball back and laid it at Chance's feet. He had his front paws stretched out and his butt in the air, wiggling with anticipation of the next throw. "As usual. Fat, dumb, and happy." She picked the ball up and tossed it.

"How's work?"

She hesitated.

As usual, her father picked up on it right away. "Spill it, girl."

Even before he'd lost his sight, Brett Cahill had exhibited an almost supernatural ability to pick up on nuances of speech and expression. It had made him a legendary interrogator in the Louisiana State Police Bureau of Investigations. It had also made it nearly impossible for Chance or her sister, CeeCee, to get away with anything as children. Unfortunately for her father, the man who put a nearly fatal bullet in the back of his head hadn't been facing him; he'd been shot in an ambush without a word of warning.

She started haltingly, but soon the words were coming quickly, the anger inside her boiling over as she described the incident with the informant. Jonas, with his own canine gift for sensing his mistress's distress, abandoned the ball and laid his head on her knee. She reassured the dog with a scratch behind the ears. When she finally ran down, her father was silent for a moment. When he spoke, his voice was dispassionate and professional. She was dismayed for a second, until she realized he was speaking to her as one cop to another. That was something not unheard of, but rare. It made her feel good.

"Undercover puts you in close relationships with people you'd normally be putting in cuffs," he said. "But you've got to remember. Some of these people are masters at manipulation. You can't get mad at 'em for that. It's what they learned to do to survive. Sometimes at Mama or Daddy's knee. But you have to learn to keep your distance. Don't let them suck you into their game." He took a deep breath, as if the words were bringing back memories he'd rather not revisit. Then some of the warmth returned to his voice. "I guess what I'm sayin', Lil' Bit, is you be careful, okay? Don't you start your heart bleedin' for an informant."

"Okay, Dad." She ran her hand through the dog's thick fur. "What about this Winslow guy?"

"The fed? He sounds like an asshole. But then, most of them are."

She laughed. "I guess what I'm asking is, how do I handle him?"

"You handle him like you handle any asshole. You stand up for yourself and you don't back down. Think you can handle that?"

She wiped her eyes with the back of her hand. "I can do that." She chuckled. "I had a great teacher."

"He anyone I know?"

That made her laugh out loud. "I love you, Dad."

"Love you too, Lil' Bit. And be careful out there, okay?"

"Always." They said their goodbyes. She broke the connection and picked up the ball. The dog wagged his tail and barked happily. All was right in his world again. Chance threw the ball. They played like that until the sun began to sink behind the live oaks.

"Where are we going?" Tyler said.

Mick was tapping out a rhythm only he could hear on the steering wheel. He shifted around in the driver's seat as if it was heating up. "My place," he said. "But I gotta pick up a couple of things first."

Tyler sagged back into the passenger seat. His mind was racing. If Mick was planning to make a stop, maybe he could get away. Call his mom and dad. No, the cops first, then his mom and dad. But first, run. Run from this strange young man Tyler couldn't even recognize as his brother.

His frantic thoughts were interrupted as Mick pulled into the parking lot of a small roadside store. A peeling wooden sign above the door identified the place as Gary's Country Market.

"What are you getting here?" Tyler asked.

He felt a twisting in his guts as Mick pulled out the gun again. "Not me, lil' bro," Mick said. "Us. You're coming inside with me." He reached behind the seat and pulled out another pistol, a massive black .45. "Take this," he said, thrusting it into Tyler's hand.

CHAPTER FIVE

Glenda watched silently as Wyatt strode back into the house, went to the kitchen fridge, grabbed another beer—his fourth of the day—and stomped back out to the screened porch that overlooked the sloping backyard. She finished drying off the dish she'd been washing, then put it back in the kitchen cabinet. She moved slowly, with the hesitation of someone stretching out a mundane task in order to delay a much more unpleasant one. Finally, she squared her shoulders, took a deep breath, and walked out to the back porch.

Wyatt was sitting in one of the iron-framed chairs with the floral print cushions that they'd picked out together at Lowe's. His gaze rested on the backyard, but his eyes were far away. Glenda had learned to dread that faraway look. She took the other chair.

"So," she said, keeping her voice as neutral as possible. "What did Carl want?"

He raised the beer can to his lips, took a drink. He didn't answer.

"Wyatt," she said, a little more steel in her voice. "I asked you a question. Can you answer me?"

He turned to look at her. She met his gaze without flinching. She'd gotten good at that.

"Tyler Welch has run off," he said at last.

She nodded. "Carl thinks it's more than that."

He shook his head. "Henry says—"

She cut him off. "*Henry.*" Her tone conveyed all that needed to be said.

"Henry's the sheriff."

"And Carl's your friend. And he wants your help." She shook her head. "I never knew you to turn your back on a friend."

His expression darkened. "Goddamn it, Glenda…"

"Don't you curse at me, Wyatt McGee," she shot back. "I won't have it."

He looked away, took another drink of his beer. "Sorry," he finally said in a low voice.

She sighed and stood up. She walked behind his chair and bent down to kiss the top of his balding head. She slid her hands down to caress his chest. "You could just ask around," she murmured. "You still know people."

He drank again. "I don't have a badge. Or a gun."

She snorted. "You don't need them. People in this county still respect you, Wyatt."

His shoulders writhed beneath her touch. "They shouldn't."

She sighed and embraced him more tightly. "Oh, honey," she whispered. "You made a mistake. When are you going to forgive yourself for that?"

He didn't answer as he took another drink. She sighed and released him. "I'm going to the store," she said. "I'll be back in a little bit."

"Okay." He took another drink. "We need more beer."

"No, we don't," she said. "But I'll get some anyway."

When he heard her car going out of the driveway, he finished off the beer. He got up and walked into the bedroom, noting the slight stumble in his gait. It made him ashamed, and the shame made him want another beer. He went into the bathroom and took a leak first.

On his way back to the kitchen, he paused by the bedroom closet. After a moment, he opened it, reached up to the top shelf, and took down a wooden box. He sat on the bed and looked at it for a moment. It was made of unfinished wood, with cheap wooden hinges. He'd made it in shop class in tenth grade for his father. His hands shook a bit as he opened the box.

Inside were two objects: One was the old .38 Police Special he'd worn in his first years on the sheriff's department, the one that had later been replaced by the sleeker Beretta. The other was a sheathed blade. The leather sheath had the globe and anchor symbol of the U.S. Marine Corps stamped into the front, and the name MCGEE burned crudely into the back with a child's wood-burning set. The knife had been his father's, the USMC-issue Ka-Bar Big Jim McGee had worn when he won the Silver Star and Purple Heart in Korea in the brutal defense against the Chinese onslaught in the snow surrounding the Chosin Reservoir. His father had given it to Wyatt when he'd first put on the khaki deputy's uniform. It had been the one and only time Big Jim had told his son he was proud of him. Wyatt had worn the blade on his own hip every day he was a law enforcement officer. When he'd been elected Sheriff, the local papers delighted in photographing him with the huge blade strapped to his belt.

In the end, that blade and his pride had been the instruments of his downfall.

He reached into the box and pulled out the sheathed knife, feeling the heft and balance of the legendary weapon, but he didn't draw it. After a moment, he put it back in the box. The box went back on the shelf, and Wyatt McGee went back into the kitchen for another beer.

Tyler stared at the gun in his hand, blinking in surprise.

"Before you get any ideas," Mick said. "It ain't loaded. It ain't even got a firin' pin. But you are goin' in there with it in your hand. Just like I'm takin' mine." He racked the slide on his own gun.

Tyler shook his head, his eyes filling with tears. "No." His voice cracked. "I'm not going to…" The pressure of the gun barrel against his forehead silenced him.

"If you don't do what I say," Mick said in a low, tense voice, "I'll go in there without you. And I'll shoot everyone in there. And that'll be on you." He took the gun away. "Now. Get out of the car. Walk in front of me. Go inside. Once you get in there, you just stand aside. But if you try to run, or if you try to stop me, I'll shoot whoever's in there. And then I'll shoot you. Understand?" Tyler could only nod. Mick raised the gun again. "Tell me you understand."

"I…I understand."

"Good. Now you go first."

Tyler got out slowly, the useless pistol limp and dangling from his hand. The store was a dilapidated wood-frame building, with peeling white paint and grates over the dirty, double-hung paned windows. An illuminated sign for cold beer shone from behind one window. Tyler heard Mick getting out of the car, the sound coming to him with unnatural clarity in the silence of the country road.

"Get goin', little brother." Tyler's feet didn't seem to want to obey him. He felt the gun barrel in the small of his back. "Move." He began to shuffle, then picked up the pace as he felt a second, harder nudge. His hand shook as he opened the screen door. There was a hand-lettered paper sign on the wooden interior door: SHOPLIFTERS! THESE PREMESES UNDER VIDEO SURVELLANCE. WE PROSECUTE. He hesitated again, then turned the knob.

Inside, the place was cramped, with aisles of candy and gum racks to his right, leading to the upright glass-doored coolers of beer and sodas that lined two walls. Neon signs for Budweiser, Rolling Rock, and Schlitz over the coolers provided more illumination than the wan fluorescent fixtures in the ceiling. To Tyler's left, a long counter took up the other wall, stacked with countertop displays for lottery tickets and vapor cigarette supplies. Behind the counter, a balding middle-aged man was slumped on a high-back wooden stool, head down, hands crossed over his ample belly. He looked up suddenly as Mick nudged Tyler closer, blinking as if suddenly awakened. His eyes grew wide as he took in the guns. He jumped off the stool as Mick elbowed Tyler aside.

"Don't do nothin' stupid, old man," Mick said. "Hands up where I can see 'em."

The man looked back and forth from Mick to Tyler, mouth opening and closing like a fish's. "I'm sorry," Tyler said softly.

"Shut up," Mick said. He moved closer to the counter, holding the gun in front of him at arm's length, wrist rotated so the butt was parallel to the floor, the way Tyler had seen gunmen hold their weapons in the movies. "Open the cash drawer," he barked. "Hurry up, goddamn it, I ain't got all fuckin' day."

The man's expression of shock and fear turned to a scowl. "You cain't talk like that in here."

Mick halted. "Seriously? *Seriously?*" He pulled the trigger.

CHAPTER SIX

The roar of the pistol in the small space nearly deafened Tyler. He screamed and came close to dropping his own gun. The sideways position in which Mick was holding his weapon may have looked impressive on a movie screen, but it pulled the barrel upwards and the bullet went over the counterman's head, shattering the plastic cigarette rack behind him. The man screamed as well, his voice high and shrill like a woman's. He ducked behind the counter, a cascade of cigarette packs falling like leaves on top of him.

Mick leaped onto the counter, swung his legs over, and slid into the narrow space. Tyler heard the man scream again as Mick stomped down. "Stay down, you old fuck." He reached over and opened the register. "Keith," he snapped. "Get over here." He clawed a sheaf of bills from the drawer and looked at Tyler. "*Keith!*" he shouted. "Come take this money!"

That's not my name, Tyler wanted to say, but Mick aimed the gun at the old man who lay whimpering on the floor. The threat was unmistakable. Tyler walked over, his eyes stinging with tears of frustration, and took the bills from Mick's hand. He noticed the black glassy eye of a small video camera behind and above the counter, focused on where he stood. He realized that this, not the money, was the point of the whole exercise. He needed to be seen on tape, with a gun in one hand and money in the other. He looked over at Mick, and the smug grin on his older brother's face fell away as he saw the hate in Tyler's eyes. Mick looked down at the old man, his gun hand never wavering.

"Don't," Tyler said, hating the pleading sound in his breaking voice. "Please."

"Please," the man on the floor echoed.

Mick seemed about to speak, then something caught his eye. He reached beneath the counter and pulled out a stubby shotgun with no stock and a pistol grip. "Well, well, old man," he said, his voice nearly purring. "What we got here? Were you thinkin', maybe, of being a hero with this here scatter-gun?"

"No…no, I swear it."

It felt to Tyler like they'd been in the cramped store, the air thick with the smell of fear, for days. "Come on. Let's go. Please."

Mick was still looking down. "I think you're lyin', old man. I think you were gonna wait till I was on my way out, then blow my ass away. Maybe come out shootin' at my brother and me. That the plan, Stan?"

The old man had gone beyond speech. He just sobbed and whimpered like a whipped dog.

Mick slid back over the counter, pistol in one hand, shotgun in the other. The smug look was back. "Let's go."

Savannah heard the front door slam and rose from the bed, her arms and stomach still aching from the beating. Charleyboy was in the living room, just flinging himself down in the creaky recliner.

"Hey," she said softly.

He didn't look at her. "Hey." He didn't sound angry any more. He sounded ashamed. Some of the tension went out of her. This was the beginning of the reconciliation, a ritual to her as familiar as the sunset. "You want something to eat?"

He picked up the TV remote and switched the set on. "Yeah. Thanks."

She went in the kitchen, found the last of the ham and a few eggs. She was standing at the stove, scrambling the eggs, the coffee maker gurgling away, when she felt him behind her. He slid his arms around her from behind and pulled her back against him. He buried his face in the hair covering her neck and kissed her there. "I'm sorry," he murmured. "I'm so sorry."

He sounded so much like a little boy, she felt the tears spring to her eyes. She couldn't bring herself to tell him it was all right, but she leaned back against him. "Go sit at the table," she murmured. "It's almost ready." He gave her a final squeeze, then released her.

She made them both plates and took them to the table, then went and fetched the coffee. They ate in silence for a few moments until he spoke again. "I know I shouldn't have lost it like that."

She was still looking down at her plate. "You hurt me, Charleyboy. Why do you hurt me like that?"

He put down his fork and rubbed his face with one hand. "I know. I know. I'm tryin' to do better. I'm just all torn up and twisted inside. But I'll make it up to you. I swear it."

She looked up at him, her anger rising. "How? What do you think you can do that makes up for you punchin' and kickin' me like I was a goddamn dog?"

He picked up his fork and took a bite, looking down sullenly at his plate. "I said I was sorry," he mumbled.

She sighed, knowing not to push it. "You want more coffee?"

He shook his head. "When we get to California, things'll be

different. I promise. We won't have all this shit hanging over us. I got somethin' in the works that'll get us out from under Mr. Luther."

She shuddered at the mention of the name. She'd only met the old man once, but that was enough. The way he'd looked at her made her feel like a rabbit being sized up by a snake. "That doesn't make me feel any better. I don't trust that old bastard."

"I don't either. But he trusts me. And…well, that's all I'm going to say about it. For now." He smiled at her, the smile that had always melted her before. "You trust me, don't you, baby girl?"

It almost worked. But she could tell he was up to something. He had a plan. That scared her. Angus Charlebois's plans over the past few years hadn't had a history of working out well.

"Yeah," she lied. "I trust you."

Later, as she'd known he would, he took her to bed. Usually, the make-up sex was the hottest, but this time her fear and apprehension muted her own responses. She did the things and said the words she knew would get him to his peak quickly, and when he was done and whispered "I love you," she whispered it back. But when he was asleep, snoring softly, she lay awake looking at the ceiling. She thought of her boys. Maybe she could leverage what little she knew of Charleyboy's plans to get Winslow more motivated to find them. And there was always the other thing. The searches she'd done online: Facebook, Twitter, Instagram…she had been to dozens of Internet support groups for parents trying to find their adopted children. She'd been intrigued by the stories of the ones who'd located them online. So she'd signed up for everything she could think of, waded through the dozens of creepy and occasionally obscene messages she was learning were the lot of every woman who put her face and name out on the Internet, and posted messages about looking for her sons.

Her life hadn't been anything close to stable to this point, but she'd built her survival strategy on her ability to read situations and plan ahead. She could sense changes coming that were going to be more cataclysmic than she'd known since the boys were taken from her. She made up her mind that, whatever happened, she was going to be standing when it was all over. And she was going to be doing it with her sons.

CHAPTER SEVEN

"You could have killed that guy," Tyler said. He was sitting in the passenger seat of the Firebird, staring down at the pile of money in his lap. Mick had taken the pistol from him and stuck it in the backseat.

Mick pressed down on the accelerator, making the car's big engine roar. "Didn't need to kill him, baby bro." There was a giddy edge in his voice as if he was about to break into hysterical laughter. "I didn't need to kill him. You know why?"

Tyler didn't want to know the reason; he knew it was something twisted. But he was afraid of Mick's reaction if he didn't answer. "Why?" he muttered.

"Because I *broke* him." Mick's tight smile was like the arc of a cut throat. "Did you see him at the end there? The fat fuck would have done anything I wanted. Anything."

Tyler shut his eyes, wishing he were anywhere else, wishing Mick would just shut up. But the robbery had his older brother as high and jabbering as Tyler imagined a gram of coke would have. "There's no feeling like that kind of power, Keith. Nothing." He fell silent for a moment. Tyler stole a glance at him. He seemed suddenly deflated, slumped in the bucket seat. "Nothing." The word came out as a haunted whisper.

"What happened to you, Mick?" The words were out of his mouth before Tyler could stop them.

Mick's face, when it turned to him, was completely blank. "Nothing. Nothing happened to me." He looked back at the road. "I just figured it out early on. Some people break. Some people do the breaking. It's better to be the one who does the breaking."

Tyler didn't know what to say to that. He looked out the window. It was getting dark outside. The miles were going by in a blur. "Where are we going?"

"My place. To get a few things. Then we get back on the road."

"The road to where? What are we doing?"

"I told you. We're going to find our Mama."

"Mick," Tyler said desperately, "how do you even know she wants to see us? And how are you going to find her?"

"I know because she's been looking for us, Keith. She wants to see us. Both of us. And I think she's in trouble. I'll explain it all when we get to the house." He smiled, and it was the first smile Tyler had seen from him that didn't terrify him. "Boy, is Mama going to be surprised when she finds out her boys are back together again."

"Wyatt." Glenda's voice came to him through a heavy mist of sleep, barely penetrating to his waking mind at first. He grunted and tried to burrow his head into the pillow and dive back down into sleep.

"Wyatt." This time she had a hand on his shoulder, shaking him gently.

He grumbled this time and moved to brush the hand away. He stopped at the last moment and opened his eyes. The morning sun was slanting through the blinds of the guest room. He'd stumbled drunkenly into the room sometime after midnight, retaining enough consideration to not want to wake his wife up with the buzz-saw snoring he knew he'd be doing after a day and a night of drinking. He raised his head slightly from the pillow and glanced at the clock: 9:46 am. Damn. In his working days, he'd never slept past six thirty, even on the weekends. It had been a habit instilled by his father, who'd lived his whole life by the Marine clock, rousting the whole family out of bed at five o'clock. When he'd gone out on his own, six thirty seemed like an incredible, guilty luxury. *Now look at me*, he thought, and that made him sit up. The motion made him wince with the sudden throbbing in his head. Glenda silently held out a pair of aspirin tablets, a glass of water in her other hand. He popped the aspirin into his mouth, then took the water before he saw the look on her face. "What?" he tried to say, the tablets still on his tongue making it come out as "Ot?"

She motioned for him to drink. The bitter taste of the crumbling tablets provided further encouragement. He downed them with a swallow of water, which set off a spasm of hacking that nearly doubled him over. When Wyatt was finally able to straighten up, Glenda was still regarding him with a thin-lipped look he didn't like. "There's someone here to see you."

He massaged his aching temples. "Who?"

She turned away. "You might want to comb your hair. And brush your teeth. Your breath smells awful."

So whoever it was had Glenda wound up pretty tight. Wyatt went into the other room and hastily pulled on a pair of ragged jeans. A look in the mirror made him nearly groan with despair. His blue eyes were watery and vague, rimmed and veined with red. His black hair, once thick and full even as it slowly became streaked with gray, was now thinning and lank. His skin looked like sandpaper, and he realized he hadn't shaved yesterday. He quickly washed his face, brushed the gummy film from his teeth, and used a brush to bring some semblance of order to his hair before pulling on a faded NC State T-shirt and heading downstairs. The scent of coffee wafted up to meet him as he descended, and he was suddenly awake. When he got to the kitchen door, however, what he saw made him stop short.

She was sitting at the kitchen island, both hands wrapped around one of his big ceramic mugs. She looked up as he came in and smiled. It was a smile he remembered well, even when he hadn't wanted to. "Hey, Wyatt," she said.

"Uh. Hum." He realized how ridiculous he must sound. "Hey, Kass." *You look good*, he wanted to say, but a glance over to where Glenda was putting something in the oven stopped him.

It was true, though. There were laugh lines around the blue eyes and the full lips he remembered all too well. There were also some streaks of gray in the blonde hair gathered back into the long braid he also remembered, but Kassidey Emmerich was still a striking woman. He realized she was speaking. "Sorry to get you up," she said. "I never knew you to sleep this late."

The stove door banged, making him jump. But when he looked over at Glenda, she had a smile of such perfect serenity on her face that anyone who didn't know her like Wyatt did would have thought she meant it. "Whoops," she said. "Biscuits'll be ready in two shakes. I can cook up some sausage and eggs to go in them, won't take a minute."

"Oh, that's fine," Kassidey said. "I don't eat meat."

"She doesn't eat meat," Wyatt said at the same time, then grimaced with embarrassment.

"Oh." The smile slipped a little. "I guess that's how you keep that figure." There was an uncomfortable silence until Glenda broke it. "Do you eat butter, then? You're not one of those, what do you call them…"

"Vegans," Kassidey said. "And no. Butter would be great. I hate to put you out like this."

"It's no trouble. At all." She looked at Wyatt. "Coffee's ready. I'll be back in a minute." As she walked past Wyatt and out of the kitchen, he could feel the tension in her. He sighed and went to pour himself a cup. He turned back to Kassidey. She grimaced.

"Well, *that* wasn't awkward. At all."

"This kind of is."

She nodded. "I know." She took a sip from her mug. "Your wife makes really good tea."

"What do you want, Kass?" The words came out more harshly than he intended.

She put the mug down. "I know Carl Welch came to see you yesterday. About Tyler and Mick."

He nodded. "Yeah. I told him there was nothing I could do."

"You sure about that?"

He noticed that his hands were trembling as they held the cup. He didn't know if it was anger or alcohol. "I'm not a law enforcement officer anymore."

"I know. But the ones who are supposed to be doing the job aren't any help. And," she hesitated, "it just got worse."

He brought the cup to his lips, willing his hands not to spill the hot liquid on him. It almost worked. A little of the hot coffee spilled down his chin. He set the cup down on the kitchen island. He didn't want to ask, but he couldn't help himself.

She spoke first. "Mick and Tyler just robbed a country store in Spencer. There's video. Tyler…Tyler had a gun in his hand."

CHAPTER EIGHT

"Oh no." Glenda was back, standing in the kitchen door. "Does Carl know?"

Kassidey nodded. "Henry told him." Her mouth tightened. "With his usual delicacy and tact."

"We need to call him, Wyatt," Glenda said. She looked at Kassidey. "How's he taking it?" Her earlier prickliness had been set aside.

"Well, you know Carl. Better than I do. He's putting all his energy into looking after Marian. She wasn't handling Tyler's disappearance well as it was. And this…" She shook her head. "After Henry came by, she took to her bed. She hasn't left it since."

Glenda looked incredulous. "Surely Henry doesn't think Tyler did this willingly?"

Before Kassidey answered, Wyatt broke in. "He can't discount it. Not without knowing more." He turned to Kassidey. "Tyler had a gun in his hand?"

"Wyatt!" Glenda's voice was outraged.

Kassidey reached over and fished in the bag that she'd slung on the back of her chair. She pulled out a cell phone that looked as big as a brick. "I have the video." She grimaced. "It was on the local news this morning."

"Oh, dear Lord," Glenda whispered. As Kassidey fiddled with the phone, Glenda went to the refrigerator. She opened it and looked inside, clicking her tongue thoughtfully, trying to absorb herself in the search for food.

Kassidey found what she was looking for and handed the phone to Wyatt. He took it as gingerly as if she was handing him a ticking bomb. "Press the play button," she said. When he still looked confused, she put her hand to her mouth to hide her smile. "On the screen. The one that looks like an arrowhead."

He did, watching the video in silence. Thanks to the cheap surveillance cameras, it was too small and jittery to tell much; he couldn't read expressions. It took him a moment to recognize Tyler, but there was no mistaking the shape of the gun in his hand. When the brief video was done, he set the phone down on the island. "I can't tell much from that."

"Except who it is," Kassidey said. "You know that's Tyler. And the dark-haired one?"

"Could be anyone."

"Could be. But we both know it's Mick Jakes."

Glenda closed the refrigerator door. "I need to go to the store," she said, "if I'm going to make something to take to Carl and Marian…" She stopped, looking back and forth between them.

Kassidey sighed. "We need to go ahead and get this out on the table, okay? Glenda, I'm not here to steal your husband."

Glenda's jaw tightened. "Well. You're very direct."

Kassidey smiled, a little sadly. "Yeah. I get that a lot."

"Then I'll be direct, too. You took him from his first wife."

"No," Wyatt spoke up.

Glenda turned to him. "So now you defend her?"

"No," Wyatt said. "I'm just telling you how it was. It's nothing I haven't told you before. I never hid anything from you. That marriage was dead before…before."

"Before Savannah Jakes," Glenda said. "And her boys. And that threw you together. And now that's happening again."

Wyatt looked over at Kassidey. She was nodding. "I understand," she said. She picked up her phone from the countertop, took the bag from behind the chair. "I shouldn't have come. I'm sorry." She looked at Wyatt and smiled. "Be well, Wyatt." She started to walk out. When she got to the door, she stopped. "There's one more thing."

"Of course there is," Glenda said.

"About two weeks ago," Kassidey said, "someone contacted Jessica at the Clerk of Court's office. Wanted to know about the adoption of Mick and Keith Jakes. They said they were with the federal government."

Wyatt frowned. "The feds? Which agency?"

"Jessica said he was, as she put it, 'real vague' about it. When she told him he'd need a court order, he got short with her. Tried to bully her. She was still upset when she talked to me. You know how Jessica hates conflict."

Wyatt nodded. Kassidey went on. "Give her credit, though. That quiet little girl can dig in her heels where confidentiality's concerned. So she called me. She was practically in tears until I told her Social Services would back her up. Then I called the county attorney. He said the same."

Wyatt picked up the coffee cup again and took a thoughtful sip. "Why are the feds interested in an adoption that happened…what, twelve years ago?"

"Thirteen," Kassidey said. "I know. It's a mystery." She smiled at Glenda. "Thank you very much for the tea. I'm sorry if I upset you." She walked out before either of them could respond.

"God," Glenda said in a tight voice after she heard the front door open and close, "she's so...so *reasonable*."

"Yeah," Wyatt said absently.

She glared at him. "You're thinking about looking into this, aren't you? You'll do it for her, but you wouldn't do it for Carl. Your friend."

"It's different now," he said.

"Right. It's a mystery."

He was preoccupied and didn't notice the edge in her tone. "Why are the feds snooping around? And what happened in Spencer? Why did Tyler Welch have a gun in his hand?" He tapped his fingers on the countertop for a few moments, then looked up and saw his wife's face. He slid off the barstool and came around the island, holding out his arms to her. She resisted for a moment, then settled against him, if a bit stiffly. As always, he liked the way they fit together, the top of her head nestled comfortably beneath his chin. "There's no one but you, Glenda," he murmured. "You're the only one for me."

Glenda was silent for a moment. Then she said in a low voice, "Do you think she's pretty?"

He weighed his answer for a moment. A facile denial would be worse than the truth. "Yeah," he said, "she's still pretty." As she began to stiffen in his arms, he finished with the rest of the truth. "But you? You're beautiful. You're always my girl."

She pulled away from him slightly, her eyes scanning his face for evidence of insincerity. Finding none, she settled back into his embrace. "I need to go to the store," she murmured. "I need some stuff to make a casserole to take to Carl and Marian. And you need a shower." She looked up, an impish look in her gray eyes. "I think the store can wait." He bent down to kiss her and she squirmed away. "The shower can't, though."

"Join me?"

She smiled. "I think that's a great idea."

CHAPTER NINE

The black Firebird rumbled down the dirt streets of the trailer park like a tank in enemy territory. Tyler stared out the window at the collection of ramshackle manufactured homes they passed: mostly single-wides, with one or two double-wides striving for respectability with wooden decks out front and concrete planters filled with struggling flowers. In one space, a rusting camper sagged on flat tires, a lantern flickering dimly within. The summer night had brought people out onto the decks and into the tiny yards, and the smell of charcoal smoke and grilling meat permeated the air. Music, a mix of heavy metal, country, and bouncy Mexican pop, blared from cheap speakers propped up behind tattered window screens.

In contrast to the carnival atmosphere of the rest of the park, the single-wide trailer Mick pulled up to was dark and silent. After he turned the engine off, he sat looking at the rusting metal walls. Tyler didn't know what to do. "So," he spoke up finally. "Is this home?"

"No," Mick said. "But it's where I stay." He got out of the car. Tyler didn't know what else to do but follow.

Inside, the trailer was dark until Mick turned on a lamp with a low-wattage bulb that couldn't disguise the shredded couch, duct-taped easy chair, and worn carpet. It also could do nothing to mask the smell of unwashed laundry and spoiled food. There was a tiny open-plan kitchen to the right, separated from the living space by a counter on which were piled empty beer cans and pizza boxes.

In their short time together, Tyler had learned to read some of Mick's body language; the tightening of his older brother's jaw and the narrowing of his eyes made him glance nervously at the gun tucked in his waistband.

"Lana," Mick called out, then louder, "*Lana!*"

There was a brief silence, then the sounds of movement and the dimly reflected illumination of a light coming on down a hallway Tyler could make out to his left. There was the shuffling sound of someone making their way slowly down the hallway, which filled Tyler with an irrational dread. The girl who eventually emerged, however, was so short and slight that Tyler almost burst out in laughter with embarrassment at himself.

She was barely five feet tall, with a short amateurish cut to her dirty blonde hair that made her look even more like a little girl. It was only when she drew closer that Tyler could see the lines in her face and the puffiness around the eyes that made her look worn and old. She clutched a ragged quilt around her shoulders that trailed to the carpet and made her look even smaller. "Hey, baby," she said in a hoarse whisper. "How was your trip?" She looked around blearily and noticed Tyler for what appeared to be the first time. "Oh. Hey." She looked back at Mick. "Is this the brother you told me about?"

Mick smiled back, seeming to relax a bit. "Yeah. This is Keith."

She walked over to him, stumbling a bit, over the enveloping blanket or her own feet, Tyler couldn't tell. He could tell she was high on something; her pale blue eyes were bloodshot and unfocused. She held out a hand. "Hey," she said again.

He took the hand, gave it a squeeze. "Hey."

She turned to Mick. "You didn't tell me he was so cute." The effect of the flirtatious words was spoiled by the lack of affect in her voice.

"Runs in the family." Mick took the gun out and laid it on the kitchen counter. Tyler glanced at it for a moment, but Mick's warning look quashed any thought he might have developed of trying for it.

Lana sniffled. "Did you bring my medicine?"

Mick shook his head. "Had to get some money first. I'll go over to Micah's and pick something up in a minute. We got anything to eat?"

Her face had turned sulky. "Look for yourself." She sank to the couch and wrapped the blanket around her, despite the warm and stuffy air inside the trailer.

Mick sighed and went to the fridge, snapping on the kitchen light as he did so. The fluorescent ceiling fixture had a slight but maddening flicker in it. Mick stared into the fridge for a moment, then slammed it. He glared at Lana.

"I didn't have no money for the store," she said, still pouting.

He snapped the flickering light off. "I left you some. What happened to it?"

She didn't answer, just looked away and looked sullenly at the floor. "Goddamn it," he said. "Micah's already been by here, ain't he?"

"I'm sick," she muttered. "I need my medicine. And you wasn't here."

Mick picked the gun up off the counter. Tyler thought for a moment that he might shoot the girl on the sofa, but Mick just stuck it back in his waistband.

"You goin' to Micah's?" Lana said. "No need. I'm okay. For now."

"Yeah," Mick said. "I'll be back in a little bit. Get dressed. And pack a bag. You're goin' with us."

She looked up, her eyes widening in alarm. "What? Where?"

"Just pack your shit. I'll be back." He looked at Tyler. "Come on, lil' bro. We gotta go see a man about a dog."

They met in a windowless conference room in one of the few actual skyscrapers in the New Orleans area. Winslow sat at one end of the table, Special Agent in Charge Salvatore Hammond sat at the other. His assistant, an officious little prick named Kimball, sat next to him. The SAC was never a patient man on the best of days, and this was not one of those. "So far, this wire we've got on Angus Charlebois's house has produced exactly jack squat on Wallace Luther's operation. Tell me in thirty words or less why I shouldn't pull the plug on it. And on your investigation."

Winslow was trying to will himself not to sweat and failing. "Charleyboy's a weak link. He's into Luther for forty grand, and the interest is mounting. Luther's sweating him for it. But he keeps telling his girlfriend he's got something big in the works. Something that'll get them out of debt."

Hammond spread his hands in a gesture of frustration. "What? Tell me what?"

"I don't know yet. But maybe if we get a tap on his cell..." The look on the SAC's face stopped him.

Hammond shook his head. Kimball mirrored the gesture. Winslow was reminded of why he'd never liked Kimball. *Fucking ass kisser*, he thought. "I'm not getting you a StingRay," Hammond said, "without more proof that this is actually going anywhere." He drummed his fingers on the table thoughtfully. "What about the girlfriend? Maybe she can turn him."

"Maybe," Winslow said. "I think I'm getting a pretty good rapport with her."

Hammond's grunt showed what he thought of Winslow's powers of persuasion. "You having any luck getting the info you said she wanted? About the sons she gave up?"

"Still trying. But the locals are stalling me. I've got someone working on it."

"How about the liaison? That female deputy from the sheriff's department?"

Winslow felt things slipping away from him. "She's only there as a courtesy. She's a mushroom. I keep her in the dark—"

"And feed her bullshit," the SAC interrupted, the cliché apparently irritating him even further. "But she's a woman. Maybe she can talk to the girlfriend. Get something more solid on what Charlebois is planning, or what's going on with Luther."

"Sir—"

"You've got a week, Winslow." Hammond stood up, followed by his silent assistant. Winslow stood as well as Hammond went on. "Get me something I can go on or I'm shutting this op down and putting you somewhere useful."

"Yes, sir."

CHAPTER
TEN

Mick strode purposefully down the darkened dirt street of the trailer park, so quickly that Tyler had to jog to catch up. "What's going on?" he asked. "Who is this Micah guy?"

"He's an asshole," Mick said in a low, furious voice, "and I told him to stay the fuck away from Lana."

"Mick, whatever you're thinking of doing with that gun…don't hurt him. Okay? Come on, we've got enough trouble."

Mick stopped and turned to look at him. He put a hand on Tyler's shoulder and looked him in the eye. "Don't worry, lil' bro," he said. "I'm not gonna hurt him. I'm just gonna teach him some respect. Okay?"

Tyler looked into that unwavering gaze, into eyes so much like his own. "You promise?"

"Cross my heart," Mick said, making the gesture. "I won't hurt him."

"Okay. But why do we even have to go, then?"

Mick sighed. "I gotta get Lana her medicine."

"You mean drugs."

Mick rolled his eyes. "No, I mean Snickers and a box of Good n' Plentys. Yeah, Keith. I mean druuuuugs." He stretched the word out with a spooky mocking quaver in his voice. "She's an addict. And part of the reason she's going with us is that if I leave her behind, fucking Micah will keep her doped to the fucking ears while he peddles her ass out of that trailer. We get her out of here, I can get her some help. But in the meantime, I can't have her going through withdrawal and puking all over my car."

Tyler shook his head like someone trying to wake up out of a bad dream that kept getting worse. He'd always avoided the stoners— "waste-oids" in the language of his clique of athletes. He'd smelled the odor of weed, or what he assumed was weed, coming from cars in the high school parking lot and at parties, but he'd never even seen the stuff. Now he was going with his long-lost older brother to make a deal for god knew what. Probably heroin. Mick was walking again, and Tyler had no choice but to fall into step.

The trailer they approached was a double-wide, much newer than Mick's. Still, the giant red Ford pickup that sat outside looked as if it might cost more. Mick climbed the short concrete steps and paused to move his pistol from the front of his waistband to the back. The door opened slightly and half a face peered out. It swung wider, revealing a tall, broad man with a wild shock of curly dark hair. He was dressed in sweatpants and no shirt, his huge belly drooping over the waistband. He had small, mean eyes sunk into the fat of his broad face. "'Sup," he said to Mick, his eyes darting back over his shoulder to take Tyler in. "Who's he?"

"My little brother," Mick said. "You been over to the house, Micah?"

Micah looked back at him. "Yeah. Lana called me. She needed some…" He looked back at Tyler.

"Yeah. I know," Mick said. "I need some, too."

Micah looked surprised. "No shit? I never knew you to do anything but some beers. And weed."

Mick shrugged. "Like I said, my little bro's in town. It's time to party."

"Yeah. Okay." Micah stepped back into the trailer. Mick followed. Tyler hesitated and looked around. He wanted to run but had no idea where he'd go. He walked up the steps.

Tyler was alone in the living room, which was much better furnished than Mick's place. A big-screen TV dominated one wall across from a big leather couch. It took Tyler a moment to make out what was on the screen, other than the word *Mute* in the corner. When he did, he gasped and turned away from the writhing bodies and skin glistening with fluids he didn't want to think about.

"Movie night," was all Mick said. He walked over to the couch and picked up the remote that lay on the coffee table in front of the couch. He pressed a button, and the air was filled with the sounds of grunts, moans, and whispers. He pressed the button again and the sounds got louder. He placed the remote back on the table.

"What are you doing?" Tyler had to raise his voice to be heard over the obscene soundtrack.

Micah re-entered the room carrying a plastic Ziploc bag full of multicolored pills. He glanced at the screen and frowned before turning back. "I got anything you need here, homes," he said, his own voice raised. "Got some oxy, some Opana, I got some Suboxone in the back if you're interested. Pick your poison."

Mick held out a hand. "Lemme see." When Micah held out the bag, Mick reached for it. He fumbled the handoff and the bag fell to the floor. Some of the pills spilled out. "Oh. Shit."

"Goddamn it," Micah grumbled. He bent over to pick it up, grunting with the effort. Mick swiftly reached into the back of his waistband and pulled out the pistol. Tyler opened his mouth to scream for his brother not to shoot, but Mick didn't fire. He raised the pistol over his head and brought the butt crashing down on the back of Micah's skull. Tyler stepped back so fast, he nearly lost his footing, the scream still stuck in his throat. Micah sank to his knees, then fell over flat on his face. Blood flowed from the gash hidden beneath the tangle of hair.

"What! What! What!" It was as if all Tyler's other words had fled.

"I told you, motherfucker," Mick whispered savagely to the man on the floor. "I fucking *told* you." He got on his knees and scooped up the bag. He picked up a few of the pills, avoiding the ones that were covered with the blood flowing across the floor. He looked up at Tyler. "Come on in the back bedroom," Mick said. "Help me find his cash." Tyler stood rooted to the spot. "Come on, Keith," Mick said. "We got to get goin'. We kinda just burned our boat here."

"That's *not* my *name*," Tyler said, the tears finally coming, streaming down his face.

Mick raised the gun, pointing at his brother's face. "I love you, lil' bro. But you got to do like I say. I'll look after you. Just like before. But you got," he bit the words off savagely, "to do. Like I *say*."

"Or what?" Tyler said. "You'll kill me? This is love to you? Mick, you're pointing a *gun* at me."

Mick stared for a moment, then swung the gun around to point it at Micah lying inert on the floor. "When he wakes up, all his shit and all his money's gonna be gone. He's gonna be looking for the *guys*," he leaned on the plural, "who took it. And if he isn't, the people behind him will. Unless..." He moved closer, drawing a bead on the unconscious fat man's bleeding skull.

"No," Tyler shouted. Mick's gun never wavered. "That's your plan, Mick? Get some drug dealers chasing us?"

"Like I said, lil' bro. Burning the boat."

"What?"

"Saw it on TV. One of those Spanish dudes who fucked over the

Incas or the Mayans or whoever. When he landed, he had his soldiers burn the boats. So they knew they weren't going back."

"Cortez," Tyler said. "And it was the Aztecs. In Mexico."

Mick grinned. "Now look at you, lil' bro. You and your education. And it turns out, that's where we're headed, once we find Mama."

"Where?"

"Mexico. Now help me get this shit up. And find the cash. We're gonna need it." He stepped over Micah's prone body and walked down the hallway toward the back bedrooms. Tyler looked at the door. It was the perfect time to run. But he was alone in a strange place, in a situation where bad people might very likely be coming to look for him soon. He followed Mick down the hallway.

CHAPTER ELEVEN

Wyatt lay awake, looking at the ceiling. Glenda lay beside him on her back, snoring softly. He reached over and put a gentle hand on her shoulder. Without awakening, she rolled to her side and the snoring stopped. Normally, this was where he'd roll over, wrap her in his arms, and drift off to sleep with her. But sleep continued to elude him, and he couldn't tell which of the many potential reasons was the right one.

For one thing, he was as sober at bedtime as he'd been in a while, which was not to say totally sober. He'd become used to passing out rather than falling asleep, and now he remembered why. Without the beer, he couldn't stop his mind from going to the places he didn't want it to go. *Savannah Jakes and her sons. Kassidey Emmerich. Morris Tyree.*

Today, after Kassidey left, he and Glenda had made love. It was the best it had been in months, the two of them rediscovering the things they'd learned about each other, the things that made them chuckle and gasp and groan with pleasure. It was a reaffirmation of the promise he'd made to her: *you're always my girl.*

Afterward, they lay in each other's arms for a long time before she'd kissed him, sat up, and stretched luxuriously. "I still need to go to the store," she'd said as she reached for her bra. "You need more beer?" It was a question asked out of habit, and he'd surprised both of them by saying no. But that hadn't stopped him from going downstairs after she'd left and quickly downing the last two left in the fridge. And none of it had stopped him from thinking about Kassidey.

They'd met the first time when he'd been called out to the scene of a Social Services investigation. Wyatt had showed up at a trailer park outside of town on a freezing evening in January to find a blonde woman in jeans and a sweatshirt seated on the crude wooden steps of a single-wide, writing on a clipboard. He got out of the patrol car, looked around, then strode over to the woman seated on the steps. "I'm Deputy McGee," he said in his best official voice. "What we got here?"

She looked up at him without speaking before she stood up. She was only a couple of inches shorter than him, and her bright blue eyes didn't show any sign of being impressed by his crisp uniform or brusque demeanor. "What we 'got,' Deputy," she said, "is two juveniles, ages five and two, abandoned by their mother. Or, more accurately, left with a friend, who herself has gone off to god knows where. Neighbor said the power was cut off a few days ago."

Wyatt looked at the trailer. "So the juveniles are alone in there?"

The woman nodded. "I checked the place out myself. They're on their own."

He scowled at her. "You went in there without any kind of backup? You know that's not the protocol."

"Yeah." She sighed. "I was worried by the report. The other on-call worker's not answering her phone. I took a chance."

"Well, don't take that chance any more. A pretty woman, going in a place like that…" He stopped, suddenly realizing what he'd just said. "It's not protocol," he finished lamely.

The corner of her mouth twitched slightly and she lowered her eyes in an attempt to mask her barely suppressed amusement. "Noted." When she raised her eyes again, though, they were serious. "So, when you go in there, there's what you might call a situation. Can I trust you not to freak out?"

"Maybe you should not talk in riddles and tell me what's going on in there so I won't."

She nodded. "Fair enough. The older kid, the five-year-old… he's very protective of his little brother. I get the feeling he's been the one left in charge way too often. And he's scared to death. When I suggested taking them somewhere else, someplace safer, with food and such, he got upset. He…he has a knife."

It took a moment to register. "A knife. A five-year-old kid is standing us off with a knife."

"Like I said, he's terrified. I want you to promise me you're not going to do anything…you know, extreme."

He stared at her, feeling is face heat up with anger. "Let me get this straight, Miss…"

"Emmerich," she told him. "Kassidey Emmerich."

"Miss Emmerich. You're seriously worried that I'm going to go in there and shoot a five-year-old?"

She rolled her eyes. "Well, when you put it like that, it does sound stupid."

"Yeah," he said. He mounted the stairs of the trailer and put a hand on the doorknob. He looked back at the social worker. "What are their names?"

"The older one is Mick. He says his brother's name is Keith."

"Really."

That quirk at the corner of her mouth, that sudden cutting away of the eyes again. "Yeah."

"So. Mama was a Rolling Stone?"

It was the first real laugh he'd heard from her, and he was hooked from the moment he heard it. "Yeah," she said. "I guess." She turned serious again. "I'll be coming in after you."

He weighed that for a minute. It was a statement of fact, not a proposal or a question. Finally, he nodded. "Way behind me. If the kid tries anything, you pull back."

"Oh, don't worry. I'm going to let you handle the five-year-old with the knife."

He was chuckling as he turned back to the door. "Mick?" he called out. "Mick, my name's Wyatt. I'm with Miss Emmerich from Social Services, okay? We're going to come in, but we just want to talk to you, okay?"

There was no answer.

"Mick? Come on, buddy, let me know you're okay."

At that moment, Wyatt became aware of a rapidly approaching squad car, blue and red flashers blazing away in a riot of color. The siren whooped once as the car rounded the corner and slid to a stop in the dirt driveway. The door burst open and a man in a deputy's uniform got out.

"Henry," Wyatt muttered. "Goddamn it."

CHAPTER TWELVE

Glenda stirred and muttered beside him. Wyatt realized that the vividness of the memory had made him speak out loud, not the exact words, but a grunt of irritation. He realized that, once again, the memories weren't going to let him sleep. He gave his wife a gentle kiss on the shoulder and slid out of bed as quietly as he could. He made his way down to the kitchen. He realized halfway down the steps that there was no more beer, and the longing he felt at the realization shocked him. *Jesus*, he thought. *I'm really turning into an alcoholic.* He popped some ice into a plastic stadium cup, poured himself a drink of water from the sink, and took it out on the back deck, overlooking the woods. He sat down and sipped, remembering that night.

Henry Caldwell had exited the patrol car, sliding his tactical baton into its belt loop. The blue and red flashers were still going. "Hey, Wyatt," he said. "What's the situation?"

Caldwell had joined the sheriff's department the year after Wyatt, and the two had never hit it off. Wyatt thought he was one of those men who'd gone into law enforcement for all the wrong reasons. He liked departmental politics, and he all too clearly liked the power his badge and gun gave him out on the street. He was a short man, already going to fat, with a perennially red face and a mustache that didn't look quite right on him.

"We got a couple of abandoned kids in the trailer," Wyatt said. "They're scared, and…" He trailed off. If he told Henry about the knife, the man was liable to do something stupid. "And those lights are liable to make things worse. Turn them off. Please."

Henry looked ready to argue, then he opened the door and leaned back in. In a moment, the lights went out.

"Trouble?" Kassidey said softly.

Wyatt wasn't about to get into discussion of another officer's shortcomings, however numerous or aggravating, with a civilian. "He's fine." He addressed Henry again. "I'm going to go in. Alone. Check for a back door and watch it in case one of them tries to do a runner." Henry didn't look happy, but he nodded and started to go around. *Shit*, Wyatt thought to himself. *I have to tell him if he's going back there alone.* "Henry," he called out softly. When the other officer turned around, Wyatt said, "One of them, the older one, has a knife. But he's five years old, okay? No need to escalate this."

Henry scowled. "I ain't puttin' myself in danger. And if someone's got a knife, he's a danger. Don't care how old he is."

"Jesus," Kassidey breathed behind him. "What an asshole."

Without looking back, Wyatt waved a hand at her to shush her. "Just don't shoot a five-year-old, Henry. The department doesn't need that kind of publicity."

That at least seemed to get through to him. He nodded, still looking unhappy, and disappeared around the side of the trailer.

Wyatt put his hand back on the door. "Mick?" he called again. "I'm coming in, buddy. Don't be scared. No one's going to hurt you or your brother." He slowly opened the door.

Inside, the layout of the trailer was familiar: entrance into the living room, a small kitchen/dining area to the left, hallways to the left and the right. The interior was dark except for a single candle lit and sitting on the coffee table in front of the couch. A boy was seated on the couch, a smaller boy lying beside him. The smaller boy was covered by a blanket. He seemed to be asleep. The boy who was awake had dark hair, and in the flickering light of the candle, Wyatt could see the whites of his eyes, wide and terrified. He was clutching a steak knife in one hand, the metal of the blade glinting in the dimness.

"Hey now," Wyatt said. "What's with the knife there, young man? No one here's come to hurt you."

The little boy's voice was thin and shaky. "You ain't takin' us. Me or my brother. We din't do nothin' wrong."

"I know you didn't, Mick. You're not in trouble. I promise. But you can't stay here. There's no food. And no lights. And no heat. Aren't you cold?" He blew out a long breath that steamed in the chill. "Look. I can see my breath. It's freezing in here."

"We're fine. Mama's comin'."

"When? How long has she been gone?"

The boy's lower lip began to tremble. "I don't know."

"Okay. Here's the deal. Let's go someplace where you can get warm and get some food in your belly. We'll try to find your mom, okay? But you need to put that knife down. You're scaring me."

The boy blinked in confusion. "I'm...scaring *you*?"

"People with knives scare me, Mick."

"But you got a gun."

"Doesn't matter. I'm still scared. How about you? You scared?"

Mick nodded, his eyes glistening with tears in the candlelight.

"So what say you put that down, we go get a burger...you like BK or Mickey D's?"

The knife was beginning to droop in the boy's hand. "McDonald's."

"Got it. And I'm in the mood for the large fries. Can I get you one?"

Mick nodded again. "And one for my brother."

"Of course." Keith, the younger boy, began to stir, as if he knew he was being discussed.

"So how about you put the knife on the table and let's go get some grub. I'm hungry just talking about it."

Mick didn't answer. He looked down over toward the back door. He was clearly considering making a run for it. If he did, and Henry saw him coming out of the back door with a knife…

Slowly, Mick turned back and put the knife on the table. Wyatt let out the breath he'd been holding. He walked over, picked up the knife, and placed it out of reach on a rusty and corroded TV stand with no TV on it. Kassidey entered as he was putting the knife down. She knelt by Mick and took his hand. "Hey," she said gently. "I'm Kassidey. I'm with Social Services. Do you guys have any stuff you need to bring with you?"

Mick nodded at a backpack that rested by the couch. Keith was sitting up, looking confused. Mick put a protective arm around him. "It's okay, lil' bro. We're gonna go get some food."

Keith nodded, never taking his eyes off his brother. "I'm hungry."

Kassidey picked up the backpack and looked inside. She shook her head and looked at Wyatt. "Not much here."

Mick pointed at Wyatt. "We're goin' with him."

"Well, no," Kassidey said, "we'll go in my car."

"*Him!*" Mick said more loudly. He looked as if whatever was holding him together was about to snap.

"It's okay," Wyatt said. "I'll take them. We'll even hit the drive-through on the way. My treat."

She considered for a moment, then smiled at him. "It's not protocol."

"I won't tell if you won't."

She nodded. "See you there?"

"See you there."

There was a bit of controversy about who was going to ride up front, resolved when Wyatt proposed Mick take the first leg of the journey, with a switch off after the burgers were obtained. Once the food was in the car, however, the deal was forgotten as both boys tore into the bags like a pair of starving wolves. Even Wyatt's fries were gone by the time they reached the Social Services building. Kassidey laughed when she met them at the door. "You too look like you've been painting one another with ketchup." She was joined by another worker, a large, middle-aged black woman with thick glasses and her hair drawn back in a bun. "Here, guys, go with Miss Treva here and get cleaned up." Sated with food and near exhaustion, the boys complied. That left Kassidey and Wyatt outside alone in a suddenly awkward silence. Finally, she spoke. "Thanks. You handled that well."

"You sound surprised."

She smiled. "Let's just say some of your colleagues are better than others when it comes to handling children in crisis."

He let that go. "What happens now?"

She sighed. "We find them a temporary foster placement while we try to run mom or dad down. I'm going to talk to the county attorney about filing a petition in the morning to take them into our custody."

"You going to keep them together? That seems pretty important to Mick."

"I know. But I've got to tell you, finding a home with two vacancies, on short notice? It's a longshot."

He grimaced. "Shit."

"That about sums it up, Deputy. So, what about you?"

"I go back, write up a report, talk to the magistrate, swear out the warrants for child abuse. I'm going to need whatever information you have on this Savannah…"

"Jakes," she said. "Can I e-mail it to you?"

"Um…" he said.

"You do have e-mail, right?"

"I think I have an account at the department. But I'm not sure."

She laughed. "Really? You know it's 2002, right?"

"Don't remind me."

"Okay. I'll call it in. What's your cell number?"

He had to fish the flip phone out of his pocket to check. She shook her head, barely containing her amusement. "Look," she said, "just call mine. I'll put your number in my phone, and you'll have mine. Okay?" She gave him the number, and he stumbled over it twice before he got it right. "It'll go to my voice mail. I'll get back to you with whatever information I can find on Savannah Jakes. And you're probably going to be a witness at the CPS hearing."

He nodded. "You'll probably be called by the DA if there's a hearing on the criminal charge."

"Looks like we're working together, then." The way she smiled when she said it made his stomach tighten.

"Yeah," He said. "Looking forward to it."

"Me too."

CHAPTER THIRTEEN

Wyatt drained the last of the water from the cup. This night was stirring up too many ghosts. Now those scared boys were young men, and they were in some kind of trouble. Some fed was sniffing around their past. And Kassidey…was still Kassidey. He needed to stay away from this whole thing. But he knew he wouldn't. He thought of the old and discredited saying Carl had used. *When you save someone's life*, he'd said, *you're responsible for them*. He didn't know if he'd saved either of the boys' lives, but he felt there was unfinished business there. And with Kass. But he wasn't going to think about that. He had a home. He had a wife who loved him waiting for him back in that bed. But for the first time in a long time, he had a reason to get out of that bed in the morning. He went back inside, put the cup in the rack to dry, and went to bed.

Back at the trailer, Mick threw himself onto the couch, fanning the wad of bills he'd located in one of Micah's dresser drawers. "Lookit this, lil' bro," he said. He sounded drunk, but Tyler hadn't seen him take any of the pills he'd carried off along with the money. "With this and the money you threw in, we're gonna have a smooth trip."

Tyler sank wearily into a cracked red leather easy chair. "To Mexico."

"Yeah. Mexico." Mick sat up straight, like he'd just gotten a shot of energy. "C'mere, I'll show you." He scooped a pile of magazines off the coffee table and pulled a black laptop computer from under the pile. The power cord to the computer was held onto the case by a web of duct tape. Mick patted the couch next to him. "Sit here."

Reluctantly, Tyler sat down. Mick opened the computer, which came to life with a soft groaning squeak that didn't bode well for the future of the device. The screen lit up and Mick pulled up the web browser. A few more keystrokes and the screen showed a beautiful emerald green ocean washing up onto a sandy beach. A low bluff rose behind the beach, surrounded by rustic-looking wooden homes amid lush vegetation. "It's called San Pancho," Mick said. "It's on the Pacific Coast. Lots of Americans live there, 'cause it's dirt cheap." He used the touchpad and keyboard to call up another photo, this time showing a low building made of what looked like pink stucco, with a deep porch and tables visible from the outside. "There's all kinds of bars and restaurants where we can find work if we need to. But mostly we can just hang out. Soak up the sun. Live like people oughta live." His voice turned wistful. "Live clean for a change."

Tyler shook his head. "And we're supposed to get there how?"

"What, you think they don't have roads in Mexico?" he pronounced it MEH-hee-co, with an exaggerated accent. "We drive, lil' bro. We drive. And we make a little detour along the way to pick up Mama."

"You don't even know where she is, Mick. Or if she even wants to see us."

"Oh, don't I?" He manipulated touchpad and keys again until he'd called up Facebook. He accessed a group called 'Birth Parents Seeking Children'. Post after post showed people of various ages looking into the camera—some hopefully, some anxiously, some holding up hand-lettered signs with the names and birth dates of their lost children. Almost all of the posts ended with some entreaty for help. Mick scrolled down and down until the faces and stories blurred. Finally, the screen came to rest on a black-and-white photograph that looked professionally done. The woman in the picture was seated in a large chair that looked like something from a Victorian library. She was dressed in a long flowing robe that fell in soft waves around her. There was an expression of defiance on her beautiful face, chin raised and thrust out, eyes pale and cool. A child was seated on her lap, looking up at her with a confused expression. She held the hand of an older boy who stood by the chair, who looked at the camera with an expression that was the twin of his mother's. The photo was staged and dramatic, like an album cover. Tyler felt a stir of recognition. "That's...us," he whispered.

"Yeah," Mick said. "And that's our mama." He scrolled down slightly so Tyler could read the wording of the post:

My children were taken from me unfairly by Social Services and a corrupt sheriff's department in 2004 in North Carolina. They were adopted out to different families without my knowledge or consent. I was then run out of North Carolina by those same people. I need my boys now more than ever. Mick, the oldest, would be 20 now, and my little Keith, the one on my lap, would have just turned 18. They need each other, and I need them. If you know where they are, please contact Savannah by direct message. I'm in the Arabi area of New Orleans. Thank you.

"See?" Mick's voice was choked with emotion. "She didn't leave us, Keith. We were taken. They tore us apart."

"That's not my name," Tyler whispered. He couldn't take his eyes off the photo. The woman in the picture stirred up emotions that confused him. She was a stranger, or he thought she was. But vague, half-remembered shreds of feelings he couldn't explain were stirring inside him.

Mick's voice was low, insistent. "That's the name she gave you, lil' bro. The name those people took from you."

Tyler closed his eyes and shook his head. "They're my parents. They were good to me. They love me."

"But they're not your blood, Keith. Not like me. Not like Mama. And she needs us. Are you going to turn your back on your mother? Your blood?"

Tyler stood up and backed away from where Mick sat on the couch. "Stop. Just leave me alone."

"Can't do it," Mick said. He began typing something on the keyboard of the laptop. "We're in this too deep, lil' bro. You owe her. And you owe me."

"You? How the hell do I owe you? You *kidnapped* me!"

"You think anyone's going to believe that? Now that you're on video with a gun in your hand? Face it, you got no one to turn to but me. And we only got one way to go. To find our mama. And then down to Mexico." Mick stood up. Tyler could see he had the gun in his hand again. "And we need to leave now. If that asshole Micah wakes up, he's gonna come looking for us. And he won't be alone."

Lana came out of the bedroom. She was carrying a ragged and frayed backpack that made her look like a schoolgirl. "Can't we wait till morning to go?" she complained. "I'm tired."

"You can sleep while I drive, baby girl." Mick sat down at the computer and began typing. Lana sank to the couch and watched him, chewing at her lower lip, her eyes uncertain. "Who's gonna look after this place till we get back? Who's gonna pay the rent?"

"We're burnin' that boat too, darlin'," Mick said, his face intent on the screen.

"What?"

Mick ignored the question. He stood up and clicked to turn the computer off. "That's it, then. We're on the road. Go on out and get in the car. I got one last thing to do." He picked up the gun. "You stay here, Keith." Lana sighed like a disgusted teenager being packed off to school, then trudged out the door. Mick stood up and walked to the kitchen.

"What are you doing?" Tyler asked.

Mick didn't answer. He opened the door of the stove and turned a knob. Then he reached down and did something Tyler couldn't see. When he straightened up, he walked over to the coffee table and plucked a candle from out of the clutter. He pulled out his lighter, lit the candle, and placed it on the floor.

"Mick…" Tyler said, but he stopped when Mick straightened up. "Now we can go."

Charleyboy was gone again. Savannah didn't know where. That was happening more and more lately, and it scared her. When he was there, he was as attentive and loving as ever, at least as attentive and loving as he was during the recovery period between violent incidents. But the disappearances were getting longer and longer and closer together. She didn't know if it had something to do with this mysterious "plan" she didn't know anything about, or if the plan involved ditching her. The thoughts and fears ran round and round in her head, making sleep impossible. Not that she could get much sleep anyway tonight, since a street party had apparently arisen a couple of doors away. It seemed like a happy group, at least for now, with the shouts and screams mostly good-natured. Savannah got up from the bed and rubbed her eyes. There was a time when sounds like that would pull her out into the street, ready for fun. But that wasn't the woman she was now. She sat down at the makeshift computer desk and woke up her aging computer. As was her habit, she opened Facebook first. The icon for the Messenger application let her know she had half a dozen private messages. She sighed. Like most women who put their actual faces up on their profile pages, she received dozens of messages a day, ranging through various degrees of creepiness all the way to outright obscenity. She opened the application. Marriage proposal from lonely Asian guy—delete. Offer to teach her to love anal sex—delete. Pitch from "really nice guy who's seeking a soulmate"—delete. And so on. She looked up at the bar running across the top of the screen and saw she had a new friend request. She got several of those a day, too, most of which she also deleted. This time, though, what she saw made her draw in her breath.

Mick Jakes.

She paused for a moment, feeling her heart thumping in her chest. It could be a trick. A troll. Some kind of sick joke. She had tried to keep hope at bay for so long, and now, here it was. But hope could deceive. If you failed to keep it away, it could tear out your heart. But…she clicked on the name.

The eyes that looked out at her from the picture that came up on the dim and faded screen of the old computer could not have belonged to anyone else. Savannah's eyes burned with tears. She put a hand to her mouth and stifled a sob. "My baby," she whispered. She clicked to accept the request with her hand shaking so badly she could barely move the mouse. There was a new message blinking in the corner of the screen. She clicked on it.

Mama. We're on our way to New Orleans. Will be in touch soon. Keith is with me.

She sat back, suddenly unable to breathe. It was him. It had to be him. It couldn't be a trick. God couldn't be that cruel. She leaned forward, hands shaking as she tried to type. After several attempts to compose something turned to gibberish, she decided to keep it simple.

Hurry. I love you both. She followed with the address. Her finger poised above the button for a moment, then she clicked send.

They'd left shortly before dawn, with Lana already curled up asleep in a nest of blankets in the backseat. Mick had left the door to the trailer open as they pulled away. "Mick," he'd said. "Why did you leave that candle burning? You could start a fire." Suddenly, he realized that was exactly the plan. "Burning the boats," he said softly.

Mick nodded, a tight, humorless grin on his face and a manic light in his eyes. "Now you're gettin' with the program, lil' bro."

"And the stove. You're trying to blow the place up." He shook his head. "Jesus, Mick, didn't you think about how someone could get hurt?"

"No one's going to get hurt. It's gonna be okay."

"You don't..." Tyler gave up. It was useless. He slumped down in the seat and watched the road appearing at the edge of the headlights and disappearing under the car, the thick trees flashing by on either side. Before he knew it, he'd fallen into an exhausted sleep.

CHAPTER FOURTEEN

Wyatt stood outside the glass doors of the new sheriff's department building and looked up. It was a slick, gleaming, two-story structure of white concrete and metal, so different from the leaky "historic" brick building where Wyatt had worked his tenure as sheriff. You could say what you liked about Henry, Wyatt thought, but the man could milk the county commissioners for money like nobody's business. He took a deep breath and went inside.

The reception area was bright and airy, with tall, tinted windows allowing the natural light in to illuminate the waiting area. *My god*, Wyatt thought, *is that a fern on the reception desk?* He shook his head and approached the counter. At least one thing hadn't changed. Freda Bufmeyer was still holding down the front, just as she'd done in the old building, although now she faced a pair of computer screens and a multi-line phone that flashed and beeped and rang with a polite chirring sound rather than the abrasive rapid-fire beeping of the old system. She clutched a headset in one hand, pressing the earpiece to her ear instead of trying to fit the band across her perfectly frosted and permed blonde hair. "Carter County Sheriff's Department," she said into the headset as Wyatt walked up to the desk, "How can I direct your call? Thanks, I'll buzz him." She reached out and touched the screen in front of her, softly, as if she was afraid she might break it. She pressed again, harder this time, then nodded and pulled the earpiece away.

Wyatt couldn't help but grin. "Look at you, all high tech."

She looked up and her plump, perfectly made-up face lit up in a bright smile. "Wyatt! Well, hey, shug!" She started to raise her ample frame from the swivel chair in which she sat, but was interrupted by the soft, insistent ring of the phone. She raised her index finger to tell him to wait and sat back down, headset held awkwardly against her ear. "Carter County Sheriff," she said mechanically. When she had routed the call, she stood back up. "Come back here, handsome. Let me hug you." He chuckled and obeyed. When they broke the hug, she sat back down, fanning herself theatrically as if overheated. He laughed out loud. It felt good to be back.

"So," Freda said, settling back into her chair, "what brings you here?"

"I wanted to talk to whoever took the report about the disappearance of Tyler Welch."

She didn't bother to check her computer. "Right now, no one."

"No one?"

She nodded. "I mean, there was a report, but the official line is he just left home. He's eighteen, and, well, you saw on the news what happened over in Spencer."

Another voice interrupted before he could answer. "Well, hey, Wyatt."

Henry was standing at the end of the desk. He'd put on even more weight in the past months, and his belly bulged against the white dress shirt he wore. His tie was knotted loosely below the top shirt button he clearly couldn't close. Wyatt pasted a smile on his face. "Hey, Henry."

There was an awkward pause as Henry looked at him with barely concealed hostility. "Can I talk to you in my office for a minute?" he said finally.

"Sure." Henry turned and walked away. Wyatt glanced at Freda, who rolled her eyes. "Asshole," she mouthed at him.

Henry's office was on the second floor, but they took the elevator. It was a short but tense and silent ride. Henry had a large corner office, with a huge plaque of the county seal hanging behind the massive oak desk where he settled his bulk. "So what's this about, Wyatt?"

Wyatt took one of the chairs in front of the desk. He noticed that it was set lower than Henry's, and one leg seemed a bit shorter than the other so that the chair was off balance. He'd read about that tactic in some magazine article and had always dismissed it as the kind of cheap trick a small and silly man would use. Nothing he was seeing so far was likely to change his mind. "Carl Welch stopped by the house. He was pretty upset."

"I imagine he is. But this is a matter for the sheriff's department."

"He said you told him there was nothing to be done."

Henry frowned. "I stand by that. There's no evidence Tyler Welch was taken. And the video from that armed robbery—"

"Shows a kid scared out of his wits. I've seen it."

Henry sighed. "Just stay out of this, Wyatt. Go home."

The tone made Wyatt want to yank him across the desk, but he kept his composure as he stood up. "One more question before I leave," he said. "You have any idea why a federal agent might be trying to find out about Tyler Welch and Mick Jakes's adoption records?"

Henry looked completely baffled. "What are you talking about?"

Wyatt figured the befuddlement was real; Henry wasn't that good an actor. "Never mind," he said. "Have a good day, Henry." Henry started to say something, but Wyatt was closing the door as he left and didn't hear it.

Back in the lobby, he passed Freda's desk on the way out. "Good to see you, Freda."

She waved him over. "I'll direct your call," she said into the headset, and touched the screen. She looked up. "I swear, I'm never gonna get used to this dang thing."

He smiled. "Looks like you've got it tamed."

She shook her head. "I want my old phone back."

"I remember you used to cuss that old system pretty bad."

"At least with that one, I could bang on it when I got mad. This thing, I'm always scared I'll break it." She looked around, checking to see who was in earshot. "So, how'd it go with Henry?"

"Not much help there."

She sighed. "Old No-Help Henry strikes again."

"That what you call him to his face?"

She raised an eyebrow. "With me three years from retirement? Do I look like a fool?"

"Never. I just wonder what you called me."

"Well, you just keep wonderin'." Her grin faded. "We miss you around here, Wyatt."

He felt a lump in his throat. "I miss you, too. All of you."

She leaned back slightly. "I bet if you were to run again…"

He put up a hand. "Put that out of your mind. And *you* help Henry. All of y'all. He's the boss now. You may not like the man, but the department needs you to back him up."

"I'll try." She looked around again. "So, I told you there was a report taken."

"Uh-huh." He leaned over the desk. "I don't suppose I could get a copy."

She started to answer, but was cut off by the ringing phone. As she picked up the headset, she nodded toward an envelope on the counter. "Carter County Sheriff's Department, how may I direct your call?"

Wyatt glanced at it. It was a plain white envelope, with *Wyatt* penciled on it in Freda's familiar sloppy hand. He smiled and picked it up.

"Uh-huh. Yes, ma'am." Freda was still on her call, but she winked at him as he left.

CHAPTER FIFTEEN

I t was almost dawn when Charleyboy slipped back into the house, but Savannah was still awake. Her thoughts had been racing around in her head since she'd gotten the message. She didn't know how to tell him. She didn't know if she should. She finally decided it would depend on his mood when he came in. And his sobriety, or lack of it.

She heard him in the bathroom, brushing his teeth. That was a good sign. When he was shitfaced, he didn't bother. She'd learned to read signs like that, the way a farmer learns to read oncoming weather.

He dropped his pants and shirt on the floor and slid under the covers. "Hey, baby," she said softly, and put her arms around him. He smelled of whiskey and cigarettes, but not too strongly.

"Hey," he mumbled in reply. "Sorry 'm so late. Business."

"It's okay." She stroked his hair, pulling him against her. He didn't seem too bad. She decided to go for it. "Charleyboy?"

"Mmmf?" He was almost asleep.

"I got some news tonight."

"S'good?"

"My sons. Keith and Mick. They...they sent me a message."

At first, she thought he hadn't heard, that he'd drifted off already. But it was just taking time to sink in. His eyes opened. "What?"

She took a deep breath. "I put a post on Facebook. In one of those groups for parents who were trying to find their kids. And... and tonight..." She was choking up again. "I got a response. From Mick. They're on their way."

He sat up. "On their way? Like on their way *here*?"

She was too emotional to do anything but nod.

He put his hands over his face and fell back on the bed. "Oh, Christ. Oh, goddamn it."

She sat up, pulling the sheet around her. "What? I thought you'd be happy for me." She felt her anger rising. "Charleyboy, this is something I been trying to do for *ten goddamn years*. Can't you be a little bit happy for me?"

He pulled his hands away from his face and sat back up. He leaned down and fumbled in the shirt crumpled by the bed until he came up with a cigarette and his lighter. "Give me one," she said. Without a word, he bent and came back up with another cigarette. He put them both in his mouth, lit them, and handed one to her. It was something he'd done on their first night together, and she'd thought at the time it was romantic, because she'd seen it in a movie one time. This morning, it took the edge off her rising anger. But only the edge.

They didn't speak until they'd both taken a few puffs. Then Charleyboy broke the silence. "It's just a bad time, baby. There's this thing going on with Mr. Luther. I can't see having kids around with that happening."

She took a long drag before answering. "Well, first off, they ain't kids anymore. Mick's twenty. Keith's eighteen. So it ain't like we're going to have to keep them in diapers and take 'em to Chuck E.

Cheese." He didn't laugh. She went on. "And what the hell is this big mysterious thing you got goin' on with Mr. Luther? If it's gonna affect both our lives this much, don't I have a right to know what it's about?"

"It's business."

"No shit, baby. And if it's your business, it's mine too, ain't it? I mean, you keep tellin' me how it's gonna get both of us out from under Mr. Luther's thumb, which I am one hundred goddamn percent for, by the way, but you act as nervous as a dog shittin' rope and fixin' to pass the hook."

That did get the laugh she was after. He always loved it when she "talked country," as he put it. The laugh died young. He leaned back against the wall, regarding her with grave eyes. "Okay," he said. "But this is something that has to stay strictly between us."

She thought of Winslow and the girl deputy. "Right. Like who am I gonna tell?"

"Yeah. Okay." He took a drag on the cigarette. "There's this guy. His name's Caspar Gutierrez. He wants in on Mr. Luther's territory."

She didn't like where this was going. "Go on."

"He's got a big shipment coming in. Tuesday. I found out where and I found out the time."

She grimaced. "Shipment. Does that mean what I think it means?"

"Yeah, baby. It means cocaine. Lots of it."

She wondered if the feds still had the house wired for sound. She assumed they did. She thought of trying to stop Charleyboy, but this was the type of thing they were after. The type of thing that might lead to them getting out of this. "Okay. So Mr. Luther's going after Gutierrez's shipment. And since you tipped him off, Mr. Luther's gonna call your debt even?"

Charleyboy shook his head. "I know him better than that. He's never going to let that go. Not as long as he can hold it over me." He put a hand on hers. "And you."

She frowned, confused. "So what…" Comprehension began to

dawn. "Oh, no. You're trying to set up some kind of double cross?"

He nodded. "Luther thinks he'll be waiting for Gutierrez. But Gutierrez'll be waiting for him."

She felt her heart breaking. This was his big plan? "Oh, Charleyboy. Oh, no."

"I know it's risky, baby. But if it works, we end up with Gutierrez in our debt, instead of us being in Luther's. We'll be free. Not only free, but rich. I can be Gutierrez's man on the ground here."

She wanted to scream at him. But he looked so hopeful, and the look on his face was a naked appeal to her for approval. She reached out and ran a hand through his hair. "It's crazy, baby." She forced a laugh. "But it's just crazy enough to work. Right?"

He nodded. "Right. But you see how it's a bad time for your boys to suddenly show up."

"I get that. I get it. But what can I tell them? They're already on the way. They're my *sons*, Charleyboy. My flesh and blood."

"Just tell them to wait a little bit, okay? You'll think of something."

Yes, she thought. *Yes, I will.* "Okay, baby. Now let's get some sleep, okay?"

He stubbed out his cigarette among the forest of butts in the bedside ashtray. "Yeah. I'm beat."

She kissed him softly. "Me, too, lover." She put her own cigarette out, guided him down to the bed with a hand on his chest, and snuggled against him. Exhaustion and drunkenness put him out like a light within minutes. She lay awake beside him until she was sure he was deeply asleep, then released him and rolled over, staring at the ceiling. *Did you get that, Winslow?* she asked silently.

CHAPTER SIXTEEN

He had. Winslow slowly took the headset off and rubbed a hand over his face. "Holy shit," he said out loud. The net he'd set for Wallace Luther had just pulled in a much bigger fish. *Caspar motherfucking Gutierrez.* A long-standing member of the Gulf Cartel, Gutierrez had been indicted *in absentia* by at least three states and four federal districts. Word was that his star was on the wane thanks to those indictments and thanks as well to the rise of some younger, more reckless *narcos*, but he was still one of the most feared men in Mexico. There'd been rumors he'd been trying to move in on New Orleans, maybe to establish a new base of operations there if he was being squeezed out of the *plazas* in Mexico. The *plazas* were established and recognized territories for the cross-border shipment of drugs and humans, hammered out by tough negotiation and sometimes brutal warfare. If Gutierrez was losing ground there, a move into New Orleans might be the kind of Hail Mary maneuver that would give him a new base of operations. And if he was actually going to set foot on American soil…well, nabbing him would be the kind of maneuver that would put Winslow's own career on a fast track. He put the headphones back on. All he could hear was soft snoring. Then he nearly jumped out of his skin as his phone rang. He glanced at the screen. The number showed the call was from the burner he'd given Savannah. He swore under his breath and answered. "This isn't safe."

"Don't worry," her voice was hoarse and weary, "he's out like a light. Did you hear?"

"Yeah," he said. "This is a big development."

Her voice sharpened. "Yeah. And did you also hear about my boys?"

He kept his own voice neutral. "I did."

"So they're in the mix now. Whatever kind of protection you're gonna give me and Charleyboy, Mick and Keith get it too. Or there's no deal."

"I don't know if I can—"

"Make it happen, Winslow. Or you don't hear another word out of me."

For a brief, reckless moment, he considered bursting her bubble and letting her know exactly how weak her position was. He already had enough to at least take Charleyboy in on a conspiracy charge and sweat him until he cracked. It would be even easier to break him down if he put Savannah in a nearby cell and let him know how close she was from going into general population with the real hard cases. But that wouldn't make bringing Wallace Luther or Caspar Gutierrez in a sure thing, and if there was one thing a U.S. Attorney demanded of an agent, it was a sure thing, a slam-dunk not even the most incompetent attorney could lose. Nothing was more embarrassing to a political appointee than parading a declared kingpin in front of the video cameras, only to have them walk down the courthouse steps as a free man a few months later. "I can make it happen," he said. "I've got to take this upstairs. But I can make it happen."

"I ain't convinced."

Winslow tried to think of what he could do to string her along. He thought of the SAC's words. *The girl deputy. Maybe she can talk to the girlfriend.* "Look, let's meet. I've got someone I want to introduce you to."

There was a short silence. "I'll call you," she said. "We'll set it up later. Right now, I need to get some sleep."

"I hear you," he said. "You've done some good work, Savannah. We're not going to forget it. We're going to take care of you." He didn't know if she'd heard his last words before he hung up. He looked at his watch. He'd been up all night, and the numbers on the cheap Seiko swam before his eyes for a moment: *6:30 a.m.* He tried to will the fatigue away. His relief should be showing up any minute. And once he did, Winslow was going to have to move fast. He decided it was too early to call his boss, but there was someone he didn't mind rousting out of bed. He dialed Chance's number.

Chance had just gotten out of the shower, sluicing off the sweat she'd worked out from a morning run with Jonas and the bug spray that made the run possible. "Who the hell…" she muttered as she picked the buzzing phone up off the bedside table, then grimaced as she saw the name on the screen. She let it ring for a moment as she wrapped herself in a towel. It may not have been logical, but there was no way she was talking with Winslow naked. "Yeah?" she said when she answered, hoping the irritation came through.

"Hey," Winslow said, "did I get you up?"

"No," she said, thinking maybe if he hadn't gotten the point the first time that one-word answers, sharply delivered, would do the trick.

"There's been a development."

She rummaged through her closet, looking for a pair of slacks. Days like this, she wished she was back in uniform. It certainly cut down on the number of clothing decisions she had to make. "What?"

"We need to meet. I can't tell you over the phone."

She wedged the phone between her shoulder and ear while she sat down to pull on her underwear and a pair of black pants. "I'm supposed to check in back at the department before I go back out with you. I'm supposed to debrief at nine o'clock, and I'm already running late."

"Cancel it."

"Winslow, this may seem strange to you, but I'm still a deputy of St. Bernard Parish. I don't work for you."

"I'll clear it with your boss. We need you to take a bigger role."

That stopped her. "Bigger how?"

"We'll go over that when we talk. I'm buying breakfast."

"Okay. Elizabeth's?" She named one of her favorite spots in the Bywater area of New Orleans.

"Where's that? Is it expensive?"

She gave him the address. "And nothing that'll break the bank."

"Okay, then," he said.

"You going to call and square it with my sergeant?"

"As soon as I get off the phone."

"See you there." She looked at the phone as he broke the connection. A bigger role? What could that mean? And why was Winslow being so secretive? Surely he didn't think her phone, or his, were being tapped? She looked at Jonas, who lay at her feet, panting happily after his run. "What's going on, boy?" The dog responded by rolling onto his back, offering his belly for scratches. She laughed. "Now there's a fellow with his priorities straight." She rubbed his tummy for a moment, causing the dog to wriggle with pleasure and wag his tail madly, before she stood up and finished dressing. She thought of calling her dad, but put aside the idea.

Winslow was obviously in a hurry, and her stomach was growling as she contemplated an Elizabeth's shrimp and tasso omelet. Having the DEA pay for it would make it taste even better.

CHAPTER SEVENTEEN

Wyatt sat in his truck and opened the envelope. The report was brief and not particularly helpful. Carl Welch had come to the sheriff's department reporting that his son, Tyler, had disappeared. The detective on duty, a guy named Lake who Wyatt remembered from his days as a road deputy, had taken down the information, but noted that the boy was eighteen years of age and that he'd taken the money he'd earned from his part-time job. "No evidence of violence or force used," Lake had written. "Subject appears to have left home." Which was a perfectly reasonable thing to have concluded, Wyatt had to admit. Unless the person making the conclusion had known Tyler Welch.

He'd followed the boy's progress since the DSS case had ended in Savannah Jakes permanently losing all parental rights to her sons, Mick and Keith, leading to their availability for adoption. It had been a two-day, contentious court hearing, with Savannah taking the stand near the end and tearfully insisting that she'd do anything, *anything* it took to be a mother to her two boys. Anything, the county attorney representing Social Services had pointed out, except turn in clean drug screens, complete her drug and alcohol rehabilitation courses, and stop living with men whose houses were raided on a regular basis by the county drug squad, as testified to by the sheriff himself, the Honorable Wyatt Cortland McGee. It had taken the judge less than a minute after the close of all the evidence and the closing argument of Savannah's well-meaning but hapless court-appointed attorney to declare that not only did sufficient legal grounds exist to terminate the parental rights of Savannah Jakes and, *in absentia*, the father or fathers she refused to identify, but also that it was in the boys' best interest that they be freed up for adoption. Preferably, the judge said while looking over his wire-rimmed glasses directly at Savannah, by people who cared more about their child's welfare than they did about their next party. That had set the young woman off. She'd raised her head from where she'd been weeping onto the counsel table, shoved her lawyer out of his chair, and charged the bench, long red hair flying and fists clenched. Wyatt had stepped into her way and almost been bowled over before he and an elderly bailiff had managed to subdue her as she kicked and spat curses. When another pair of deputies showed up to cart her off to jail, Kassidey had come over to where he sat on one of the courtroom chairs. "That's a pretty nasty scratch," she said.

He was wiping the blood from his arm with his handkerchief. "Yeah."

She'd leaned over to whisper to him. "Let me take you home and patch you up."

They'd been seeing one another since two weeks after the incident where they'd picked the boys up. They thought their affair was under the radar, but Wyatt was to find out within a month of the hearing, on the day he was served with divorce papers, that it was the least well-kept secret in the county. At the time, though, the thrill of what Wyatt thought was secrecy made their meetings all the sweeter.

Wyatt shook his head and tried to put that history out of his mind.

Savannah had spent thirty days in jail for contempt and had dropped off the radar as soon as she got out. Mick, the older boy, had been hard to place. He was a wild one, prone to sudden outbursts of physical violence that disrupted every home and several facilities where he'd been placed. Wyatt had eventually lost track of the various placements. Keith, however, was quickly adopted by his foster parents, Carl and Marian Welch, who renamed him Tyler, all record of his prior name and history blotted from public records. He'd grown up to be a straight-A student, a talented athlete, and a dutiful churchgoer. Every time Carl or Marian had run into Wyatt in town or at some social function, they were overflowing with the news about their boy and with gratitude toward Wyatt, who they credited in large part with making his good life possible. It seemed improbable that polite, well-behaved Tyler Welch would just up and leave like that, without so much as a goodbye to his doting parents. It seemed even less likely that he'd be involved in a robbery like the one up in Spencer. Unless, he thought, he'd been more like his mother and brother than anyone suspected.

Wyatt frowned. Had Tyler really gone willingly with his brother? Wyatt had seen the gun in his hand, but did that necessarily mean that Tyler wasn't under duress? He needed to talk to whoever was investigating the robbery up in Spencer. He knew the sheriff there, but not well. It wasn't a sure thing that anyone there would talk to a retired lawman, especially one who'd left under the cloud he had. *What the hell*, Wyatt thought. *The least they can do is tell me no.* First, however, he needed to fill in the gaps in his knowledge about where Mick had gone. He started the truck.

Tyler sat up, blinking in confusion. It was daylight. Out the window of the car, green fields rolled by on either side. His neck was sore from the awkward position he'd slept in. He looked over at the other seat. Mick had his eyes locked on the road, staring straight ahead, his hands clenched tight on the steering wheel. As Tyler watched, his head began to droop forward, his eyes slowly closing.

"Mick," Tyler said.

Mick's head snapped up, his eyes widening.

"You need sleep," Tyler said. "You've been up, what, a day and a half now?"

"Two." Mick's voice was low and raspy with exhaustion. "But I'm okay."

"Bullshit. You're not okay! I just saw you nearly nod off. You're going to get us all killed!"

Lana spoke up from the back seat, her voice slurred and sulky. "What's going on? Where are we?"

"South Carolina, baby girl," Mick said. "You hungry?"

"I guess."

"I got sandwiches. Pass Keith up his. It's got his name written on it."

"Seriously, Mick," Tyler said. "You've got to pull over and get some sleep."

"I'm fine. I took a little something from Micah's stash. Just waitin' for it to kick in."

"Great." Tyler sighed and looked out the window again, nervously chewing at his lower lip. Lana passed a package wrapped in white paper up between the seats. Tyler hesitated, especially when he saw the name *Keith* scrawled in a ragged, childish hand, but his stomach was beginning to growl. He took the sandwich and unwrapped it. It was a sub, made with various cold cuts. In a moment, Lana also passed up a bottle of water, also tagged with the name *Keith*. He wanted the water more than the sandwich, but he quickly downed both. When he was done, he started again. "Look, Mick. I know you're afraid I'll run off if you stop and get some sleep. But I promise. I won't."

Mick smiled tightly. "I know you won't. I took care of it."

"What are you talking about?"

"You'll see. Soon."

Tyler stared at him. "Mick. What did you do?" Mick didn't answer. Tyler sat back in his seat, his panic rising.

"Put on some music," Lana demanded.

Mick reached over and turned on the radio. It scanned through the stations, finding only commercials and preachers at first before Mick finally stopped it on a staticky classic rock station out of Atlanta. They passed the next few minutes to the sounds of REO Speedwagon and Foreigner. Tyler began to feel dizzy, then a heavy lethargy began to creep up on him. The music on the radio began to take on an odd echo, as if he were hearing it inside an empty airplane hangar. He looked over at Mick, who seemed suddenly blurred and fuzzy. "You…" He couldn't seem to form the next word. "You," he said again. Then the world slowly faded to gray, then black.

He looked over to where Keith slumped in the seat again. He'd hated to use the roofies he'd found among Micah's stash, but Keith had been right. He needed sleep, and he didn't have any faith at all in Keith's promise not to run off. That would ruin everything. Everything he'd dreamed of. Everything he was risking so much for. That didn't even deserve thinking about. Never had failure been less of an option.

He rubbed his eyes. Now to find a cheap motel and lay up for a few hours before the drugs wore off.

"Lana, baby?" he said to the backseat.

She leaned over the back. "Yeah?"

"Did you get some rest? Because I need you to do something for me."

A green interstate sign promised LODGING. Exit 34A. He took the exit.

"I'm gonna stop for a little bit at this motel here. I need you to watch my brother while I get some shut-eye. If he starts to wake up, you wake me up, okay?"

He looked in the mirror and saw her nodding. "Can I have some of my medicine? My back's hurtin'."

"When we get inside, yeah. But only a little, okay? I need you to stay awake."

"Okay, baby. I promise."

He spotted the faded sign, peeling wood placards beneath the turned-off neon MOTEL logo promising air-conditioned rooms and free TV. He pulled in.

CHAPTER EIGHTEEN

Wyatt arrived at the Department of Social Services building a little after 11:00 a.m. The outer waiting room was filled with people, mostly women. Some were alone, sitting and staring into space, lost in their own thoughts while waiting for their names to be called. Others had brought families, and it was those groups that provided most of the din in the brightly lit waiting area. Children darted here and there, pursued by snapped orders or mothers scrambling to catch up. Wyatt navigated his way to the sliding glass window at the front of the room. The receptionist was skinny and snaggle-toothed, with reading glasses on a chain around her neck. "Name?" she said without looking away from her computer.

"Wyatt McGee," he said. "I'm here to see Kassidey Emmerich."

She still wouldn't look at him. "D'you have an appointment?"

Wyatt was beginning to think aggravation was going to become his permanent state. "No. Please just let her know I'm here. It'll only be a minute."

Only then did the woman turn and look at him, a look of exasperation more eloquent than words. "You don't have an appointment?"

He was holding on to his temper with both hands and it was slipping from his grasp. "No, ma'am. Just please let her know I'm here."

She let out a sigh so heavy Wyatt could imagine the floor sagging under the sheer weight of it. "Can I tell her what this is in reference to?"

Out of habit, Wyatt reached for the pocket where he kept his badge and county ID in its leather wallet before remembering he didn't have it anymore. "She'll know, ma'am."

The woman looked at him blankly. "She'll know."

"Yes, ma'am."

She continued to stare long enough to make clear how hard it was for her to believe that anyone could impose on anyone this much. Wyatt stared back. Finally, the woman sighed again, picked up her phone, and muttered, "Have a seat. I'll see what I can do."

"Thank you." Wyatt walked over and took one of the plastic chairs that were bolted in rows to the Formica floor. He shook his head. While he was sheriff, people recognized him, deferred to him, fell all over themselves to accommodate him. Now, he was just another face. He began to look at the people around him in a new light. This was the kind of petty, obstructive bullshit they probably had to put up with every day.

After a few minutes, the door to the waiting room opened and Kassidey motioned him toward the back. Wyatt tried to ignore the resentful stares of the people still waiting their turns. She led him back to an office that, judging from its size, might have once been a janitor's closet. The desk was piled high with files. "Nice place," Wyatt said without irony. "A step up from the cubicle, at least."

She dropped the file she'd been carrying on her desk and sat down. "Perks of being a supervisor."

"Congratulations."

"Thanks," she said. "So, what's up?"

"I'm just trying to fill in some things I don't remember. Like where Mick Jakes went after Savannah's rights got terminated."

She looked surprised. "So you're really looking into it?"

"I guess I am."

She smiled. It was a smile he remembered all too well. Then it was gone, replaced by an appraising look and a slight tilt of her head. "And how does your wife feel about all this?"

"She's okay." He laughed, and it sounded insincere even to him. "She's just glad to get me out of the house."

"Uh-huh." She didn't sound convinced. She picked up a file from the stack. The manila folder was yellowing and frayed at the edges. "I had to look it up myself, actually." She opened it up and paged through it. "We've been trying to digitize all this stuff," she muttered, "but it's been kind of a nightmare." She found the page she was looking for. She read it and grimaced. "Worse than I remember. Mick went through eighteen placements in the thirteen years we had him."

Wyatt shook his head. "Eighteen."

"Yeah." She sighed. "It's hard to place a kid, even a young one, with the kind of problems Mick had. He'd be doing fine for a while, then he'd go off the rails. The first year, when we could keep the boys together, was the most stable. But when we had to split them up, he lost it. He started stealing, fighting other kids, running away. And then, of course, he discovered drugs and alcohol in junior high."

"Like mother, like son," Wyatt murmured.

"I guess. But that had him bouncing back and forth between detention, foster care, and inpatient treatment. He'd been through detox and rehab twice by the time he graduated high school." She put the paper down, a look of pain on her face. "Some of the foster placements were...not ideal."

"What does that mean?"

She didn't look at him. "One foster home lost its license when we found Mick and another foster child locked in a coat closet. Together. The foster parent did it because he said he couldn't control, and I quote, 'those little bastards' any other way. Mick was thirteen. The other kid was fifteen and…" she took a deep breath, "…awaiting trial as an adult for sexually abusing his seven-year-old sister."

Wyatt felt cold twisting in his gut. "Was Mick…" He trailed off.

"We don't know," Kassidey said. "Mick never would say. And, of course, neither would the other kid."

Wyatt's shock was turning to anger. "And who the hell had the bright idea to put those two in the same house?"

She looked at him for the first time since opening the file. "Me." When she saw the look on his face, she flushed. "You don't know what it was like, Wyatt. We didn't have a whole lot of options with Mick."

"Okay, okay." He took a deep breath to calm himself. "So I guess what I need to know is, where was the last place that the agency knew he was?"

She opened the file again. "The two years before he turned eighteen and aged out were relatively stable, if you don't count the thirty days he spent in jail on his first adult charge after he turned sixteen."

"Wait, how did a sixteen-year-old get active time on his first charge?" North Carolina was only one of two states that began trying defendants as adults at age sixteen, but juvenile records were supposed to be sealed, and what was technically a first offense should have resulted in probation, not jail time.

She checked the file again. "Got thirty days suspended on a carrying a concealed weapon charge, then told his probation officer to 'suck his dick' at the intake interview."

"That'll do it."

She nodded. "But going to adult jail seems to have been some kind of wake-up call. When he came out, we started him on an independent living plan, to get him ready to live on his own. He didn't get in any trouble after that, at least nothing he got picked up for. The foster parents we found for him that last time seemed to be a good fit. Or at least if Mick gave them problems, they didn't let us know."

"Can you give me a name?"

She chewed her lip and looked at him uncertainly.

"Look," he said, "I know it's against the rules. But you asked me to look into it. And if this family is someone Mick might have been in contact with, they may have some idea where he went."

She nodded. "I know. I did ask you. But I didn't really think you'd do it."

He laughed. "Me either."

"I don't know. I'll have to call and ask. I think only one of them's still alive, though."

"The husband or the wife?"

"I guess you'd have to ask him."

"What?"

"It was two men. A gay couple."

He frowned. "You put a messed up teenage boy with a couple of—"

She cut him off. "You're showing your age, Wyatt. These two men were some of our best foster parents. They'd take the kids no one else wanted. And there was never a whisper of anything inappropriate. And you know what? I'm getting a little tired of you judging my decisions when you—"

He held up his hands, taken aback by her sudden anger. "Okay. Okay. I didn't mean anything by it."

She'd risen partway from her chair as her voice rose. Now she sank back into it, rubbing her eyes tiredly. "Yeah. You did. But let's not have that argument right now. I've already said too much." She looked up at the clock, then back at him. "You free for lunch?"

He was. And he wanted to have it with her. But something inside told him it would be a bad idea. "No," he lied. "Sorry. Got an appointment with the sheriff up in Spencer."

She smiled sadly. He remembered that she always used to say what a terrible liar he was. His first wife had said the same thing, but with more heat. "Okay. Some other time, then."

"Yeah. Some other time."

He walked out past the noisy chaos in the lobby to his truck. He sat in the front seat for a while, contemplating his next move. Appointment or no, he could drive on up to Spencer, talk to the investigators up there. Or he could talk to the surviving foster parent who'd been with Mick before he'd dropped off the radar. The mention of lunch, however, reminded him that he was hungry. And thirsty. He knew just the place.

Val's was a classic roadhouse, dirt parking lot, neon beer signs and all. But they served the best burger in the county, and it was, after all, on the way to Spencer, along what everyone called "the old highway." Wyatt slid into a booth. Val herself, all three hundred pounds of her, came over to the table. "Well, hey, stranger," she said as she put a menu down. "Long time, no see. You by yourself?"

Wyatt remembered with a jolt that this was one of the places he and Kassidey had come when they were seeing one another. They'd held hands across this same booth. "Uh, yeah," he said. "I don't really need a menu."

Val grinned. "Double ValBurger, American cheese, hold the pickles, fries, shot of Jack, PBR chaser."

Wyatt looked around. It was barely noon, but the day drinkers were already beginning to congregate at the rickety bar along one wall. He started to amend his usual order to cut out the alcohol, but all that came out of his mouth was, "Yeah, that'd be good."

CHAPTER NINETEEN

Winslow was pacing back and forth on the concrete walk in front of the restaurant, glancing uncomfortably from time to time at a group of black patrons who stood chatting a few feet away. He was dressed in a brown leather jacket, t-shirt, and jeans that looked as unnatural on him as a clown outfit. Chance hurried across the street from the parking lot in the shadow of the Mississippi River levee. "Hey," she said. "Waiting long?"

"This place looks like a dump," Winslow said in a low voice. Not low enough, it seemed: a couple of members of the nearby group looked over at him and frowned.

"Seriously, Winslow," Chance whispered. "Try not to act like a goddamn tourist." She led him inside, where a skinny white hostess with a purple streak in her hair and colorful tattoos snaking up both arms led them upstairs and seated them at a table. Brightly colored artwork covered the walls and the tables were covered with equally cheerful tablecloths. "So," she said, opening a menu, "what's going on?"

He opened his own menu, still glancing around. The place was noisy enough to provide privacy, but he still acted jumpy. Finally, he took the plunge. "Last night, Charleyboy told Savannah what he's been up to." He started to go on, but was interrupted by the arrival of the waitress. Once they'd ordered coffee and the waitress had bustled away, Winslow filled Chance in on what he'd heard.

"Wow," Chance said. "That's…pretty major. And a little above my pay grade. I think we need to get my people in on this."

Winslow shook his head. "I don't think any of this is going down in St. Bernard Parish. It's south of the city. Down in," he hesitated, trying to remember the local geography, "Terrebonne."

"So we need to let those guys know."

"No," he said. "We need to keep this on a need-to-know basis. We don't know if Luther's got people in law enforcement down that way."

Chance was liking this less and less. The coffee arrived and they placed their orders, Chance going for the omelet she'd been looking forward to, Winslow hesitating before picking the "Basic Breakfast" designated on the menu. Chance sipped her coffee, trying to think of the best way to say what she needed to say. "I'm not so sure I like keeping my fellow cops in the dark on this."

Winslow took a sip from his own cup, his face carefully expressionless. "Suit yourself, *Deputy* Cahill." He leaned hard on the word "Deputy," making it seem like something trivial and pointless. "But an operation like this could be a major opportunity for you."

She tried to compose her own features into the same bland mask. She didn't know if she was succeeding. "What exactly does that mean?"

"I think you know." He sipped his coffee. "I don't know, maybe when this is over, you want to go back to being a road deputy, busting drunk drivers and breaking up the same domestic disturbance between the same peckerwood dipshits every Saturday." He put the cup down. "Or maybe you want to go after the major bad guys. The guys like Luther and Gutierrez who fuck up the lives of thousands, maybe hundreds of thousands, without thinking for a second about the damage they cause." He slid out of the booth. "Think about it. I need to take a leak."

As he walked away, Chance stared down at her coffee cup. She knew Winslow was trying to play her. She knew he was pushing her buttons, playing to the desire that had caused her to put on the uniform in the first place. The desire to help people. To make their lives better. Freer from fear.

The thing was, it was working.

The waitress arrived again, bearing plates. As she slid Chance's omelet in front of her, she leaned in. "Are you okay, sweetie?"

Chance blinked at her. "I'm sorry?"

The waitress indicated the direction Winslow had gone with a quick motion of her head. "That guy you're with. I'm getting a bad vibe from him. You need to get out of here?"

Chance stared at her for a moment, then stifled a laugh. "No. No, thanks. It's fine."

The waitress looked dubious. "You sure? If he's makin' you, you know…do things you ain't comfortable about, we can get you straight out of here, by the back door. We've done it before." She looked around. Chance noticed the hostess, standing by the stairs. She gave Chance a knowing nod. The waitress spoke up again. "Thing is, honey…I think he's a cop."

Chance did laugh then. "Thing is, honey, *I'm* a cop."

This time it was the waitress's turn to look confused. "Say what?"

"We both are. But…"

The waitress straightened up, her face hardening as she saw the amusement in Chance's face. "Okay. Sorry."

"No. No," Chance said quickly. "Really, thank you." She looked at the hostess, flashed her a quick thumbs-up. "You guys keep looking out for people, okay? It's important." The waitress nodded stiffly and bustled off.

Winslow was returning to the table. He saw the look on Chance's face. "What?"

She choked back the laughter that threatened to bubble up. "Nothing." She composed herself and picked up her fork. "So what is it that we're talking about here?"

He looked suspicious, but went on. "I want you to talk to Savannah. Become the main contact with her."

Chance frowned. "Me? I don't have any experience in…" She put down her fork, her frown deepening. "Wait a minute. Is this because I'm a woman?"

"Well, yeah." He took a bite of his own food. "Hey, this is really good." He stopped when he saw the expression on her face. "What?"

She shook her head. "Wow. Okay."

He looked puzzled. "I mean…we just thought a new approach might—"

"We?"

"Well, of course, I ran it by the agent in charge."

"Of course." She shook her head and went back to her meal.

"Is there something wrong?"

She remembered the waitress's words. *If he's makin' you do things you ain't comfortable about, we can get you straight out of here.* She wished it were that simple. "No. Nothing's wrong."

He apparently took her at her word and returned to his meal. "Anyway," he said after another couple of bites, "we'd like to set up a meeting with Savannah. With you there."

"To do what, exactly? Convince her to keep playing ball? Even if you can't arrange protection for her boys?"

"We just need to get her settled down. Everything's kind of in a state of flux right now."

"Are the boys getting protection or not?"

He shook his head. "We're working on it. But I've got to tell you, it's kind of a longshot. The older one, Mick…he could be a problem. He's a loose cannon, from what I hear."

"So by 'get her settled down,' you mean you want me to lie to her." Chance put her fork down, her omelet half finished. The fact that Winslow was ruining a meal she'd looked forward to was making her even angrier.

Winslow put his own fork down and looked at her steadily. "She's an informant, Cahill. Informants are to be run. To be managed. And you know why that is? I really shouldn't have to tell you. It's because they're on the other side." He picked up his fork again. "Maybe you've lost sight of who the good guys are."

"Yeah. Maybe I have." More than anything at this moment, she wanted her father's advice. "Let me get back to you."

"No." The blunt finality of the word startled her. She stared at him, suddenly apprehensive, as if he might spring across the table at her. "This thing's moving too fast. I need an answer now, or you can go back to St. Bernard today and get back in uniform." He finished the last of his eggs and pushed the plate away. "Are you in or are you out?"

She picked up her fork and pushed her food around on the plate. She didn't want to go back. Winslow, prick that he was, had summed up how she'd felt about being a road deputy. She wanted out, and up, and this was opportunity knocking. And in the end, Winslow was right about Savannah. However sympathetic she might be, thanks to her efforts to dig herself out of the hole she was in, it was still a hole she'd dug for herself. Her father's voice came back to her. *You have to learn to keep your distance. Don't let them suck you into their game.*

"Okay," she said, "I'm in."

CHAPTER TWENTY

Wyatt came to not knowing where he was. He hated when that happened. The answer was usually nowhere good. He raised his head slightly, the skin on his cheek peeling away from a sticky leather surface. His mouth felt as if someone had scoured it with sandpaper. Slowly, he levered himself up to a sitting position, biting back a groan at the pain in his joints, then giving in and letting the groan out as the change in position made him realize the even worse pain in his head. He blinked as he looked around the dark room before realizing he was in his own living room, on his couch. He saw a blanket on the floor. Glenda must have tried to cover him. *Oh god,* he thought, and then the nausea hit. He staggered to the downstairs bathroom, fell to his knees, and got the toilet lid up just in time for the first convulsion to hit. The vile odor of his spew set off another spasm, then another, until all he was bringing up was a thin yellow bile. He hit the lever to wash the vomit away. His stomach rebelled again. He felt a presence behind him and started to get up, but another retch drove him to his knees. He saw Glenda's hand reach around and place something on the toilet seat—a washcloth soaked in cold water. He picked it up in shaking hands and wiped the spittle and vomit from around his mouth. He heard her place something on the vanity beside the toilet, then she was gone. He reached for the glass of cool water he knew would be there, took a mouthful, and rinsed the vile taste from his mouth. It might have been another few minutes before he knew the sickness had passed. It might have been an hour. He thought of just sinking to the cool, inviting tile floor and sleeping the rest of his life there, but the awful clarity of his position made rest impossible. He flushed again and pushed himself painfully up. He downed the remaining water in a gulp, then pulled out the drawer of the vanity until he'd located an old tube of toothpaste that was rolled up almost to the top. There was no toothbrush to be found, so Wyatt managed to squeeze a dollop of cement-like paste onto his index finger and rub it over his teeth and gums until his mouth felt less like an untended dumpster. He'd been trying not to look in the mirror over the sink, and when he did, he wished he hadn't. His face was pale and drawn, and there was a cut over one eye, blood crusted over a wound he had no idea how he'd gotten. "Shit," he said out loud, and it came out as a deathbed croak. He stumbled out of the bathroom like a man who'd forgotten how to walk and saw that things weren't about to get any better for him. The light was on in the kitchen, and he could hear the sounds of Glenda moving around. He took a deep breath and walked toward the light like a man headed for a date with the noose.

She was seated at the kitchen table, a cup of steaming tea in front of her. She wouldn't look at him. He was surprised to see a cigarette dangling from between the fingers of one hand.

"I thought you'd quit," he said, sliding into the wooden chair across from her.

She looked him in the eye then, her eyes narrowed and furious, her brows drawn together. "You really think this is a good time to bring up *my* bad habits?" She flicked her ash into a saucer she'd pulled out in lieu of an ashtray, as if daring him to make a further comment.

"I know. Sorry." He looked over to the kettle on the stove.

"There's more tea," she said. She didn't offer to make it. He got up, still shaky, and prepared himself a cup. Neither of them spoke. He poured the water over the teabag and spooned in two heaping tablespoons of sugar before he took his seat again. She was back to not looking at him again.

"At least tell me I didn't drive home like that," he said finally.

"No." She stubbed the remains of the cigarette out in the saucer. "*She* brought you home."

There was no doubt from the venom in Glenda's voice who *she* was. "Oh, damn," he said. Then he added desperately, "Look, honey—"

"Oh, I know. Nothing happened. She said it, you said it, and from how messed up you were, I sure believe it." She took a sip of tea and he saw that her hands were shaking. "That doesn't change the fact that you called your old lover to come get you instead of your wife." She looked at him, her eyes brimming with tears. "You told me it was over. You told me..." She set the cup down, no longer able to control the shaking. She took a deep breath. He could see her drawing herself together with sheer force of will. "I thought looking for Tyler Welch would help you. Give you something to do besides drinking yourself to death. But I was wrong. It's making you worse."

"Glenda," he said, "it's not your fault."

She looked at him as if he'd started babbling in Ancient Greek. "I *know* it's not my fault, Wyatt. You don't have to tell me that." She shook her head and closed her eyes for a moment. When she opened them again, she looked at Wyatt with quiet determination. "We've both been married before, Wyatt. I came into this knowing we both had some baggage. Some damage. I thought we could make it better for each other. And you've made it better for me. Mostly. But…" She stopped, choking on the next words before going on. "I guess I can't fix everything that's wrong with you. You need help, Wyatt. You need AA, or rehab, or something. Some kind of treatment that's beyond me. And you…you need to decide who you want to be with."

"You," he said immediately. "I want to be with you, and nobody else."

"Then prove it," she shot back. "Get the help you need."

He got up and went to where his tea was steeping. He pulled the bag from the hot water and put it on the saucer as he considered his next words. "Finding Tyler is the help I need," he said.

She shook her head. "I can't believe you…"

"No, hear me out. Please." He took a long drink. The sugar seemed to hit his system almost immediately. "If I find Tyler, I find Mick. And I failed Mick."

She frowned. "What in the world are you talking about?"

"I put all my interest in helping Tyler. I found him a new home. A place where he could have a new life. Even a new name. But Mick? I just let him go. I don't know why. I guess I thought Tyler was the one who was salvageable. And I gave up on Mick. Now look what's happened."

"Wyatt…"

"It all comes back to you. It always comes back. All the things you've done wrong, all the mistakes you think you got away with. You haven't. They're still out there. Waiting. Waiting for you to make it right. Or pay the price."

She blew out an exasperated breath. "You're still drunk."

"A little," he confessed. "But I know this is something I have to do. And I need you to know it too."

"Do what, exactly? Find Tyler. And, I guess you're thinking, Mick Jakes, and then…what? Fix it all for them?" She got up and came around to stand behind him. She slid her hands down his chest and rested her chin on the top of his head. "You think if you can save Mick, it'll make up for Morris Tyree."

The name took his mind back to that cramped interrogation room, the smell of fear-sweat, of anger, the dizzy feeling of crossing every line of civilization and knowing he was completely in the right to do so. He saw his hand pinning the right wrist of skinny, shaking, contemptible Morris Tyree, who'd been the last person seen in the vicinity of four-year-old Rachel Wagstaff, to the table. He saw his other hand, holding his father's shiny, legendary Ka-Bar knife, laid across Tyree's frantically squirming fingers. He heard a voice that he'd never imagined would come out of his own throat, low and terrifying. *You sign that confession, boy*, the voice had said, *or you say goodbye to these fingers.*

The thing was, he had *known* Tyree was guilty. He had known beyond any reasonable doubt that Tyree, a convicted sex offender with a folder full of candid pictures of beautiful blonde Rachel on his old and barely functioning computer, was the one responsible for leaving her battered and violated body lying in a ditch alongside State Road 113. He had known it with such complete conviction that when the weeping and sniveling Tyree had insisted he'd had nothing to do with the girl's death, it was more than just a challenge to Wyatt's interrogation skills. It was an outrage too great to be borne. So the knife had come out. Morris Tyree, fully cowed, had signed the confession that would send him to death row.

Nine years later, a DNA match had conclusively proved that while Morris Tyree might have been Rachel's stalker, her killer had actually been a homeless drifter with a long history of violent mental illness named Judah Cuddahy. Before being finally run to ground, Cuddahy had committed two other murders of young girls, inflicting exactly the same sort of grotesque injuries he'd committed on Rachel Wagstaff. The day the State Supreme Court issued the order for Tyree's release, Wyatt turned in his resignation as sheriff, headed straight for

Val's, and stayed drunk for a week. He and Glenda had been married for three years at that point, and he expected her to leave him. In a way, he'd wanted her to. He'd wanted her to pack up, to leave, to show him and the world he really was as big a monster as he now knew he was.

But she didn't leave. She didn't even complain. She listened to his drunken diatribes, held him when he wept, and rode out the storms of his self-loathing. Finally, in one of his more lucid intervals, she'd sat down across the kitchen table from him and calmly said, "Okay. You messed up. You messed up bad. What are you going to do now?"

In the two years since, he hadn't come up with an answer to that question, but while he looked for an answer, he'd managed to keep the drinking under control. Or so he thought. The revelation of what had happened to Mick Jakes, something to which he'd given little or no thought in the intervening years, had made him realize that there were more failures in his career than just Morris Tyree. The county had done a good job of covering up the Tyree fiasco. A generous cash settlement with an ironclad confidentiality agreement had kept Wyatt out of the public eye. But he couldn't hide his failure from himself. Now more of his failures were coming back to haunt him.

"Maybe I do," he said in a low voice. "Glenda, I've screwed up. In so many ways."

"Horse puckey." The vehemence of her voice combined with the awkward half-curse made him laugh in spite of himself. She glared at him, then she had to smile, too. He rose from his chair, the two of them wrapping their arms around each other and holding on tight. She shifted around to settle onto his lap. "The first time I met you," she whispered, "you were larger than life. Everybody treated you like a superhero. You were Wyatt by-God McGee. You were a rock star, and I was like a teen-aged girl."

"Sorry to disappoint you."

She pulled back slightly and cuffed him lightly on the side of the head. "Be quiet and listen to me." She nestled back against him. "Imagine my surprise when I found out you were just a human being after all. And imagine my surprise when that made me love you harder."

All he could think of to do was hold her tighter. All he could think of to say was, "I love you, too."

"Good." She pulled away. "So. What do you do now?"

That question again. This time, he answered without thinking. "I need to find Tyler. And Mick. Not because of Tyree. For them. I need to try to bring them back. Bring them home. Not for my sake. For theirs."

She nodded as if this was the answer she'd been working toward all along. "There's my superhero." She lifted her head and fixed him with a steady gaze. "But I want you to know something. I'm not saying for sure it's the last time I'm ever going to put up with something like what happened last night. But it might be. I've got my limit, Wyatt. And you coming home drunk in another woman's car—a woman you used to be involved with—that came pretty close. Right up to the edge. Do you hear what I'm saying?"

He nodded. "I do. I don't want to lose you, Glenda."

"Then don't." She slid off his lap. "Now. You may not feel like it, but you're going to eat some breakfast. You've got some traveling to do."

CHAPTER TWENTY-ONE

Even though she'd grown up in and around New Orleans, Chance had never been a huge fan of the Café Du Monde. Sure, the famous restaurant down by the French Market had good beignets and coffee, but there were plenty of places that made both as well or better and that weren't crowded, noisy, and overrun by tourists. Still, if that's where the informant wanted to meet, that's where they were going to meet. Winslow told them to grab a table while he fetched them breakfast from the place's limited menu.

"So," Savannah said, not looking Chance in the eye, "I guess they figured a woman might handle me better."

Chance felt completely out of her element. A couple of conversations with her dad and some admonitions from Winslow had done little to prepare her for handling informants. She decided to try honesty. "Yeah. Maybe." She leaned forward. "But this shit Charleyboy's trying to play? Trying to play Luther off against Gutierrez? Honey, that's fucking nuts. You're all going to end up in prison. Or dead, more likely." She paused, took a deep breath. "And your sons are going to get caught in the middle of it."

Chance felt slightly guilty for how well that shot struck home. Using Savannah's children as a means of leverage left a bad taste in her mouth. Savannah only nodded. "Everything I do," she said, "I'm doing for them."

"Right," Chance said, although she didn't entirely believe it. In her career in law enforcement, she'd heard people try to justify some pretty heinous behavior by claiming they were doing it for their children.

At that moment, Winslow appeared bearing a tray burdened with plates of crisp, heavily sugared beignets and cups of coffee. "Ladies,'" he said in a smarmy voice that made Chance roll her eyes as he distributed liquids and pastries. "So," he asked when he was done, "where are we?"

Savannah spoke up first. "We're waiting to see what you can do about protecting my boys."

Winslow nodded. "We're working on that. But as a gesture of good faith, if you could maybe give us a date when the delivery is supposed to be made. A time. A location…" He trailed off, looking at Savannah expectantly.

She smiled without a trace of warmth. "The date is the twelfth of fuck you. The time is fuck you o'clock. The location is fuck you street, fuck you, Louisiana." She took a sip of her coffee. "You get shit until I cut a deal that provides safety for me and my boys."

Chance's voice was gentle. "What about Charleyboy?"

Savannah took a sip of cafe au lait, not meeting Chance's eyes. "If we can get him out of this…well. That'd be good."

"But it's not a deal breaker."

"No."

"So, when this is over," Chance said, "do you see you and Charleyboy together or apart?"

Savannah looked her in the eye for the first time. "I don't know," she said.

Chance nodded. "I get it. I don't know if I'd want to stay with a guy who—"

"You don't get shit, lady," Savannah flared up. Even in the noisy restaurant, her voice was intense enough to draw stares. She settled back down and crossed her arms across her chest. "You don't know me. You don't know my life. So stop trying to pretend you do. And stop trying to get close to me. You're not going to be my friend. Not now. Not ever. This is business. So let's do business."

"Okay," Winslow broke in, his voice low but harsh. "Fine. Business. You know one thing they say in business? The person who has the power in a negotiation is the person who can walk away from the deal. We can walk away from this. What we have already is enough to snap up you and Charleyboy and put both of you away for a while. If I have to be satisfied with that, I will."

"Bullshit," she said. "You want Luther and Gutierrez so bad you can taste it."

Winslow shrugged. "Sure. I'd love to sew up one or both of those two assholes. But they're assholes. They'll always be assholes. If I don't get them this month, they'll fuck up some other way and we'll get them then." He leaned forward. "We're the U.S. Government, sweetie. We've got all the time in the world. You? I don't know, Savannah. What's the sell-by date on an aging drug whore?"

"Goddamn it, Winslow," Chance burst out.

Savannah half rose, picking up her coffee cup as if she meant to throw it at him.

Winslow regarded her coolly. "Go ahead. Storm out. Throw that cup at me. I'll have agents at the house before you get home. And your boys can come visit you in the roughest federal penitentiary I can find to put you in."

She froze. If looks could kill, Winslow would have left the Café du Monde in multiple body bags. After a moment, she sat back down. Chance could see the tears in her eyes.

"Good," Winslow said. "Now that we understand one another, I need something concrete by this time tomorrow. I'll keep working on the deal for you and your boys. But if you don't call me tomorrow with something I can use, we're going to have to re-think this relationship."

"Okay," Savannah muttered. Then she looked up. "But not you." She jerked her chin at Chance. "I talk to her. Only her from now on."

Winslow gave her a condescending smile, the smile of a man granting a meaningless concession to a beaten foe. "Sure. Whatever." He stood up. "Call Deputy Cahill tomorrow." He got up and walked away. Savannah slumped in her chair, staring into her coffee cup.

"If it's any consolation," Chance said, "I think he's an asshole, too."

"It's not."

"But he has a point, Savannah. You thought you could play us. Am I right?"

Savannah didn't answer at first. Then she said, "I guess you put me in my place." She looked up, the tears coming to her eyes again. "People like you been putting me in my place all my goddamn life."

"People like..." Chance stopped, confused.

Savannah went on. "It was people like you who took my boys away from me in the first place."

"I can't answer for that. I wasn't there. I don't even know what happened."

Savannah's jaw tightened with remembered anger. "I thought I'd left my boys with someone I could trust. She left them alone. But it was me who took the blame. Was that fair?" Before Chance could answer, Savannah went on, rushing to tell the story the way she'd undoubtedly honed and polished it in front of any number of listeners over the years, carefully editing and crafting it to make herself the victim. Chance had heard variations on the story before, in the backs of patrol cars, in interrogation rooms, in court. Then Savannah came up with a detail she hadn't heard before. "And you know the really fucked-up thing? The cop and that bitch social worker who ganged up to take my sons away? They were fucking. The whole time. And he was married." She smacked her coffee cup down for emphasis. "Bitch was judging me. Judging my goddamn life. While she was fucking a married man." She looked up at Chance. "I ask you, is that right?"

Chance didn't know what that had to do with anything, but she just nodded, trying to look sympathetic. She tried to get the conversation back on track. "The question is, what do you do now? You've got a chance to get out of this life. You've got a chance to be reunited with your sons. But for that to happen—"

Savannah broke in. "All I have to do is betray the man I love." The tears were brimming in her eyes again. "I know," she said. "Yeah. He loses his temper sometimes. He goes over the line. But you don't know what he used to be like. Charming. Funny. He could be in a crowd and look at me across a room full of people and make me feel like I was the only girl in the room." She smiled wistfully. "And oh, how that boy could dance."

"Not much dancing going on now, though," Chance said.

The smile faded. "No." She stood up. "Give me your number. I'll call you tomorrow if I can find out anything. And keep that shithead away from me."

Chance took a notebook out of her bag and wrote her cell number down. "I'll do what I can. But he's the one running the investigation."

"Whatever." She walked away without looking back. Chance took a last sip of her coffee and grimaced. It had gone cold.

CHAPTER TWENTY-TWO

The scrambled eggs and bacon had been tough to choke down at first, but Glenda had been right. Breakfast and a shower had put Wyatt back to something resembling functional. He'd come up with a plan over the breakfast table: talk to the detective who'd investigated the robbery in Spencer, then see if he could track down Mick Jakes's last foster parents. They might still have contact with him, or at least know where he might be. Glenda had taken him to recover his truck from Val's, where it was the lone vehicle left in the dirt parking lot. He'd given his wife a long, deep kiss before getting out of her Subaru and trudging to his vehicle. When he got in, he saw his phone, still plugged in. He picked it up and grimaced. There were four messages from Kassidey, beginning at seven in the morning. He considered not answering, but then it occurred to him that he needed to talk to her in order to get the name and possibly the address of that last foster family. He grimaced. "Shit," he muttered out loud. Awkward didn't even begin to cover what this conversation was going to be. He hit the button to dial her back.

She answered on the first ring. "Hey."

"Hey."

"Are you okay?"

"Yeah." He hesitated. "Thanks. For bringing me home, I mean."

"Yeah. It wasn't the most comfortable evening I've ever spent."

"I know. I'm sorry."

"I know you are. You kept saying it. You said it a lot."

"Well, I am. I had no right to ask you to—"

Her voice rose for the first time. "Damn straight you had no right." The force of her anger silenced him. "Jesus Christ, Wyatt, do you have the slightest goddamn idea how humiliating that was? To have you ring me up in the middle of the night, drunk off your ass, like I was some kind of *booty call*?"

"It wasn't that. I swear it."

"Oh. So you called me up for the express purpose of taking you home to your wife? Even if I believed that, would you expect that to make me feel even a little bit better? God*damn* it, Wyatt!"

He leaned forward and rested his head on the steering wheel. "What can I say other than I'm sorry?"

"Nothing. Don't say another goddamn thing to me. The only reason I didn't tell you to fuck off last night was I was afraid you'd try to drive in that condition and kill yourself."

"Well, you don't want me dead. That's something." Gallows humor had always brought them together. It didn't work this time.

"Do not even try to be funny, Wyatt. Do not." Her voice was shaking with rage. "The worst part was having to deal with Glenda."

He sat up, alarmed. "Did she…"

"She was as nice as she could be, Wyatt. I expected her to try to claw my eyes out. But she was totally polite. Even thanked me. Several times. And that made me feel even worse. She couldn't have made me feel more like trash if she'd set out to do it. But I know she didn't. She doesn't have it in her." Kassidey paused for a moment, and then he heard her take a deep breath. "Don't call me anymore, Wyatt. Drunk, sober, whatever. We're done. I didn't break up your first marriage, although everyone thinks I did, and I've been living with that in this goddamn county ever since. And I'm not going to be blamed if your second marriage goes down the tubes, either. Just don't, okay?"

"Okay," he said. "But I need one more thing."

She was silent, disbelieving. "Jesus, Mary, and Joseph," she finally said. "You are the most..." She sighed. "Okay. What is it?"

"I need the name and contact information, if you have it, for Mick Jakes's last foster family."

"What?"

"I'm going to try to find Tyler. He's with Mick. Maybe Mick's ex-foster family might have heard from him."

"That sound you hear," Kassidey said, "is me grinding my teeth. I already told you I can't release that information. Not without violating about ten different regulations and several laws of the State of North Carolina."

"No one has to know."

"Yeah. Seems like I've heard that before."

"You said you could call the guy. Ask him if it was okay."

She sighed. "Hang on a minute." She put him on hold. An earnest recorded voice reminded him that the mission of the Department of Social Services was to assist people with life's challenges and strengthen the community through high quality social services. A lengthy recitation of the various ways DSS could aid the challenged followed, then a reminder that Wyatt's call was important and that he should please stay on the line. He'd heard the message play through four times by the time Kassidey came back on the line. "Okay. Got a name, got a phone number. The name's Delwyn Chandler." She read off the number as Wyatt scrambled for a pencil and paper in the truck's center console. "And he's willing to talk to you."

"You spoke to him? Just now?"

"I wasn't going to give this to you otherwise."

"Okay. Thanks for making the call." Something occurred to him. "You said Mick was placed with a couple."

"Chandler's partner died about two years ago. Cancer, I think. Sounds like Delwyn's still taking it hard, so you might want to stay away from that subject."

"Got it. And thanks, Kass."

"Don't mention it."

"And…I really am sorry about last night."

"Don't mention that, either. Ever. Good luck, Wyatt. And goodbye." Before he could answer, she'd hung up.

He looked at the number he'd scrawled on the back of a Walgreen's receipt. It was another piece of the puzzle, another stepping stone toward the truth. He felt a faint shiver of the thrill he'd used to experience when he realized he was on the way to solving a crime, taking one more step in the darkness, not knowing where the next step would lead him, but knowing, deep in his heart, that he was going to put things right. Then he remembered how that feeling had led him so badly wrong, how that feeling of needing to take the next step toward the truth had led him to pull his father's legendary knife from his belt and torture a confession from an innocent man.

The sound of an engine broke into his reverie. He looked up and saw a dented and dirty Ford pickup pulling into the parking lot. Val had come to open up. He knew he could get out of the truck, cross the lot, and Val would pour him a "freshener," a "hair of the dog what bit you," an "eye opener." She had an inexhaustible store of terms for the first drink of the day. She wouldn't judge, wouldn't urge him, wouldn't make any comment beyond, "You want another?" Or maybe, much later, "You want me to call somebody?" He watched Val shift her bulk out of the front seat. She noticed him sitting in his truck and gave him a cheery wave before turning and trudging to the front door. Yeah, he thought. Val would take care of him. Right up until the day he died.

He started the truck and headed up the road to Spencer.

CHAPTER TWENTY-THREE

Tyler didn't know what he was looking at. He seemed to be hovering above a rough, flat desert liberally strewn with rocks, mottled brown and dirty white. He blinked once, twice and then with a nauseating swoop, his perspective changed and he realized he was looking up, not down. The barren landscape he was surveying was a stained and crumbling popcorn ceiling. As more of his awareness returned, the nausea intensified. He let out a low groan and tried to sit up. The effort nearly made him puke. He fought it down, mostly because he didn't know where to find a toilet or even a wastebasket in which to spew. Once he'd struggled to a sitting position, he saw that he was perched on the edge of a bed. The bed was covered with a thin, scratchy spread.

A godawful sound split the air. It was a grotesque gurgling, rattling noise, like a tiger trying to roar while drowning in its own phlegm. Tyler snapped his head around to see Mick lying on his back on a twin bed on the other side of the room. His mouth was open and his eyes were shut tight.

"I don't know how anyone can sleep through that," a female voice said. Tyler's head wasn't going to take many more sudden changes in perspective. He squinted across the dimly lit room and saw Lana sitting in a chair, at a table, by a window. The window was covered by a thick curtain that only let in a thin sliver of sunlight from outside. He realized he was in a motel room. A dirt-cheap one from the looks of things, with the emphasis on dirt.

"Morning, sunshine," Lana said. She took a drag off her cigarette. Her other hand rested on the big revolver on the table.

"What happened?" Tyler groaned. "Where are we?"

She shrugged. "Georgia, maybe. Maybe Alabama. I don't know. I ain't the captain of this ship. He is." She nodded at where Mick still lay sprawled on his back. As Tyler watched, he gave a great snort and rolled over onto his stomach. Mick began to breathe deeply and evenly, without snoring. "Thank god," Lana said. "I was about ready to shoot him myself."

Tyler wanted to reply, but another wave of dizziness overwhelmed him. He leaned over and put his head in his hands. He heard Lana moving about, but didn't have the energy to look up and see where. The bed creaked and sagged as she sat down next to him. "Here," she said gently, handing him a paper cup from the bathroom, "drink this."

His first instinct was to shy away, but when he took a sip he realized it was just water. It tasted of rust, but he drank it down, grateful for the relief to his dry mouth.

"I told Mick he was givin' you too much," she said. "But he'd been up for two days and he wanted to make sure he could get some sleep."

Tyler shook his head. "You two *drugged* me."

She shrugged and took the cup from him, putting it on a scarred and battered bedside table. "I know. Kind of fucked up, ain't it? Him bein' your brother an' all. But you have to admit. If he'd fallen asleep while you was awake, you would have been out of here like a rabbit. Am I lyin'?"

"I guess not." The dizziness was subsiding slowly, but Tyler still felt as if he'd been clubbed in the back of the head.

"So what's the deal with you and Mick?" Lana asked. "He said the county pulled you two apart. Kept you from each other, and your mama."

"I don't know," Tyler said. "I was, like, three years old. I don't remember any of it. All I know is what my parents told me."

"Your parents." The words came out flat and expressionless, but there was a world of contempt in her expression.

"They raised me." Tyler felt defensive, then resentful for feeling that way. "They're the only family I ever knew."

"So you never saw Mick after that? They didn't let you see your own brother?"

Tyler searched his memory. He could remember nothing clearly; just vague flashes of a dark-haired, dark-eyed boy, a little older than him, a thin arm across his shoulder, a voice in his ear. *We're gonna be together again, lil' bro. You, me, and Mama. Real soon now.* "I think I saw him, some. Early on. But I really can't remember."

"That sucks," Lana said. "I remember my brother. He was my best friend."

"Was?" Tyler asked.

She drew herself up onto the bed, her knees to her chest, her back against the headboard. "He got killed in Iraq. Blown up. Or shot through the head when his Humvee got blown up. We never did get the whole story. All we know is he came home in a casket they told us it was best not to open."

Tyler didn't know what to say, so he fell back, as he'd been taught, on comforting clichés. "I'm sorry for your loss."

She frowned at him. "You didn't even know him. You don't know me."

"I—"

"Tell me this. Before he picked you up, did you even remember Mick's face?"

He didn't want to have another glib answer slammed back at him, so he thought for a moment. "I don't think so," he finally admitted.

She shook her head. "I don't get that. I can remember everything about my brother. His face. His voice. I think about him every day."

"I was just a little kid," Tyler said.

"So," another voice said, "did your *parents*," he leaned on the word with contempt, "not tell you anything about you having a brother?"

Tyler shifted around to look at the other bed. Mick was awake, sitting up, looking at him. His brows were drawn together in the angry expression Tyler was already learning to dread. "They did," Tyler said. "I just…after a while…"

"After a while I just faded away."

"I didn't say that."

Mick stood up. "You didn't have to. Well, lil' bro, like the song goes, it's better to burn out than to fade away. But I ain't doin' either one." He hitched up his pants. "I gotta take a leak. Then it's time to get back on the road." As he headed for the motel room's small bathroom, Tyler noted that the gun was on the bed nearest him, with Lana on the far side of the room. He tensed, waiting, nearly vibrating with the strain until the door closed. Then he bolted for the door, yanked it open, and stumbled out into the daylight.

CHAPTER
TWENTY-FOUR

The town of Spencer, North Carolina had once had two industries keeping it alive. One was Spencer Fabrics, a sprawling complex of mostly windowless brick buildings by the railroad tracks on the outskirts of town. That was where most of the town's population wove and shipped denim for cheap jeans and rougher, sturdier cloth for car seats. The other was county government, as practiced in the old courthouse in the center of town and the municipal complex across the street. In the 1980s, the fabric business went to Mexico and the town discovered, to its surprise, that being the county seat wasn't enough of a draw to keep a town alive. Vacant, dusty storefronts lined the main street, interspersed here and there with small storefront law offices near the courthouse and bail bondsmen clustered around the decaying jail on the next street over. The jail had been the subject of a report on a Raleigh news station detailing its security problems after two pairs of inmates managed to escape on two separate occasions within ten days of one another. There'd been talk of refurbishing the old structure, or even tearing it down for a new one, but no one could seem to find the money. Wyatt felt for Sheriff Elon Pratt, who he'd met at various law enforcement conferences; he'd known what it felt like to be caught between the public's demand for safety and its unwillingness to spend any money for it. Politicians like Henry could navigate those waters; lawmen like Wyatt McGee and Elon Pratt never seemed to get the knack.

Wyatt pulled his truck into the parking lot of the Spencer County Public Safety Building, a mid-sixties structure that spread out in two long wings on either side of a central entranceway. The white paint was old and cracking on the building's facade, but the strip of grass in front and the hedges beneath the office windows that looked out onto the parking lot were immaculately trimmed, most likely by inmates from the jail.

The heat of the day hit Wyatt hard as he got out of the truck. He broke into a sweat immediately. The sweat and his roiling stomach let him know he wasn't fully recovered from last night's binge. He leaned on his truck for a moment before heading inside.

The air in the building was frigid from an air conditioning system cranked to full blast, and he was shivering by the time he got to the front desk, where a short, cheerful young woman looked up and gave him a big smile. "Can I help you?" she said.

Yeah, Wyatt thought, *can I just lie down on this cool floor and sleep for a while?* "Wyatt McGee," he said. "To see Sheriff Pratt."

The smile never wavered. "Do you have an appointment?"

"I, um, called ahead." It was technically true. He'd used his cell phone to call the number he still had in his contacts for Pratt's personal number, but had only gotten voice mail.

"I'll check," the woman said, but as she reached for her phone, a voice from behind her boomed, "Well I'll be damned. Wyatt McGee."

Wyatt looked up as the young receptionist looked around. Elon Pratt loomed in the space behind the desk, a broad grin on his ruddy, weathered face. Wyatt was a big man, but "Bear" Pratt, as he was known to close friends and voters who saw his campaign posters, was a giant, nearly seven feet tall and weighing over three hundred pounds, most of it muscle.

"Hey, Bear," Wyatt said. "Don't know if you got my message."

Pratt shook his head. "Hell, I can't figure those damn phones out. Can't hardly work the buttons." He swallowed up Wyatt's hand in one of his huge ones and smacked him on the shoulder. "Whatever, it's good to see you, brother. How's retirement treating you?"

Wyatt couldn't help but smile back. To be in Bear Pratt's presence when he was in a good mood was to be buoyed up on a wave of good cheer. Wyatt had heard that to be on his bad side was utterly terrifying. He hoped he never had to find out. "Retirement's good," he lied. "But I'm working on something. A favor for a friend."

Bear inclined his head quizzically, looking at Wyatt with narrowed, suddenly shrewd eyes. "Okay. C'mon in the house."

Sheriff Pratt's office was large and untidy. The head of a moose that he'd shot on a vacation in Alaska hung on one wall. Another wall was decorated with pictures of his children and grandchildren, hung in such a haphazard fashion that it must have been done by Pratt himself. The big man settled himself into a desk chair that creaked alarmingly under his weight. "So," he said, folding his hands across his massive belly, "what can I do for you?"

"You had an armed robbery a couple days ago," Wyatt said. "A store out in the country. I saw some video."

Pratt grimaced. "Yeah. It was on TV."

"So do you know who the subjects were?"

Pratt's earlier bonhomie was gone. "Do you?"

"I think. One of them was a boy named Mick Jakes."

"Hold on." Pratt leaned over and punched a button on his desktop phone. "Alicia," he rumbled. "Is Garcia in the building?"

There was a brief pause and the front-desk girl's voice came back, distorted through the tiny speaker. "Yes, sir."

"Ask him to come in." He leaned back and regarded Wyatt. "Garcia's the detective assigned to the case," he said, "Mexican. But he's a smart little fucker. And you know how those people love to work. Makes him a damn good detective."

"Um," Wyatt said, unsure of how to deal with casual racism and effusive praise in the same statement. His confusion was cut short as Garcia arrived at the office door. He was a short, round man with a military crew cut and a serious face.

"You wanted to see me, Sheriff?"

"Yeah." Pratt motioned at Wyatt. "This is Wyatt McGee. Used to be sheriff in Clark County. He may know something about the robbery at Gary's."

Garcia looked dubiously at Wyatt. "Yes, sir."

Pratt levered himself ponderously out of his chair. "You fellas share what you have." He grimaced. "I got a meeting with some empty suit from some bullshit governor's crime commission. Just close the door when you leave." He sighed and lumbered out the door.

Garcia watched him go, then turned back to Wyatt. "I'm sorry, sir," he said with careful politeness, "but I'm not sure what your position is here."

"I don't have one," Wyatt admitted. "I'm trying to find out something for a friend."

"Yes, sir," Garcia said, still noncommittal and trending towards uncooperative.

Wyatt sighed. "Look, Detective, in your shoes, I wouldn't trust me either. But here's the thing. I know Mick Jakes was one of the robbers. I think the other was a kid named Tyler Welch."

For the first time, Wyatt saw a glimmer of interest in Garcia's eyes. "And you know this how?"

"I recognized him. On the surveillance video."

"Yes, sir." Garcia pulled a small notebook out of his back pocket. "Can you tell me how you know him?"

"Yeah," Wyatt said, "I helped take him away from his mother."

CHAPTER
TWENTY-FIVE

Savannah paced the floor, waiting for Charleyboy to get home. Across her shoulders, she wore her favorite shawl, a black lace number that an old and nearly forgotten boyfriend had bought for her at a street fair because, he told her, it made her look like Stevie Nicks. That was a lot of years and a lot of miles ago, but somehow the feel of that soft, delicate cloth draped on her skin always brought back good memories and made her feel calmer. It was working today, to a point, although she still caught herself chewing nervously on one of the ends. She took it out of her mouth and sighed. She couldn't figure out how she was going to get Charleyboy to tell her more about the upcoming meeting between Luther and Gutierrez without tipping him off to the conversations she'd been having with the feds. *Maybe,* she thought, *I should just tell him. Pull him into what I'm doing. Maybe I can make him see…* She shook her head angrily at her own foolishness. He'd never go for it. He was too in love with what he thought was the cleverness of his plan. He'd freak out if he thought she'd betrayed him. At best, she could expect another beating. At worst…the thought stopped her. Did she really believe Charleyboy would kill her? Sometimes, when he was in one of his true rages, she wondered. Maybe that's why she'd told the female cop that Charleyboy not getting out of this wouldn't be a deal breaker. She was a mother. She had to look after herself. And her boys.

That thought sent her back to the computer to check her messages. No new ones, just the one that had made her heart leap. She scrolled to it again. *Mama. We're on our way to New Orleans. We'll be in touch soon. Keith is with me.* She'd hoped for some further word, some idea of when they'd arrive. She sat down at the keyboard, hesitating a moment before she punched in the address of the house. *Can't wait to see you,* she added.

The sound of footsteps on the front stoop made her leap up, her heart pounding. Could it be them? She shook her head. No, it couldn't be. Not so soon. It was Charleyboy. She pasted a big smile on her face anyway. "Hey, baby, how was your…" The look on his face stopped her. "What?"

"You look nice," he said as he stood in the doorway. "That's good. We're going to have company. Is there anything in the fridge?"

"Some beer," she said, "and the rest of that bottle of wine. But who…" She heard the tread of other footsteps as Charleyboy stepped aside. She stepped back, feeling the blood drain from her face.

Mr. Luther stood in her doorway, leaning on a silver-headed cane. She could see the two hulking figures behind him on the stoop.

"Well, hey there, gal," he said in a cracked and reedy voice. He smiled, revealing a mouthful of misaligned and yellowed teeth. "Been wantin' to meet you in person for a while now."

"Oh shit," Chance said as she saw the big black Escalade pull up behind Charleyboy's Mercedes. A lean, weathered-looking redneck in jeans, a red wife-beater, and the kind of mullet Chance hadn't seen since the turn of the twenty-first century got out of the front passenger's side and opened the door. A second man, twin to the first except for his green sleeveless t-shirt, got out of the driver's side and walked over to where Charleyboy was waiting. The first man went to the back door and opened it.

"Mr. Luther," Winslow said in a low voice as he saw who was slowly getting out of the vehicle. "As I live and breathe." He picked up the camera lying on a nearby table, focused the long lens, and began taking pictures.

Chance reached down for her sidearm. "This can't be good." She pulled it from the holster and worked the slide.

"Maybe," Winslow said, still focused on the tableau on the sidewalk, "or it may be the break we're looking for." He noticed what Chance was doing. "Put that damn weapon away, Deputy," he snapped. "What the hell do you think is going to happen here?"

Chance nodded toward where the four men were forming up, with Charleyboy in front, Luther right behind him, and the two guards behind him, and heading for the front door. "You think those goons and Mr. Luther are here to deliver the mail?"

Winslow shook his head. "If someone kills our assets, Deputy Cahill, I guarantee you Mr. Luther will be miles away, with a roomful of witnesses who'll vouch for him being there all night. And the bodies will never be found. That's how he works." He raised the camera again and snapped off some more shots. "Make sure that recorder's running. Luther's not dumb enough to kill someone in broad daylight, even if he thinks they're turning on him. But he is old and cocky enough to say something stupid."

Goddamn it, Chance thought. *He's right. And I hate it when he's right.* She picked up the headphones, put them on, and made sure the recorder was running.

"Yes, sir," Luther said, looking Savannah up and down in a way that made her skin crawl. "I'd heard you was pretty. But Charleyboy didn't do you justice." He turned to where Charleyboy stood, off to the side and looking as if he was going to throw up. "You been hidin' this light under a bushel, ain't ya? I guess I can't blame ya, pretty lil' thing like 'at."

Winslow, you motherfucker, you'd better be watching over me, Savannah thought. The idea helped her find her voice and her smile. "You're so sweet. Would you like something to drink, Mr. Luther?"

He turned back to her, swiveling his whole body as if he had trouble turning his neck. "Well, now that you mention it, darlin', I am a little parched."

"We have beer, wine...I could make some iced tea?"

"Beer would suit me fine," he said, "as long as it ain't some fancy brew like those man-bun-wearin' faggots is drinkin' these days."

She kept smiling. It was starting to hurt her face. "Well, it is local."

Luther snorted. "Ain't been a decent local brew since Dixie Brewery moved to goddamn Wisconsin." He shook his head. "But I'm bein' rude. Whatever you got will be fine."

"How about your, ah..." She looked at the two bodyguards, still standing stone-faced with arms crossed behind Luther.

"They're workin'," Luther said. "They'll be fine."

"Okay. Charleyboy?"

He couldn't meet her eyes. "Sure."

Without another look at him, she went to the kitchen. She opened the door of the old, rusted, and creaking refrigerator and leaned on it for a second, trying to get her legs to stop shaking. *Deep breaths. Deep breaths. You're not going to die today. Not before you see your boys again. That won't happen. God isn't that cruel.* She opened three Abita beers with the opener attached to the side of the fridge and took them out.

When she got back to the living room, Luther was seated on

the couch, flanked by his two bodyguards. The two men, who were clearly brothers, never took their eyes off her. It was creeping her out the way they followed her every move, like the attack dogs they were. She handed a beer to Charleyboy, then crossed the room to Mr. Luther and handed him his beer, relieved to see her hands didn't shake. As she took her own seat in the easy chair, she saw that one of the bodyguards was sitting on the couch cushion under which she'd hidden the burner phone she used to communicate with Winslow. For a moment, she thought she could see an edge of the phone peeking out from between cushion and frame and something in her died a little. But then Luther distracted her by raising his bottle. "To family," he said in his dry, raspy voice, then turned his beer up and drank deeply.

"To family," Savannah and Charleyboy murmured, both confused.

Luther tipped his bottle back down and grimaced. "Well, it's cold," he said. It took a second before Savannah realized he was talking about the beer, and that he was less than satisfied.

"Would you like something else?" she asked.

He ignored the question and fixed her with eyes bright and sharp and sunk in his wrinkled skin. "Family's important, don't you think? Most important thing in the world, really."

She took a drink of her own beer, positioning the bottle in a way she hoped would obscure her face. *Oh god*, she thought, *what does he know about Mick and Keith?* "I do," she said. "I mean, I really do. I think it's the most important thing in the world."

"Good, good," he said. "'Cause I know we're not blood kin. But if me an' Charleyboy are gonna do this business like I think we are, we're gonna be like family. That makes you family, too. Doncha think?"

"I'm…I'm flattered." She took another drink. "Sure. Absolutely." She smiled brightly, wishing she had something sharp nearby to plunge into his heart.

He took another drink. For someone who clearly didn't like the beer, he was sucking it down at a good clip. "I unnerstand you been lookin' for your boys. The ones the gummint took."

Her hand tightened on the worn arm of the easy chair, fingers nearly digging through the threadbare fabric until she willed them to relax. She took a sip of her beer to catch her breath before answering. His sharp eyes were focused on her, the eyes of a hunting hawk perched on a dead branch and waiting for the rabbit to break cover. She wasn't going to give him the satisfaction. She smiled and inclined her head, raising her beer in a salute. "You're very informed."

His smile was as insincere as hers, but not nearly as charming. "I have to be, in my line of work."

"Hmmm," she said. "I never really got what your line of work was."

"Bullshit," he said, the word making Charleyboy flinch a little. "I know Charleyboy here. He can't keep his damn mouth shut. Not when he thinks something big is about to happen. He can't resist braggin' about it."

"I didn't," Charleyboy protested. "I swear."

"Uh-huh. I don't believe you, boy. But you okay, as long as you keep it to pillow talk, Charleyboy. 'Cause now that I met your lil' gal here, I feel a lot better. I think she's got sense enough to keep her mouth shut. Ain't that right, Savannah?"

"Absolutely, Mr. Luther." She gave him another smile. "Besides, who would I tell? I don't have many friends here."

He drained off the last of his beer and stood up, leaning hard for balance on the silver cane. "You got one now, gal," he said. "You got one now. You need any help, for findin' your boys or anything else, you just call Mr. Luther."

She stood up as well, hoping her long skirt kept anyone from seeing how her legs were shaking. "Thank you, sir. I'll keep that in mind."

"Good." He advanced on her, his two goons behind him. "Now c'mere and hug my neck."

Oh god, she thought, then steeled herself. *It'll be like hugging Aunt Jessamyn when you were little*, she tried to tell herself. *The one with the warts and the chin hairs. You just have to get through it.*

It was worse, much worse. The hug went on about ten seconds too long, and it ended with a shaky, guttural "mmmmhmmmmm" of pleasure that made her crave several long, hot baths. But she endured it, and when he broke away she managed not to gag on the sour, medicinal old-man smell and give him the most difficult smile of her life so far. "Thanks for coming, Mr. Luther," she said.

He smiled back, his point made. "Any time, gal. Any time."

CHAPTER TWENTY-SIX

Garcia stopped writing. "Excuse me?"

"Before I was sheriff," Wyatt said, "I was a patrol officer. I investigated a child neglect call. Two young kids were left alone in a trailer with no electricity, no food, no nothing."

Garcia's only reaction was a slight nod. He'd undoubtedly seen the same thing or worse. Wyatt went on. "The older boy was Mick Jakes. The younger was his brother, Keith."

Garcia inclined his head quizzically, but didn't speak. Wyatt recognized the old interrogator's trick: let the subject fill the silence. He smiled slightly with appreciation and continued. "Both kids were taken by DSS. After the mother failed to make any progress getting her life together, the court terminated her parental rights, and the boys were adopted out. Well, Keith was. His adoptive family changed his name to Tyler. Tyler Welch."

Garcia wrote that down. "You said Keith—Tyler was adopted out. What about Mick?"

"Mick was a tougher case. He had some, I guess you could say, behavioral issues."

Garcia shook his head. "Yeah. I checked the record. Assault, drugs, arson. All as a juvenile. Then a concealed weapon charge as an adult."

"So you can see how he'd be hard to place for adoption."

"Right." Garcia scratched his chin. "So suddenly Mick Jakes and the younger brother he hasn't seen for years are back together again. And they're robbing country stores."

"Yeah. Strike you as a little strange?"

"More than a little." Garcia was beginning to relax in Wyatt's presence as he pondered the new information. "So I'm getting that you don't think Tyler's, or Keith's, or whatever his name is...you don't think his participation in this robbery was voluntary."

"I don't," Wyatt said. "He's been a straight arrow. For years. He was literally a Boy Scout, for god's sake."

Garcia tapped his pen on the edge of his notebook and looked off into the middle distance. "I don't know. You know what they say. Blood will tell."

Wyatt frowned. "What, you think after all those years of being a good kid, straight-A student, his true nature suddenly busted out and he turned into a criminal like his brother?"

Garcia looked at him calmly. "I'm saying anything's possible." He leaned back and closed his notebook. "Sheriff, let me make a guess. You said you were looking into something for a friend. I'm thinking that's the boy's father. Or his mother. Am I right?"

"Yeah," Wyatt said.

"They're good friends. Good people. People you'd hate to give bad news to."

"Well, yeah. But..." He stopped.

"With all due respect, Sheriff, I think you may be a little too close to this." He stood up. "Still, you've given me some good information, and I appreciate it."

Wyatt stood up as well. "So do you have any idea where they are?"

Garcia hesitated.

"I just need to be able to tell the family something," Wyatt said.

"No," Garcia said. "They're in the wind. But if you do catch up to them, tell them to come in. ASAP. Tell them they'll be safer with us than they are on the street."

Wyatt felt a chill on the back of his neck that had nothing to do with the cranked air conditioning. "What does that mean?"

Garcia looked at him soberly. "It means that before the two subjects left, they burned Mick's trailer to the ground. But not before they cracked the skull of a local dealer named Micah Culp and made off with his entire stash."

"Did they kill him?"

"No," Garcia said. "He's in ICU, though. And word is that Culp's suppliers are not pleased about losing a fresh shipment."

"Or one of their people."

"They can replace a dealer any day," Garcia said. "They probably have already. But a lost stash of pills? That's serious money. Losing money makes them mad. And, Sheriff, these are not people you want to have mad at you."

Wyatt grimaced. "Damn." Then Garcia's words reminded him of something that had been lurking in the back of his mind. "That reminds me. One more thing. It's a weird loose end, and I'm not sure what it means." Garcia gave him that quizzical head tilt again, and Wyatt almost laughed. *The kid's got promise*, he thought, *but he needs to come up with some different moves.* "Not too long ago, some guy claiming to be from the federal government called the Clerk of Court's office in my county, asking for details on the adoption of Tyler Welch."

Garcia frowned. "The adoption? Why?"

"He wouldn't say. So the assistant clerk told him she wasn't going to say anything without a court order."

"Of course not," Garcia said absently. He drummed his fingers on the desk he was standing beside. "A fed, you say."

"Yeah," Wyatt said. With elaborate casualness, he added, "could be just a coincidence."

That snapped Garcia out of his reverie. He raised an eyebrow at Wyatt. "You believe in coincidences, Sheriff?"

"No," Wyatt said, "I surely do not."

Garcia nodded. "Me either. You or this assistant clerk have any idea who this fed was?"

"I don't. But I can ask."

"It'd be a big help."

"Okay." Wyatt extended a hand. "Nice to meet you, Detective Garcia."

Garcia took it. "Same to you, Sheriff."

As the handshake ended, Wyatt said "Oh, one more thing, while I'm up here."

Garcia had half turned away. He turned back, a look of impatience on his face. "Yes, sir?" he said, clearly having to make an effort not to snap at the old man who seemed determined to keep him from getting back to work.

"Delwyn Chandler," Wyatt said. "Mick's last foster placement. You interviewed him yet?"

Garcia's brows drew tighter together. "Of course. He didn't know anything about where Mick had gone. Hadn't heard from him in a year or more."

"Okay," Wyatt said. "I just didn't want to get out ahead of you if you hadn't—"

"Sheriff," Garcia said. "Again, all due respect. But I'd really appreciate it if you didn't get out ahead of me, or behind me, or anywhere around my investigation."

"You want me to just go home. And call you with what I find out about that federal guy."

Garcia nodded. "Yes, sir. I'd appreciate that." He smiled thinly. "Enjoy your retirement."

As he turned away, Wyatt had to choke back the impulse to smack the young detective on the back of the head for the condescending tone. But again, he had to admit, he'd have most likely done the same thing in Garcia's position. It still wasn't going to stop him from talking to Delwyn Chandler.

CHAPTER TWENTY-SEVEN

The sudden blast of heat and sunlight after the cool dimness of the motel room stopped Tyler in his tracks. He looked around in confusion, trying to get his bearings. The fear rising in him was screaming in his head. *Move. Somewhere. Anywhere. Just run.* He spotted the sign that said *Office* a long way down the concrete walkway where he stood. There'd be a phone there. He could call the cops. He headed that way at a dead run, his heart racing, the blood pounding in his ears. The door slammed open behind him. "Keith!'" Mick's voice called, then he bellowed. "*Keith!*" Tyler didn't turn. He ran past the rows of closed doors and windows with their thick curtains drawn against the outside world, straining every muscle like he was pounding toward a goal line. There were no other cars in the parking lot other than Mick's Trans Am.

He reached the office door and grabbed the knob frantically. It turned, slippery in his sweaty palm, but the door wouldn't open. Tyler sobbed with terror and frustration. It was only then that he noticed the Post-it note attached to the door. *Back in 5 min. - MGR.*

"No," Tyler groaned. "No. No. No." He turned to run again. He had no idea where. All he knew was that a man with a gun was behind him and every door in front of him was locked. It was a moment out of nightmare, made even more surreal by the bright and sunny day.

A car pulled into the parking space in front of the office, a bright red Ford Focus, as shiny as if it had just come off the lot. Tyler stole a look back to see Mick advancing down the row of doorways, his pistol held out in front of him. Tyler ran to the side of the car just as a short, pale man with dark hair and a pronounced five o'clock shadow was getting out, holding a bag that said *Zaxby's* in one hand and a set of keys in the other. He looked startled at Tyler's sudden appearance by his vehicle. "Can I help you, sir?" he said, in an accent that Tyler couldn't place.

"Call the police," Tyler gasped. "I've been kidnapped."

The man blinked. "Kidnapped?" He dropped his bag of food and his hand went to his throat as if he was choking. Blood began spurting from between his fingers just as Tyler registered the bang of Mick's gun. A second report shattered the silence of the summer afternoon and the man sagged back against the car, another red bloom spreading across his chest as he slid to the ground, an expression of shock and terror on his face. Tyler staggered backward, nearly falling as he tried to backpedal away from the horror unfolding before him. He was stopped from crashing down by Mick's arm as he came up from behind Tyler, the pistol still held on the man dying on the ground in front of them.

"Awwww, lil' bro," Mick said in a voice of real regret. "Look what you made me do."

"No," Tyler sobbed. "I didn't."

"You did." Tyler wouldn't look at Mick, but the voice in his ear was insistent. His arm tightened around Tyler's shoulders. "I told you what would happen if you tried to get away, Keith. I guess you thought I was just bullshitting. But you were wrong. And look what being wrong can do." The man on the ground was convulsing, his legs kicking as his body fought a losing battle for life. "I think you owe that guy an apology, Keith. Don't you agree?"

Tyler didn't answer; he was stunned and terrified beyond speech. Tears ran down his face as the hotel manager ceased his kicking and lay still. "I'm sorry," he finally choked out. "I'm so sorry."

"It's okay, lil' bro," Mick said softly, giving Tyler's shoulders a squeeze. "We all fuck up. It happens. But the important thing when you fuck up is to learn from it. You get what I'm saying?"

Tyler shook his head. He seemed incapable of forming a sentence. "I," he said, then stopped. "How. What."

"Here's what you learn from this, Keith," Mick said, and he brought his lips so close to Tyler's ear that Tyler shuddered. "You don't ask for help from strangers. Strangers will fuck you over. Every goddamn time. The only people you can trust are family. And not some fake family. Your own blood. You get me?" Tyler didn't answer until he felt the pressure of the gun barrel against the soft hollow behind his jaw and beneath his right ear. "I said, you get me?"

"Just kill me," Tyler sobbed. "You're going to do it anyway."

Tyler felt the pressure relax. "What?"

"Sooner or later, I'll do something that pisses you off and you'll pull that trigger. So just get it over with."

Suddenly, the gun and the confinement of the arm around his shoulders were gone. Tyler turned to look at Mick. His brother was standing, the gun down by his side, looking at him with real hurt in his eyes. "Is that what you think of me, lil' bro? You think I'd kill my own flesh and blood? After all this time apart, you think I'd do anything to hurt you?"

Tyler grabbed his head as if he was afraid of it exploding. "I can't believe you!" he shouted. "Mick, you were just holding a goddamn *gun* to my head! Just now! Do you not even realize that?"

Mick looked at him, then looked down at the gun. "Aw, lil' bro," he said. "I'm sorry. I just get worked up sometimes. I don't mean it."

Tyler heard the roar of a big car engine. He turned to see Mick's Trans Am pull up behind the red Focus. Lana leaned out the driver's side window. "Get in," she barked. "We need to haul ass outta here."

"No," Tyler said. "I'm not leaving. I'm done with this. I'm done." As if to prove his point, he sat down on the hot pavement, sitting tailor fashion and crossing his arms over his chest.

"Well, Keith," Mick said. He pulled a blue bandanna out of his back pocket and took the pistol by the barrel. He began carefully wiping down the grips and trigger of the gun. "I suppose I could leave you here with the dead body and the murder weapon. And you could try and convince people that I was the one who shot that poor fucker lying there. But if they ever catch up with us, Lana and me will say we're running from you after you went crazy on the drugs they'll find in your system."

Tyler was stunned. "You gave me those. You slipped them to me."

"So you say, lil' bro. So you say. But you'd most likely be locked up while they sort all that shit out. And maybe they'll believe you. Maybe they won't." He laid the gun gently on the pavement. "Or maybe you'll end up dead in a jail cell in whatever bumfuck town is nearby." He straightened up. "Or you could come with us. Your family. And we'll keep you safe."

"And this is what you call love, right Mick?"

Mick smiled. "Tough love, lil' bro. Tough love. That means it's for your own good."

"Come *on!*" Lana insisted.

Tyler felt as if his head was coming apart. He looked over at the dead man, into his blank and staring eyes. He looked back up at Mick, who was holding out a hand.

"I hate you," he whispered, but he took the hand and let Mick haul him up.

"I know, lil' bro," Mick said. "I know. Tough love is like that. But that'll change. You'll see."

Never going to happen, Tyler thought. He got in the car anyway. Mick slid into the backseat behind him. He pulled out his phone and began tapping on it.

"What are you doing?" Lana said from the front seat as she stomped on the gas. The tires squealed as the car accelerated away from the scene.

"Lettin' Mama know we're coming." He smiled. "It won't be long now."

CHAPTER TWENTY-EIGHT

As soon as Luther was out the door, Savannah turned on Charleyboy. "You *asshole!*" she raged. "What did you *tell* him?" She raised the empty bottle in her hand as if to fling it at him.

He backed up, hands raised in front of him. "Nothing. I swear it. I didn't tell him nothing about your boys."

"How am I supposed to believe that, Charleyboy? Luther's right. You got a big mouth. You love to play the fucking big shot. And now you may have put my sons in danger. My *sons!*" the last work rose to a shriek that left Charleyboy backed against the wall. Normally, a confrontation like this would begin with her berating him for some offense or slight and end with his own anger rising, shoulders and arms grabbed to the point of bruising, punches thrown, all by him. But this enraged woman was a stranger to him. The look in her eyes made him fear for the first time that she might actually kill him. She stood there, eyes wild, red hair disheveled and tangled about her beautiful face.

Suddenly, he felt his rising anger collapse, replaced by a sorrow so profound he felt as if it would crush his heart. How had it ever come to this? There had been so much love, so much promise when they'd first met. Their favorite song had been the one by Robert Earle Keene whose chorus they'd always sung along to while clinking the their long-necked beers together: "The road goes on forever, and the party never ends." Now, a few years on, he could see the end of the road, and it didn't end anywhere good. While he wasn't looking, the party had ended. If she didn't hate him already, she was getting there quickly. "I didn't talk about you, baby," he said softly. "At least I tried not to. I know what Luther is like. He'll find what you care about and use it as a handle on you."

"Yeah, no shit," she said. "Now he thinks he's got a handle on *me*."

"I thought you were going to call them off. Tell them not to come."

She shook her head. "That's what you thought. But I never said I'd do it. If you'd fucking *listen* to me…"

It was an old argument, and it steered him back into one of the old grooves that led to the old bad places. "Listen to you? Jesus Christ, when do I do anything else? You never shut the fuck up. Especially about those brats of yours." It may not have been a good place they were in, but it was one he knew how to navigate. Or so he thought.

As he advanced on her, ready to do what it took to shut her up, she didn't back away, fearful and suddenly placating, the way she'd always done before. She stood her ground, eyes blazing. "You touch me," she said in a low, vicious voice, "you're going to find out I have friends of my own."

That stopped him, but only for a moment. He laughed derisively. "You think Mr. Luther is your friend? You think he's going to protect you? Jesus, you really are a stupid bitch."

She stunned him again when she smiled. "No. Not him." She raised her voice. "*Winslow! Cahill!* It's time we all had a talk."

"**G**od*damn* it!" Winslow ripped the headphones off. "What is that crazy bitch doing?"

"She's playing her trump card," Chance replied. She took off her own headphones. "We need to go in and talk to Charleyboy. Bring him to our side." She stood up and headed for the door. "On second thought, not us. Me." She gestured toward the street. "We don't know that Luther hasn't set up his own surveillance on this place. And no offense, but you can't help but look like a cop." She barked out a laugh. "Me, I've been told for years I don't look like one. Besides, I don't have a lot of rapport with Savannah, but I've got a damn sight more than you."

Winslow shook his head, but the frustrated expression on his face showed he didn't have a better idea. "Just be careful," he muttered.

"Why, Agent Winslow," she said. "I'd almost think you cared."

He smiled weakly. "I just don't want to have to do the paperwork if you get yourself killed."

"Now there's the Winslow I know and really don't love." As she moved to the door, he spoke up. "You can't go out on the street with your sidearm. If Luther's people are watching, it's a dead giveaway."

She looked down. "Shit." In deference to the heat and the lack of air conditioning, she'd worn jeans and a thin t-shirt. There was no credible place to hide her service weapon once she took off her gun belt. She unbuckled it and handed it to Winslow. "If any shit starts—" she began.

He cut her off. "Deputy Cahill," he said, "I know you think I'm an asshole. In many ways, you are absolutely correct. But one thing I will never, *ever* do is fail to back up a fellow officer."

She nodded. Something passed between them in that moment, and she knew he was sincere. "Got it. Thanks."

"Here, take your earpiece," he said, handing it to her. She looped it into her ear as he went on. "And I'm calling in some backup. Just in case. Don't know when they'll get here." He shook his head, as if he couldn't quite wrap his head around what was happening. "Things, ah, sort of moved faster than I expected."

"Yeah. Me too. Let's just hope things don't go south here."

He solemnly held up his right hand, index and middle finger crossed. She laughed and slipped out the door. It was only when she was in the street that she thought about the double meaning of crossed fingers. One meaning was a wish for luck. The other was the betrayal of a promise.

Charleyboy stared at her, dumbfounded. "Baby. Baby. What did you *do*?"

"What I had to do, Angus," she said. "What I needed to do. For all of us." She walked over to the couch and pulled the burner phone out from under the cushion. She held it up for a second.

"Oh, fuck. Oh, Jesus, Mary, and motherfucking Joseph." He ran his hands through his hair. "You can't be serious."

"A lot more goddamn serious than this fucked up scheme you had to play Mr. Luther and Caspar Gutierrez off against one another." She slid the burner into her purse.

"You know that's probably why he came by here, right? Because he knew you were talking to the law."

"If he knew that," she said, "we'd both be dead now. Or dying, very slowly and painfully." She shook her head. "He knows something's up, sure. So he was hoping to rattle you—us—into wondering how much he knows."

"I'd say he did a hell of a job."

"Not really. We know now that he doesn't know about what you're playing with Gutierrez. Or about me talking to the feds."

"Because we're not dead or dying," he said bitterly.

"Yeah. Exactly because of that."

There was a knock at the door. They looked at one another, frozen.

"If it was Luther," Savannah whispered, "he wouldn't be knocking."

Charleyboy's face was pale. He looked like he might pass out any moment. "We hope."

A voice came through the door. "This is Deputy Chance Cahill. St. Bernard Parish Sheriff's Department. Let me in."

CHAPTER TWENTY-NINE

Delwyn Chandler lived in a small, neatly kept house on a dead-end street on the outskirts of Spencer. He greeted Wyatt on the tiny front porch, rising slowly from a light green rocker. He was tall and slender, with a lined face and kind eyes. An ancient spaniel lying beside the rocker raised his head and gave a half-hearted "woof" before settling back down, snout between his paws, and going back to sleep. Chandler regarded the dog with fond exasperation. He extended a hand to Wyatt. "Delwyn Chandler," he said.

Wyatt took the hand. The skin felt thin over bones that felt as if they might break at a firm pressure. "Wyatt McGee."

"Would you like some iced tea?" Chandler gestured at the pitcher and glasses already set out on the side table. Cut lemons waited in a dish by the pitcher.

Wyatt was still a little parched from his hangover. Iced tea was just the remedy he needed. "I'd love some," he said.

After he'd taken a seat in a rocker that matched Chandler's and fortified himself with a tall glass of tea, Wyatt didn't know how to begin. Chandler noticed his discomfiture and filled in the gap. "You're here to ask about Mick."

"Yes, sir."

Chandler sighed. "Such a sad and tragic boy." He looked at Wyatt sharply. "Don't read too much into that."

Wyatt was even more uncomfortable. He didn't say anything because he didn't know how.

Chandler shook his head, more irritated than angry. "Sorry. We got a lot of nasty talk and innuendo, Merle and I. I got tired of it. Still am."

Wyatt found his voice at last. "Merle?"

"My husband," Chandler said. "Didn't the sheriff's department tell you anything?"

"Not his name," Wyatt said.

"He never…" the words caught in Chandler's throat, "never lived to see the law recognize what we were. Are." He stopped, looked away, and took a deep breath before turning his attention back to Wyatt. "Sorry. I'm wandering."

"I'm sorry for your loss." The prescribed words of sympathy were the easiest part of this conversation yet.

Chandler's eyes narrowed as if he'd detected mockery. Then he relaxed. "Thank you," he said.

"So how did Mick come to live with you?" Wyatt asked.

"It was Merle's idea," Chandler said. "He always wanted children. At the time, though, adoption was out of the question for people like us. So we volunteered to be foster parents. But, of course, most social services departments were reluctant to place damaged children with the likes of us. Until they got desperate. Like Kassidey."

"She'd run out of alternatives."

Chandler nodded. "Yes. Even the inpatient mental health facilities had turfed him out." He shook his head. "What kind of mental health system kicks a mentally ill child out of a facility for acting mentally ill?"

Wyatt had no answer for that question. He'd seen the same thing over the years. "So how was Mick when he came to live with you?"

The answer came back without thought or hesitation. "Angry." Chandler shook his head. "Mick Jakes was the angriest person I'd ever seen. And really, who could blame him?"

The dog by Chandler's rocker gave a long, shuddering groan in his sleep and rolled over on his back. Chandler gave him an affectionate smile and reached down to scratch his belly. "Merle was so good with him. Even when I was about to tell the Social Services people we'd had enough, Merle convinced me to give him another chance." He looked up at Wyatt with tears welling in his eyes. "I think Merle knew what being abandoned felt like. When he came out to his parents, they kicked him out and never spoke to him again. He was fourteen."

Wyatt tried to keep focused on Mick's story. "So how did Mick respond?"

"Slowly," Chandler answered. "But he did respond. He stopped sneering and rolling his eyes at everything we said. He stopped lashing out in therapy. He stopped sneaking out to smoke weed with his stoner buddies."

"Did he ever talk about his brother?"

"Oh, Lord," Chandler groaned. "Did he ever. He was furious that they were being kept apart. He was going to get them back together. He was going to find their mother, and they'd be..." Chandler stopped for a moment. "A real family," he said at last.

"And you thought you were a real family."

Chandler reached down again to rub the sleeping dog's stomach. "Mr. McGee," he said, "do you know what it's like to love someone with all your heart, and to have it not be enough?"

The question staggered Wyatt for a moment. He thought of his first wife, Vanessa, who he'd left for Kassidey. Kassidey, who he'd left to try to reconcile with Vanessa, but who he still felt drawn to, and so that reconciliation had failed. And now Glenda, who he loved, but… had he inflicted that pain on them?

Chandler didn't seem to notice Wyatt's reverie. "We gave that young man all the love we had to give, and more. But he could never stop thinking about the family he couldn't have."

Wyatt cleared his throat. "So, have you heard from him?"

Chandler shook his head. "Not recently. When he turned eighteen, he wasn't in Social Services custody any more. They offered him help for independent living, but he seemed to want to put that relationship behind him. Again, who can blame him? He kept trying to find out what had happened to his brother. Social Services wouldn't tell him."

"Did he leave?"

"Eventually, yes. We let him know he could stay here as long as he wanted. He did, for a while. Then he got a job in Tennessee."

"Tennessee?"

Chandler nodded. "Some sort of marketing thing. Merle and I thought it was a scam. But I think Mick just wanted out of North Carolina." He sighed. "He sent us some e-mails. A couple of texts. Said he'd made some friends. One in particular. A guy named Kevin something. He called Kevin his 'brother from another mother.'" He sighed. "See? Even then, he was still looking for a family." He shook his head. "Then the e-mails stopped. I tried to get in touch with him when Merle got sick, but…" he shrugged, "…there was no answer and the number he texted from had gone out of service."

"Were you surprised when you found out he was back here?"

Chandler nodded. "Surprised and hurt. I thought he was happy here. But he didn't call. Or come by." He looked away. "It was like he didn't want to know us. Or like he never knew us."

"I'm sorry," Wyatt said.

Chandler looked back at him. "You know, I think you actually mean that."

"I do. So you never saw Mick when he was here?"

"Well…" Chandler hesitated. "There was one time I thought I did."

Wyatt leaned forward. "Really? Where?"

Chandler shook his head. "It was in the parking lot at the Food Lion. There was this boy, getting into a car with a girl. I could have sworn it was Mick. But he looked at me, and there was no recognition at all in his face. I just stood there as he drove away. When I got home, Merle told me I was imagining things. After all, he said, if it had really been Mick in town, he'd have…" Chandler stopped and took a long drink from his glass. When he finished, he said in a small voice, "He'd have acknowledged me. Acknowledged us. Unless…" His face began to crumple with sorrow as the implication hit him, probably not for the first time.

Wyatt broke in. "Have you seen the video? Of the robbery?"

Chandler regained his calm. "I heard about it. But no, I couldn't stand to watch it. I couldn't bear the thought of Mick…" he broke off. "Excuse me." He stood up and went inside. The dog rolled over, then sat up, blinking, obviously confused. He looked at Wyatt and gave another lackadaisical "woof" before rising to his feet with a groan and ambling over to Wyatt's chair. Wyatt reached down and scratched the dog behind the ears. Chandler came back, red-eyed but composed.

Wyatt stood. "Thank you for your time, sir. And for the tea."

"You're very welcome. And, Mr. McGee? If you find out anything about Mick, please let me know."

"Yes, sir," Wyatt said. "I'll be sure to do that."

As he walked back to the truck, his cell phone rang. He glanced at the screen. It was Kassidey. By the time he'd gotten back in the truck, the call had gone to voicemail. He redialed and she picked up on the first ring.

"Wyatt. Where are you?"

"I'm up in Spencer. Talking to Mick's last foster parent." He looked over to the porch where Chandler was tidying up the tea pitcher and glasses. He moved like a man grown old before his time. "It was a dead end."

"I checked Facebook," Kassidey said. "I found Savannah Jakes. And, Wyatt...I think Mick did, too."

CHAPTER THIRTY

Chance took the big easy chair. Savannah and Charleyboy sat together on the couch. Savannah tried to put her arm around his shoulders, but he shrugged it off, not looking at her, and moved away. He sat with his head down and his hands dangling between his knees. Savannah sighed and looked at Chance.

"Look, Charleyboy," Chance said, "I know this isn't what you planned. But you want to get out from under Luther's thumb, right?"

"Go to hell," he mumbled.

She ignored it. "This stands a better chance of that than this complicated double cross you're setting up. And you won't be switching one owner for another."

He looked up, his eyes narrowed. "No one owns me."

Chance leaned forward and spoke softly but firmly. "Wrong, Angus. Right now, I own you. The both of you. Me and the United States government."

"Right," he sneered. "And who's holding your leash?"

"No one I can't walk away from. Which is different from where you are right now, isn't it?"

He didn't answer.

"Baby," Savannah spoke up from the end of the couch, "you know she's right. We need to get out of here. Out of this life. Not deeper into it."

He shook his head. "I'm not a goddamn rat."

Chance shrugged. "Maybe not. You can choose to walk out that door, but it'll be in handcuffs. We've got enough for a conspiracy charge that'll put you away for a while." She looked over at Savannah. "Both of you."

"Bullshit." His voice didn't sound nearly as confident as his words. "She didn't have anything to do with...with anything."

"Well, we can let the court sort that out. But you'll spend some time in custody first. And maybe Luther or Gutierrez will believe that you'll stay quiet. But I've looked at the DEA files, and I do know that Gutierrez, for one, isn't known for taking chances. The last associate of his that got locked up in Texas disappeared right after he made bail. He turned up three weeks later in an abandoned house in the Mexican desert. What was left of him, at least. They'd tied him to a chair and tortured him with a power drill, probably to find out what he'd told the cops. They don't think he was dead when they left him. Think about that, Charleyboy. They left him to bleed out, then to rot in the heat. Apparently, the Mexican authorities still talk in whispers about where they'd put that drill. And they're not easy people to impress."

Winslow's voice came through her earbud. "Damn, Cahill, you're getting good at this." She ignored him.

Savannah had gone white. "You're full of shit," Charleyboy said, but he was looking pale as well.

"Guess we'll see." Chance stood up. "But if I walk out that door, any deal you might make goes with me. The next ones through it will be a DEA strike team."

"Strike team?" Winslow said.

Chance ignored him. "And we'll let the chips fall where they may." She started for the door. She was almost there when Charleyboy spoke up.

"Wait."

Chance paused to compose herself and start breathing again before she turned around. "Yes?"

"Okay," he said, still looking down. "Okay."

"Wait," Savannah said. "Any deal has to give some kind of protection to my boys."

Charleyboy looked up at the ceiling. "Oh, for god's sake."

"I'll see what I can do," Chance said. "But Charleyboy's right about one thing. The best thing you can do right now is call them off. Tell them not to come. Until things settle down."

Savannah shook her head. "I can't do that."

"You know how Luther is. He'll use what you love to hurt you."

"You can protect them."

Chance was getting frustrated. "I can." She still didn't know if that was true, but she was not going to give these two informants a chance to get off the hook. "But to make that happen, I need to talk to the people higher up. Call them off, Savannah. At least until we can make arrangements. Once we get that done, I'll do everything I can to get you back together. I promise."

"That doesn't mean shit to me," Savannah flared up. "Once you people get what you want, you'll move on. You won't help me. Your kind never has." She turned to Charleyboy. "Don't tell them shit, baby. Not until they—"

"Baby," Charleyboy interrupted her, "fuck you."

She reeled back as if she'd been slapped. "What?"

"You got me into this, bitch," he snarled. His eyes were slits of rage. "I trusted you. I fucking *trusted* you, and you put me into this box where I don't have any choice but to try to cut a deal. Now you want to tell me what deal to cut? Fuck you, and fuck your two brats."

She started for him, and he looked ready to go for her as well, when Chance spoke up. "*Hold it!*"

They stopped, glaring at each other like prizefighters pried out of a clinch. "You need help?" Winslow said in her ear.

"I got this," Chance answered. She got between Savannah and Charleyboy. "We're going to have some ground rules here. Rule one is no more hitting. I find so much as a bruise on her, Charleyboy, and all deals are off. You go into custody, and we see what happens after that."

"Cahill," Winslow said, "You don't have the authority to..."

She was back to ignoring him. "We have an understanding here?"

"Sure," Charleyboy said. "Best way to avoid that is for her to get the fuck out. I don't want to even fucking see that bitch anymore."

"Fine." Savannah walked off toward the bedroom. "I'll get my stuff."

"You have any place to go?" Chance called after her.

"I'll find something." She disappeared into the back of the house.

"Shit," Chance said. She spoke to the hidden mike. "Winslow, we got any place for her to stay?"

Charleyboy looked around. "Who are you talking to?"

"We don't have any safe houses in place," Winslow responded. "If we had a little more warning..."

"You're wearing a wire, aren't you?" Charleyboy said. "You're wearing a goddamn wire."

"Of course I'm wearing a wire," Chance said. "Now shut up and let me think." She didn't have any alternative but one. When Savannah came out of the bedroom, dragging a roller bag behind her. Chance told her, "You're staying with me."

Savannah was still fuming. "Like hell."

"Unless you have some other friend that you won't mind putting in danger if Mr. Luther comes looking for you..." Chance trailed off.

Savannah clenched her jaw. "Fine. Whatever." She walked toward the door. Before she got there, she turned. "I got one last question, Charleyboy. How did Luther find out about my boys? Did you tell him?"

He looked stricken. "I didn't. I swear it."

She started for him, but Chance barred her way. "Either you're a lying sack of shit," Savannah whispered savagely, "or he's got us wired, too. Either way, you fucked up and put my boys in danger. I could kill you for that."

"Have a nice life, you fucking whore," Charleyboy said, but it came out sounding week in comparison to Savanah's fury.

Chance had heard enough. "Come on. Let's go." She turned to Charleyboy as she reached the door. "Oh, and, Angus? Don't even think of running. We'll have people on you. You may not see them, but they'll be there. You try to rabbit, you'll be in a federal cell so fast it'll make your goddamn head spin." She didn't wait for a response as she pushed Savannah out the door. "You need to get some people on him," she whispered into the mike as she marched Savannah across the road.

"Well..."

"Damn it, Winslow," she snapped. "Can I get a little fucking cooperation here?"

"I'll see what I can do."

"Yeah. You do that."

He'd made it back home in what must have been record time, until he was back in Kassidey's tiny office, seated across the desk from her. She was typing away on a laptop computer.

"Sometimes I forget how much of people's lives go on Facebook now," she was saying. "Anyone who has a grievance can't help but air it out for the entire world to see. So if you're looking for someone who's looking for someone…" She finished typing and turned the computer around. The screen showed a Facebook group page. 'Birth Parents Seeking Children', the title of the group read, and Kassidey had scrolled down to the black-and-white photo of Savannah, seated, with her boys beside her. Wyatt felt his throat tighten at the sight.

"Check the message under the picture," Kassidey said.

Wyatt scrolled down again. *Thank you 2 the group*, the last message read. *My boys are in touch and on their way to me in Arabi, New Orleans. God is truly good.*

"New Orleans," Wyatt said. "They're headed there."

Kassidey took the computer back. "Right. And I didn't know what Arabi meant, so I looked it up. It's in something called St. Bernard Parish. So what we need to do is contact the New Orleans PD or St. Bernard Parish Sheriff, tell them they have a couple of fugitives headed their way, and let them handle it."

"Yeah."

"Wyatt," she said, "are you listening to me? We need to turn this over to the locals."

He wouldn't look at her. "Sure. You should probably do that."

She gaped at him for a moment. "Jesus H. Tap-dancing Christ," she said. "You're going down there."

"I didn't say that."

"You didn't need to. I know that look in your eye, Wyatt. And I know this is a really stupid idea."

"Yeah. It is."

"There's nothing you can do that the locals can't do."

"Most likely."

"In fact, they'll tell you to go home and get out of their way."

"Yep."

"You know, Wyatt, there are a lot of things you used to do that drove me up the wall. But probably the biggest one was this thing you did…that you still do…where you agree with everything I say, then go and do whatever you were going to do anyway."

"I can see how that would be annoying." He looked at her blandly until they both burst into laughter. When it ran down, she shook her head. "Seriously, Wyatt, what in the *hell* do you hope to accomplish here?"

It took a long moment for him to pull his thoughts together. Finally, he spoke. "If I find them, or, more likely, if someone else finds them, they're going to be a long way from home. They'll be strangers. Unknown. Maybe I can make things a little easier for them."

"If the locals will listen to you at all."

"I'm law enforcement. I know I may not have felt much like it recently, or acted like it. But I can still talk to officers in language that'll reach them. And I know the subjects. They'll listen."

She raised both eyebrows at him. "Uh-huh. And how much of this, Wyatt, is you trying to work out a boatload of old guilt? Not just the Jakes boys, but Morris Tyree as well?" She sighed. "Don't even bother to answer. You're going to do what you're going to do. Aren't you?"

He smiled. "I usually do."

She waved him away. "Just go, Wyatt. Go do whatever you need to do."

As he got up to go, he said, "I'm glad you're not still mad at me."

She'd turned back to her computer. "Who says I'm not?"

CHAPTER THIRTY-ONE

"So," Hammond said, "you brought in Charlebois." He shook his head. "Hell of a risk."

There didn't seem to be disapproval in the SAC's voice. "Yes, sir," Winslow said.

Hammond went on. "And the woman. Have they given you anything useful yet?"

"We're setting up a debrief with each of them," Winslow said. "Tomorrow morning at the latest."

The SAC nodded. "We've got a clock ticking here. Our sources in Mexico say Gutierrez is itching to make a move. We need to know when and where he's trying to come into Louisiana and we need it fast."

"You'll get what you need." Winslow wished he was as sure as he sounded.

"I understand Cahill, the local deputy, is managing the woman."

"Yes, sir." Winslow hated what he was about to have to say.

"Which brings up an issue."

The SAC looked over the papers he'd been perusing, his eyes expressionless. "Right. Savannah Jakes's sons."

"Yes, sir." Winslow didn't like the look on the SAC's face. "Deputy Cahill," he said, carefully distancing himself, "thinks that Savannah Jakes will be more cooperative if we can insure the safety of her sons. One was adopted out, but his brother found him. Apparently, the two of them are on their way here."

He took off his glasses and stared at Winslow. "The only problem is this, Agent Winslow. We have, at your request, been putting on a full search for Mick and Keith Jakes. You're right that the younger brother, Keith, was adopted. We've hit a wall, apparently, with some officious local clerk. We can't get any information on that without a court order, and I can't take this to the U.S. Attorney without something a little more concrete."

"But that should be a moot point. Mick informed Savannah that they're together and they're on their way here."

"Well, that's very interesting. Because Mick Jakes was a lot easier to track, thanks to his record. He had a lot of run-ins with the law. We followed that trail right to its end."

"It's…end?"

"Mick Jakes has been dead for over two years. He was killed by another inmate in a county lockup in Gatlinburg, Tennessee."

Winslow sat back down, his head feeling like it was going to explode. "That's…there must be some mistake."

Hammond shook his head. "No mistake. Jakes was drunk. They either didn't have a single cell for him or just didn't care. He got into a fight with some other redneck drifter and got his head banged off the edge of the metal bed enough times to fracture his skull. He died on the operating table. The sheriff's department caught some flak for it in the local papers, but one lowlife killing another apparently wasn't a story that grabbed the public's attention. Imagine that." Hammond punched a button on his phone. "Kimball, could you come in here, please? Bring the Jakes sub-file." In a moment, Kimball came in carrying a couple of file folders. He handed one to Hammond, who opened it. "Here's where it gets interesting," he said. "This 'dead man' now has warrants out on him for an armed robbery, assault, and arson. All in North Carolina. His brother, too. The brother apparently goes by the name of Tyler Welch now, by the way." He handed a photograph across the desk. Winslow took it. It was a still from a security camera. The picture was grainy and blurry from the movement of the subjects in it, but Winslow could make out the features on the two young men. "The one with the brown hair is Tyler Welch. The one with the shotgun is the one who rented a trailer in some hick town out there under the name of Mick Jakes. Apparently, he'd been on the radar of the local cops for a while, but they never could hang anything on him. Until a few days ago, when he did this. After which he beat the hell out of a local drug dealer and ran off with the stash. Oh, and on the way out of town he burned down his own house."

Winslow handed the picture back. "And now they're on the way here."

Hammond nodded. "We've alerted the locals. If they show up, we've asked them to hold them, oppose bail, keep them bottled up." He gave Winslow a tight smile. "That's technically keeping them safe, right?"

Winslow thought of Mick Jakes getting his head bashed in in a jail cell far from home. "So who is the guy claiming to be Mick?"

Hammond looked over at Kimball, who spoke up for the first time. "Best ID we have on him is a habitual thief and small-time drug dealer named Kevin DeWalt. He and Mick Jakes were cellmates at Hardeman County Correctional in Tennessee for about six months." Kimball opened the file he'd kept and handed a picture to Winslow. It was a prison mugshot marked *DeWalt, Kevin.* Same dark hair, same eyes, same build. The resemblance was remarkable. Kimball went on. "After they got out, the two of them apparently moved up to Gatlinburg. Shared an apartment for a while."

"How do you know that?"

"Same address on the misdemeanor warrants each of them kept picking up. Then Mick Jakes got picked up again. For the last time. When he died, DeWalt dropped off the radar."

Winslow nodded. "Taking Mick Jakes's identity with him." He shook his head in amazement. "So, what do I tell Savannah?"

The SAC looked at him with an eyebrow raised, as if he couldn't believe the stupidity of the question. "Well, you certainly don't tell her one of her sons is dead. From the sound of things, she's not that stable to begin with, and this could send her completely off the rails. We need her cooperation. Not as badly as Charlebois's, but she's still an asset. And you'd best not tell the deputy, either. What she doesn't know, she can't spill by accident."

Winslow frowned. "I don't like lying to my…" he almost said "partner," but realized that it wasn't actually true, since she wasn't DEA, "to another officer," he amended.

Hammond waved a dismissive hand. "We keep the locals in the dark all the time, Winslow. You know that. You even said it."

But this is different. Winslow thought back to the moment that had passed between him and Cahill before she'd gone into the house with Savannah and Charleyboy. He found that he actually liked Cahill. He respected her. He didn't believe for a moment that she'd spill the beans by accident. Still, orders were orders.

"Yes, sir," he said.

"Here we are," Chance said as she pulled the pickup into the patch of earth beside the trailer. From his pen beneath the trees, Jonas set up a joyful baying. Savannah regarded the place without expression, then gave a heavy sigh and opened the door.

Well, fuck you too, honey, Chance thought as Savannah got her bag out from behind the seat. Like the dump where she'd been living was any better. Chance walked over and let the dog out. He paused for only a second to receive his welcoming pat, then bounded toward the new stranger, tail wagging furiously.

Savannah stepped backwards at first, clearly apprehensive, but when Jonas stopped, hindquarters raised and front paws stretched out in front of him, tail still going a mile a minute, she broke into a smile. She put down the bag and crouched down, holding out a hand. "C'mere, puppy," she crooned. When Chance walked over, Jonas was receiving a thorough scratching behind the ears, tongue lolling from one corner of his mouth in ecstasy.

"World's worst watchdog," Chance said with a laugh.

"He's a big ol' sweetie," Savannah said. "Aren't you? Aren't you?" The hard look on her face had softened, and Chance could see what she must have looked like as a young girl.

"Come on in," she said. "I'll see what's in the fridge for dinner."

Savannah picked up her bag. "Thanks. I know I've been kind of a bitch about this." She put a hand on Chance's arm. "But I really do appreciate it. I don't know where I'd be right now if it hadn't been for you, Deputy Cahill." That wide-eyed, guileless look threw Chance for a moment.

Call me Chance, she wanted to say. Then she remembered her father's words. *You have to learn to keep your distance. Don't let them suck you into their game.* She gave the hand on her arm a pat that turned into a brush off, but a gentle one. "Don't mention it. Part of the job."

Her dad. Shit. It was her night to call him. She wondered what he'd say about her bringing a CI home with her. Nothing good, she figured. "There's a spare bedroom down that hall," she said as they entered. "I'll get some sheets and a blanket out of the closet once I check out the food situation."

"Is there a guest bathroom? I need to freshen up."

"Yeah. Towels are hanging up. Let me know if you need more." Savannah nodded and disappeared down the hallway.

Chance looked in the fridge. "I got some pork chops," she called out. "That good?"

"I don't eat pork," Savannah called back.

Of course you don't, Chance thought. "Only other choice is chicken."

"Fine."

Chance pulled the frozen chicken tenders out of the freezer, wondering how many would be enough. She wasn't used to cooking for anyone else, and most nights she just curled up with a mug of soup and a book or the TV. Her phone rang as she put the tenders on the counter. It was Winslow. She tucked the phone beneath her chin as she opened the package. "Hey."

Winslow got right to the point. "We scheduled her debrief for nine thirty tomorrow. A half hour after Charlebois gets here."

"Yeah," Chance said. "Probably best that they not see each other. That situation's what you might call a little tense."

"A little, yeah."

Chance frowned. Winslow sounded strange. Not himself. "Everything all right, Winslow?"

"Yeah," he said. "Just busy trying to get this together. You going to have any problem getting her there?"

"Not that I can think of. You got any word on the boys?"

There it was again. That slight hesitation that made the back of Chance's neck tingle. "Nothing," Winslow said. "If Savannah gets something, let us know. If we can find them, we can bring them in."

"Bring them...you're talking about taking them..." Chance looked up to see Savannah entering the room. "Text me, okay? I gotta make dinner."

"Yeah. Okay." Winslow hung up.

"What's going on?" Savannah asked.

"We've got a debrief at nine thirty tomorrow morning."

"A what?"

"You'll sit down with a couple of DEA agents. They'll ask you what you know. I don't think I need to tell you how important it is to tell the truth. They'll be cross checking what you tell then with what Charleyboy says. If they think you're bullshitting them, it's not going to end well."

"Will you be there?" Savannah asked in a small voice.

"I don't know," Chance confessed. "Seriously, though, I doubt it. I'm not DEA. I'm the local yokel. I think once this thing really gets going, they're going to take the ball and run with it."

"I'd really like it if you were there," Savannah said. She stepped in closer, her eyes wide and glistening with tears. "I really need a friend." She put a hand on Chance's arm. "I'm sorry about what I said earlier. Back in the café." She began rubbing the arm softly and moving closer.

Jesus, Chance thought, *is she coming on to me?* She pulled her arm away. "We need to get something straight, girl. You were right the first time. I'm not going to be your buddy here. And I'm sure as hell not going to be your girlfriend."

Savannah looked crushed for a moment, her face crumpling like that of a child about to cry. When she saw that wasn't working, the mask dropped away, her face turning to stone. "Sorry," she said. "The way you got your hair cut, well, I figured…" She didn't go on, just walked away, threw herself onto the ragged couch, and picked up the TV remote.

Chance's first instinct was to argue, *No, I like men, it's just…* But she realized that her being on the defensive was just what Savannah… *the informant*…wanted. Chance shook her head and went back to making dinner.

CHAPTER THIRTY-TWO

They came into New Orleans like a rocket shooting down I-10, blasting past Slidell so fast that Tyler was sure they'd get pulled over. But they made it through, across Lake Pontchartrain, taking the exit through Chalmette, passing through mile after mile of industrial blocks and poor areas that were nothing like the New Orleans he'd seen in the movies or in magazines. The houses were jammed together, all of them looking ragged and run down. It was getting dark, and Tyler was getting apprehensive about being in this sketchy area after dark. "Where are we going?" he finally asked.

Mick didn't answer at first. He seemed suddenly nervous, nowhere near as self-assured as he'd been all the way down. Finally, he pulled over in a vacant concrete-covered lot with weeds poking up from between the slabs. "I need to let Mama know we're here," he muttered.

"Wait," Tyler said. "You don't know where she lives?"

"Somewhere around here," Mick said impatiently. "I just need to get the address."

"You don't already have it?" Tyler's voice was rising. Lana reached out from the backseat and put her hand on his arm to calm him. "Is she even here?" Tyler demanded. "I mean, Jesus, Mick, does she even exist?"

"Of course she fucking exists!" Mick's scream was ear-splitting in the confined space of the car. Tyler recoiled back against the door. Mick leaned toward him. "You think I'd bring us all the way here if she wasn't real? I've dreamed about this day, lil' bro. Dreamed of when we could be together. Be a family. Be…" He got hold of himself with difficulty. Tyler stayed pressed back against the door. Mick shook his head and reached down to pull his phone from the center console. "Relax, Keith," he said. "It won't be long now."

W yatt had never liked airports, and New Orleans' Louis Armstrong Airport seemed more confusing than most, especially when it came to finding ground transportation. Eventually, after retrieving his checked bag, he found the desk for the rental agency where he'd booked a car. After verifying he was who he said he was, he asked for directions to the hotel he'd booked in Chalmette. She began to explain, but when she saw Wyatt's evident confusion, the clerk just sighed, gave up, and showed him how to program the destination into the car's GPS. He fervently hoped he'd never have to do it again; he didn't trust vehicles with computer screens where instruments and knobs should be and dreaded the day when he'd have to abandon his old truck for a model that gave him no choice but to adapt. The trip took about a half hour and wound through the midtown, the Ninth Ward, then through Arabi to Chalmette. The neighborhoods were run down, and in some areas Wyatt could still see devastation from the 2005 hurricane. The GPS kept speaking up, making him jump every time. It would warn him of upcoming turns, remind him of them as he drew closer, then tell him again when it was time to make the turn. It got on his nerves from the beginning. Along the way, Wyatt kept checking his phone, looking for a reply to his calls to the New Orleans Police Department or the St. Bernard Parish Sheriff. Before he took off from Raleigh-Durham airport, he'd even gritted his teeth and tried to tap out some e-mails. It was the first time he'd tried that on his phone rather than a desktop computer at the station. It didn't matter. He'd gotten nothing back. He kept thinking of his last conversation with Glenda.

"New Orleans," she'd said in the neutral voice that meant he was in trouble from the beginning.

"Yeah."

She arched an eyebrow at him. "And do you know anyone in New Orleans?"

This was shaping up to be the same conversation he'd had with Kassidey. "No. But, you know. Brotherhood of the badge and all that." He tried to keep the words lighthearted, almost self-mocking, but they landed like lead.

"Uh-huh," she said. Then she surprised him by putting a hand on his. "You're afraid they're going to kill Tyler, aren't you?"

He nodded. "That's been worrying me, yeah. Word comes down he's a violent armed robber…" He paused and took a breath. "All it'd take is one scared rookie to put him down. I couldn't face Carl Welch if I didn't try to do something."

Glenda nodded, her face set in that blank expression that meant she was thinking something through. "Well, we've got some money put back. This isn't how I meant to spend it. I was thinking of a new roof, you want to know the truth. But if you're careful and don't eat at Chef Whoever's every night, we can swing it." The distant expression went away and she looked at him with the direct gaze that had attracted him when they first met. "Just don't do anything stupid, okay? If…stuff gets bad, stand back and offer encouragement and good advice. Don't get into the middle of anything. You know what

I mean."

"I do. And thanks."

She snorted. "You don't need to thank me for telling you that it's okay to do what you were going to do anyway, Wyatt."

"I know," he said, "but thanks anyway."

She kissed him. "You'd better go pack. Will they let you take your bulletproof vest on the plane?"

"I doubt it."

"So, what I said earlier still stands, okay?"

"In one hundred and fifty yards," the cheerful computer voice interrupted his memory, "your destination will be on your left."

He pulled into the parking lot of a Best Western. He didn't know what he expected—Spanish moss hanging off live oaks in the parking lot, maybe, but there was none of that. It looked like every other hotel of its type in the United States. He found a parking space and got out. As he walked into the lobby, dragging his roller bag behind him, his phone vibrated in his pocket. Cursing under his breath, he fumbled it out and answered. "Hello?"

"Mr. McGee?" a female voice, all business and clearly not up for any nonsense, came over the scratchy connection.

"This is Wyatt McGee."

"Mr. McGee, this is Sergeant Delphine Cormier of the St. Bernard Parish Sheriff's Department. What can I do for you?"

There was a small sitting area a few feet away from the front desk. A slim young black man stood behind the desk, looking skeptically over a pair of reading glasses at Wyatt. He pulled out the printout Glenda had made of his reservation and waved it at the young man. The clerk gave him a professional smile, nodded, and returned to his computer screen. Wyatt took a seat. "Thanks for returning my call, Sergeant. I'm a law enforcement officer...well, retired...from North Carolina."

"Yes, sir." Cormier's voice was getting more disinterested with every word.

"I've got some information about a couple of…um, suspects… from North Carolina who may be coming to New Orleans. Specifically, to your county…sorry, parish."

"Sir, we haven't heard anything about any fugitives from North Carolina."

"I'm telling you now. There are two young men coming to town who are wanted for an armed robbery and arson in North Carolina."

"Yes, sir. And why are they coming to St. Bernard Parish?"

"They're looking for their birth mother. Savannah Jakes."

"Yes, sir," Cormier said, the automatic politeness like a brick wall. Then her voice sharpened. "Wait. Did you say Savannah Jakes?"

Wyatt's heart skipped a beat. "You know the name?"

There was a brief pause that seemed to stretch out for minutes. "Mr. McGee? Will you be at this number for an hour or so?"

"Yes. Yes, I will."

"Okay," Cormier said. "I'll get right back to you." She broke the connection, leaving Wyatt staring at his phone in bafflement.

"Ready to check in, sir?" the desk clerk called to him.

Wyatt stood up. "Yeah. Thanks."

In the room, he lifted his roller bag onto the bed and unzipped it. He looked down at the objects that lay on top. He had debated bringing them along, seeing as how he had no official status here. Carrying weapons also required him to check his bag and leave it to the mercy of the airline, something he loathed. But the thought of going unarmed into a situation with this much uncertainty was intolerable. That explained the Beretta semi-auto and the shoulder rig. The knife…that he had more trouble explaining, even to himself. He picked the sheathed blade up for a moment and regarded it, turning it over to read the burned-in name on the back. His thumb unsnapped the safety strap and he wrapped his fingers around the hilt. He hadn't drawn the knife in years, even to look at. It occurred to him that it would probably look ridiculous strapped to the JC Penney belt that held up his khaki pants, with his dark green polo shirt pulled over it. He put the knife back into the suitcase and picked up the holster.

CHAPTER THIRTY-THREE

Chance was putting away the dinner dishes when her phone rang. She picked it up off the kitchen table and checked the screen. It was work. "Hello?" she said.

"Hey, Chance, it's Delphine."

She relaxed slightly. She'd always liked Delphine. Short, round, dark-haired, with a dry yet bawdy sense of humor that had reduced Chance to tears of helpless laughter on more than one after-hours outing, Cormier was one of the few officers in the department with whom she felt totally comfortable. "Hey, girl. What's up?"

"Aw, you know how it is. Hey, *cher*, I just got a weird call."

Chance sat down at the kitchen table. "Go ahead."

"Isn't the lady in that case you're working with the feds named Savannah Jakes?"

Chance looked over to where Savannah was slumped on her couch, stone-faced and watching *Wheel of Fortune*. "Yeah. Why?"

"Some old guy, said he was from North Carolina, has been

calling. Says he used to be sheriff in one of the counties up there."

Chance turned away slightly. "Go on."

"Well, he's here. Says Savannah's sons are on their way."

Chance felt her heart speed up. "What did he know?"

"I didn't go into it with him. I figured I'd let you know first, since it's your case and all."

"Not really mine. I'm just the liaison with the feds."

"As far as I'm concerned, *cher*, it's yours. Fuck the feds. What have those sumbitches ever done for St. Bernard?"

Chance had to laugh. That was Delphine all over. "I heard that."

"You want his call-back number?"

"Yeah." She searched for a pencil and a scrap of paper and a pencil in the kitchen junk drawer. "Shoot."

Cormier read off the number to her. "And the name is McGee. Wyatt McGee, if you can believe that."

"Thanks, Delphine." She stole another glance at Savannah. This must be the sheriff Savannah had been so bitter towards. She didn't know how she was going to handle this.

"No problem, girl," Cormier said. Her voice went from lighthearted to serious. "You need any kind of backup on this? Seriously. Anything."

"I'll keep you on speed dial," Chance said.

"You do that."

"Thanks, Delphine. I owe you."

"Hey," Delphine said. "We ladies don't look after each other, who will?"

"You got that right. See ya." She broke the connection and looked over again at Savannah. As if sensing her disturbance, Savannah looked away from the TV for the first time since their silent dinner and regarded Chance suspiciously. "What?"

Chance decided to be upfront. "That was one of my co-workers." She hesitated, trying to think of the best way to broach the subject.

"Someone called her. Said he has some information about your boys."

Savannah jumped up. "Who? Who was it?"

Chance took a deep breath. "I think it was that sheriff. From back in North Carolina."

Savannah's face went blank for a moment, then her eyes narrowed and her lips drew back in a snarl. "What's he saying? More lies? I know it's lies. He just lies." She was working herself up to a full-blown rant.

"Easy," Chance said. "We don't even know what he has to say."

Savannah began to pace. She rubbed her hands together in agitation. "Whatever he says, you'll believe it. You stick together. All you bastards stick together. All you fucking cops."

"*Hey!*" Chance barked. Savannah stopped and looked at her, wide-eyed. "Stow that shit, okay?" Chance said. "I don't know this guy from the man in the goddamn moon. I'm going to hear what he has to say. He may be as bent as you think he is. I'll keep that in mind. But here's the thing, Savannah. I don't totally trust you, either."

She looked stunned, then as if she was about to cry. "Why wouldn't you believe me?"

Chance rolled her eyes. "Oh, please. Spare me, okay? I'm going to call this guy. I may even meet with him."

Savannah looked alarmed. "Wait. He's here?"

"Somewhere in the area, yeah."

Her mouth drew into a tight line. "If you meet him, I want to go with you. I want to look him in the eye and ask him why he lied. And then I want to spit in his face."

"That doesn't exactly make me want to bring you along. But I'll talk it over with my partner. We've still got to get you to your debrief tomorrow morning, and me having to book you for assaulting a law enforcement officer with bodily fluids might slow that down."

"Fine." Savannah stomped off down the hall and slammed the door to the guest room. Chance shook her head. She'd be glad when this babysitting job was over. She thought for a moment about who to call first, Winslow or this McGee. She decided to find out what McGee's game was first. Then she and Winslow could decide what to do. She walked down the hall toward her own bedroom at the other end of the trailer, dialing as she went.

Wyatt was hanging his shirts carefully in the hotel room's tiny closet when his phone rang. He picked it up, but didn't recognize the number. "McGee," he answered.

"Mr. McGee," a female voice said. "This is Deputy Chance Cahill of St. Bernard Parish Sheriff's Department. How can I help you?"

"Thanks for calling me back so quickly, Deputy Cahill. Did the sergeant fill you in?"

"Sergeant Cormier said you had some information on Savannah Jakes. And her sons."

He sat on the end of the bed. "Yeah. I know her sons are on the way. And…" He hesitated. "Do you mind if I ask what your connection is with Savannah?"

"Yes, I do mind, sir," Cahill said. "For the moment, at least. Sorry, but I need to know what your interest in this matter is."

Wyatt was getting irritated. Then he picked up on what Cahill had just said. *This matter.* There was clearly something going on, Savannah was involved, and everyone was more than a little touchy about discussing it. He felt the tension creeping up his back and neck, the same tension he'd felt on the job when going into a house or bar on a call, not knowing what was waiting beyond the door. He decided to lay his cards on the table, and hope Cahill would do the same. They were, after all, on the same side. He hoped.

"Okay," he said. "I know the boys. I'm the one who first picked them up from their mother. The younger boy, Tyler, was adopted by friends of mine. I know the boys are headed here to try and meet up with their mother. Savannah. But there was some trouble along the way."

A brief pause on the other end. Then, "Go on."

"The boys were involved in an armed robbery. At least, they were both there. I think Mick, the older boy, may have put Tyler up to it. Then, as they were leaving to come here, one or both of the boys assaulted and robbed a local drug dealer. Then Mick appears to have burned his own house down."

"Ooooh-kay," Cahill said. "So, are you here to bring them back?"

This time, it was Wyatt's turn to pause. "I don't have that authority," he said finally. "I'm just here to try to help them. I…I feel a certain amount of responsibility for them."

Cahill's voice, when she spoke again, was softer, less formal. "I guess I get that. But you have to understand, Savannah doesn't exactly trust you."

Wyatt laughed ruefully. "I guess in her position, I wouldn't either. I take it you've been dealing with her."

"Yeah."

"She's an informant, isn't she?"

"I can't really say…"

"Come on, Deputy," he said impatiently, "I'm not some rookie. We both know Savannah. The only way she'd be dealing with you, a law enforcement officer, is if she was an informant. And the only way she'd be doing that is if she was in deep shit. And now we have her sons, in deep shit of their own, about to enter the mix. There's no way this ends well for anyone unless we all get together and get on the same page."

There was a brief commotion on the other end, as if Cahill had dropped the phone. He thought he heard a curse, but it was too muffled to make it out. When she came back on the line, Cahill sounded slightly breathless and her voice was tense. "Okay. Let's meet. But you'll need to come to me."

"What? Why?"

"Because that fucking bitch just stole my truck."

CHAPTER THIRTY-FOUR

Chance paced back and forth in the narrow confines of the trailer's tiny living room, cursing bitterly under her breath. Jonas sat on the couch, following her with his eyes and occasionally thumping his tail anxiously. She paused from time to time to reassure her dog with a scratch behind the ears, then returned to pacing.

How the hell could I have been so careless, she thought. Then another part of her mind took over and tried to defend what happened. She'd only turned her back on Savannah for a moment. How could she have known? Then again, she should have known better. Savannah was an informant. Informants will burn you given half a chance.

It seemed like longer to her, but it only took a minute or so before Chance made her decision. She went back to what she'd learned from her father. *You screw up, Lil' Bit*, he'd told her, *you own up. Then you step up. You do what it takes to make it right.* This was something exponentially worse than losing her dad's favorite cufflinks or denting the car, the two major times she could remember her dad imparting that lesson, but it still stuck. She picked up the phone, tapped it a couple of times against her hip, then took a deep breath and dialed Winslow. "Savannah's in the wind," she said as soon as he answered.

The response was immediate. "How long?"

She was humiliated at how grateful she was that he wasn't berating her. "About fifteen minutes. Give or take a minute. I was on the phone with this ex-sheriff from North Carolina. He's been tracking the boys. When I turned my back for a second, she took my keys, slipped out the door, and hit the road."

"Okay. Only one place I can think of that she'd be going."

Chance got it immediately. "Home. To Arabi."

"That's where the boys would be heading. It's the address she gave them. And I'm still set up on that house. I've got eyes on it right now."

"Wait," she said. "Alone?"

"Well, you did kind of advance things faster than anyone was anticipating. But we'll cover it. I've got a relief coming. Eventually."

"What happens if she tells them to meet her somewhere else?"

"Don't know how she'd do that," Winslow said. "And her computer's still in the Arabi house."

You know she can access it from her phone, right?"

"She can?"

Chance shook her head and moved on.

"Is Charleyboy still there?"

"Yep," Winslow said. "Obviously, I'd rather have him in a safe house, but…"

"I know. I moved up the timetable."

"Yeah. But he knows better than to try to run."

"Okay. She could be figuring out some place else to meet the boys, but this is the only meeting place we know of so far. We start from there and figure out where to go from that."

"Yeah."

"Okay," she said. "So. When your relief comes—"

"You need me to come out and get you."

She sighed. "No. I made arrangements. And, Winslow?"

"Yeah?"

"You can give me as much shit over it as you like, okay? Just do it later."

"Oh, you can count on that." He chuckled. Then his voice grew serious. "But yeah. Later."

"Thanks."

"Wait one. Someone's rattling the back door. Maybe some kids trying to get in. Or my relief's early."

"Okay." She tucked the phone under her ear and went to fetch her sidearm. She made sure she had extra magazines. A minute passed. Then another. "Winslow?" she said. There was no answer. "*Winslow?*" she demanded.

There was no one there.

Savannah drove blindly, tears stinging her eyes. She didn't know where she was going. The only place she wanted to be was away. She remembered a phrase Charleyboy used to use: "We'll cross that bridge when we burn it behind us." Tears sprang to her eyes as she thought about him. All her bridges were an inferno flaming behind her. Charleyboy had betrayed her. The cops were trying to use and discard her. Her boys were on their way, and she didn't know how to find them. She didn't know how long she drove before the realization hit her. She'd given them the address on Esteban Street. That's where they were supposed to find her. But she couldn't go back there. Not with Charleyboy there. And the cops. Possibly Luther even had people watching the place. They were headed there. She pulled over and pulled out her phone. The only way she had to contact Mick was via Facebook message. She should have gotten a number, but things had turned so frantic, she'd never gotten back to that. She called up the Facebook application on her phone and swore when she saw how weak the signal was. She was still out in the sticks. All she could do was punch in a quick message. *Don't go to Arabi. Send me a phone #.* She pushed send and hoped for the best. Then she pulled back onto the road and headed for the house. Maybe she could head them off.

Winslow heard the rattling at the back door again. He checked his watch. His relief, a young agent named Causey, wasn't due for another hour and a half. He shook his head, thinking about his own rookie years. Had he ever been that gung-ho? He supposed he had. Or maybe it was some homeless guy trying to get in. Or kids looking for some place to get high. That thought made him smile. Wouldn't it just fuck with some stoner's head to be looking for a place to blaze up, and get greeted at the door by a DEA agent? He walked to the back door, through a kitchen stripped of all appliances by the last occupants, and looked out. He frowned. There was no one there. He could swear someone had knocked. He opened the door and looked out. *That rookie had better not be playing with me.* When he stepped out onto the concrete slab of the back stoop, he sensed rather than saw the presence standing to one side. But it was too late. He reached for his sidearm, only to feel a gun barrel jammed into his side. "I wouldn't," a voice said. Winslow froze, his knees feeling suddenly weak. "Reach down," the voice said. The accent was straight out of the bayou. "Two fingers. Take that there gun out nice an' slow." Winslow hesitated. "Don' fuck around," the voice warned. "This shotgun'll blow your spine right in two."

"I'm a goddamn federal agent, dumbass," Winslow said. His ears were buzzing from the adrenaline coursing through his system, so he couldn't tell if he was keeping the fear out of his voice. He hoped he was. "Believe me, you don't want to do this. You are about to bring a mountain of shit down on you."

"'Zat so?" the voice said. The man sounded amused. "Maybe I should just shoot your ass right now an' run off. Cut my losses." He shoved the shotgun into Winslow's side harder.

"Don't," Winslow hated the way his voice cracked, hated the chuckle from the redneck with the gun.

"Get the pistol out, motherfucker. I ain't tellin' you again."

He reached down, pulled the gun out of his hip holster with two fingers, but hesitated. Everything in his training told him not to let go of his sidearm. But he wanted to stay alive. Maybe, if Causey showed up early, he could warn the kid. Keep him from walking into an ambush. Or maybe, he thought, he was just rationalizing. But he wanted to live. He tossed the gun into the yard.

Charleyboy sat on the edge of the couch. The room was darkened except for the glow of the TV. He stared at the screen, unseeing, wanting to look anywhere but at Mr. Luther seated in the easy chair or one of the twins—he thought it might be Zig—leaning against the jamb of the kitchen door, a cigarette dangling from the corner of his mouth and a shotgun dangling from his right hand.

"Don't look so glum, Angus," Mr. Luther said. "You made the right choice, tellin' me what's goin' on, then tellin' us the way to get here through the neighborhood so that fucker across the street didn't see us coming." He took a drink from a silver flask he'd produced from a back pocket. "I knew somethin' was up from the way you was actin'. I woulda found out eventually, and then I might not be in such a forgivin' mood."

"Remember our deal, though," Charleyboy said. "Savannah doesn't get hurt. She didn't know what she was doing. She thought the feds would help her find her sons. So just let her go. Let her walk out of this. You promised."

"Yeah," Luther said. "I did say that, din't I?" He took a cigar from a shirt pocket and regarded it thoughtfully, rolling it between his fingers. "And here I was thinkin' you'd hate her for what she done."

I don't, Charleyboy thought. *Even after all she's done, all the things I told her, I can't stand to see her hurt. I still love her.* But he knew better than to tell Luther that.

The old man went on. "Understand, that's not normally how I do things. Someone turns traitor, they got to pay. They got to pay for a long, long time, till I get tired of makin' 'em pay." He produced a lighter, lit the cigar, and took a puff. He smacked his lips in satisfaction. "An' everybody got to see how much they paid, so they ain't tempted to do the same. That's just good bidness."

"You promised," Charleyboy said, his voice cracking on the second word. He cleared his throat. "Being known as a man of your word. That's good business too. Right?"

Luther looked at him without expression. Then he laughed in a ghastly, wheezing cackle. "Damn, boy, you can sling some bullshit, I'll give you that." He leaned forward. "You're right. So I ain't gonna hurt your lil' redhaired gal, much as it's gonna disappoint my nephews." His face hardened and his eyes bored into Charleyboy's. "But she's still gotta pay. So when she's done tellin' me everything she told the feds, I'm gonna let her live. But I'm gonna take something from her. Something she cares about." He leaned back and took a drag off the cigar. "I'm gonna make her choose which of her brats gets torn apart by my dogs."

Charleyboy felt like he was going to throw up. He took a deep breath, trying to keep his dinner down, when he heard the back door open. The other twin, Zag, came in, pushing a short, balding man in a navy-blue windbreaker before him. "Look what I found," he said with a grin.

Luther stood up. "Well, well," he said. "How are you this evening, Mr. DEA? That is who you're with, ain't it?"

"His name's Winslow," Charleyboy said. "I heard…" he hesitated, "…I heard Savannah mention his name."

Winslow looked at Charleyboy, hatred twisting his face. "You son of a bitch," he said in a low voice. "You know you're not going to get away with this. You are in for a world of hurt."

Zag smashed the butt of the shotgun into the back of Winslow's head, driving him to his knees. He groaned with pain and put his hand to the back of his head. It came away red and sticky with blood.

"Seems to me, Mr. Winslow," Luther said, "that you're the one gonna be doing some hurting. How much hurting you do depends on how much you tell me about what you know." He jerked his chin at the back room. "Zig. Take Mr. DEA in the back room. See what he has to say."

Zig grinned. He motioned toward Winslow with the shotgun. "C'mon, boy," he said. "Up an' at 'em."

"Fuck you," Winslow said. Zag smashed him in the back of the head again. This time, Winslow fell forward on his face, out before he hit the floor.

"Damn, bro," Zig complained. "Now we got to drag his limp ass back there."

"No," Luther said. "You do." He turned to Zag. "Get in that place across the street. Keep a watch. Anyone who shows up, bring 'em in here. Bring 'em to me."

CHAPTER THIRTY-FIVE

"**W**inslow!" Chance yelled into the phone. Still no answer. "Shit." She broke the connection, her gut twisting in fear. Something was wrong. She had to let someone know. She'd given McGee her address, but she didn't know how long it would be before he arrived, and it might be as much as another half hour back to Arabi. She needed to call Winslow's people at the DEA. She pulled up the number she'd been given at the beginning of the investigation. Someone picked up on the third ring. "DEA. Special Agent Kimball."

"Agent Kimball," she said, "This is Chance Cahill with the St. Bernard Parish Sheriff's Department. I've been working with Agent Winslow."

The voice was cool and uninterested. "Yes?"

"He's set up on an informant, doing surveillance. I was just on the phone with him, and I lost contact."

There was a pause. "Probably a dropped call."

"Maybe." She was trying to contain her anxiety and frustration. "But I haven't been able to raise him again."

"Have you talked to your own people? They're nearer."

She gritted her teeth. "Yeah. I'm getting ready to call them. But I thought you need to know."

"We do. And thank you. We'll send an agent to look in on him. But call the locals."

"Right. I will, but he said he'd heard…" He hung up before she could go on. Chance sighed. She knew who she had to call, and it wasn't going to be easy. But…*own up, then step up.* She hit the number in the recently called queue on her phone.

Delphine picked up on the second ring. "Hey, shug, what's up?"

"Delphine, that DEA guy I was working with? I need someone to go by and check on him."

Her voice sharpened. "Check on him? Where is he?"

Chance gave her the address of the Arabi house. "He was doing surveillance from across the street. I was on the phone with him. He said he heard someone at the back door. Then we got cut off."

"Huh. And you don't think it was just a dropped call."

"No. He'd—"

"He'd have called you right back. Okay. I'll get a patrol car out there to check it out."

"Thanks. Tell them to be careful. I've got a bad feeling about this."

"Oh, I will." When Chance hesitated, Delphine asked, "Is there anything else?"

"Yeah. There's something else. They need to keep an eye out for Savannah Jakes. She's driving my truck."

There was a brief pause on the other end. Then, "Oh, Chance. Oh no. She didn't…"

"Yeah. While I was on the phone, the informant I was supposed to be watching stole my truck."

"This is bad, hon. This is really bad."

"Tell me about it."

"I ain't tryin' to be smart, Chance, but I have to ask…"

"She doesn't have my gun. Or my badge."

"Well, praise Jesus for small favors," Delphine said. "Okay. I'll tell 'em to watch out. You need someone to come get you?"

"No. Someone's on his way."

"That sheriff who called?"

"Yeah."

"So, I guess I need to tell the deputy to look out for those boys he was talking about, too. He said they had warrants on them out of Carolina." Delphine chuckled. "Damn, girl, you are makin' life way too interestin' for everyone."

Even through her fear and shame, Chance had to laugh at that. "Sorry."

Delphine's voice grew serious. "You just hang in there, Chance. You're gonna get through this. I got your back. And I ain't the only one."

She felt her throat tighten. "Thanks, Delphine. I needed that."

"You're welcome. See ya."

Chance looked at the phone, checking the time. It was still going to be a while. She dialed her father.

"Hey, Lil' Bit," he answered. "How's it going?"

"Not good, Dad," she said. "I screwed up."

"Personal or professional?"

"Professional."

He became all business. "Tell me."

She explained the situation, her voice catching from time to time as she tried not to cry. "I guess I screwed any chance I have of getting on with the feds, huh?" she said finally. There was a long silence. "Are you disappointed in me, Dad?"

"Yes," he said, "but not for the reason you think." He continued talking over her attempt to respond. "You've got a partner missing.

And you're thinking about your career?" His voice was quiet and measured rather than angry, but the words couldn't have hurt worse if he'd screamed them at her.

"I…" She stopped. He was right.

He went on, his voice softening. "You did exactly the right thing in calling the DEA, then calling your friend and filling her in. That's looking after your partner. It was your first instinct, even though it'll probably get you in hot water. But looking after your partner is *all* you need to be doing. It doesn't matter that he's an asshole, it doesn't matter if you don't like him. He's your partner. He's one of us. Everything else is secondary. No. Not secondary. Everything else is got-damn *irrelevant*. Got that?"

"Yeah. I do."

"I knew you would. You're a good officer, Lil' Bit."

She heard the sound of an engine coming up her driveway and went to the window. A nondescript beige sedan was pulling up.

"I've got to go, Dad. My ride's here."

"Good. Be careful out there, okay?"

"I will. And, Dad, thanks for the kick in the ass."

He laughed. "What else is a dad for? Now go kick some ass of your own. Go find your partner."

Wyatt was getting out of the rental, looking around the property. He took a deep breath of the humid air. There was a swamp nearby, and the air carried that familiar aroma that smelled of life and rot at the same time. From inside the trailer, he could hear a dog barking. As he approached the trailer, the door banged open and a young woman emerged, dressed in jeans and a New Orleans Saints t-shirt. A gun belt was incongruously strapped to her waist. She barely came up to Wyatt's chin, but she was striding with an angry determination that made him stop and extend a hand. "Hi," he said,

"I'm Wyatt McGee."

She took the hand briefly, gave it a quick shake, then slipped past him and headed for the car. "Chance Cahill," she said over her shoulder. "Okay if I drive? I know the way."

"Oh. Sure," he said. Despite his longer stride, he had to hurry to catch up. She was already in the front seat, adjusting seat and mirrors, when he clambered into the passenger seat.

"Sorry to be so abrupt," she said in a voice that told him he was anything but sorry, "but we got a situation here." She started the car. "After we talked, I called my partner. Well, a DEA guy I've been working liaison with." She whipped the car around in the narrow parking area so quickly Wyatt had to grab the handle above the door. He stifled a gasp as she punched the accelerator, throwing up a plume of dust behind him. "He's been set up watching the house where Savannah's been living with her boyfriend, a lowlife named Angus Charlebois. He told me to wait a minute, there was someone at the door. Then, nothing. He never came back."

She hit the hard road at the end of her driveway with a squeal of tires and headed down the narrow track at a speed that made the rental car's engine strain. He saw her grimace. "You couldn't have rented anything with a little more speed?"

"Sorry," Wyatt said. "They didn't have any police cruisers at the Hertz counter."

She glanced at him, then back at the road. She chuckled. "Okay, fair enough."

Wyatt's head was reeling, trying to keep up. He hadn't expected things to move this fast. "You think this Charlebois character ambushed him?"

She shook her head. "Hard to imagine that Charleyboy—that's what they call him—would have the stones. But they're running with some pretty bad people. That's why we flipped Savannah. After that, Charleyboy didn't have much choice."

"You think these 'bad people,' as you put it, got to him? And your partner?"

"I don't know." She barely paused at a stop sign, then picked up speed again. "Could be nothing. His battery may have died. Or his service dropped out."

"That's not what you think happened."

"I said I don't know," she snapped. Then she took a deep breath. "Sorry. I'm a little tense."

"No need to be sorry. You think your partner's in danger. Can't blame you for that."

She looked at him again, then made a turn onto the highway leading into the city. "Yeah," she said. "Thanks."

He reached into the back. "Hope you don't mind that I brought this, then." He pulled the pistol in its shoulder out and held it in his lap.

Her jaw tensed at the sight. "Mr. McGee, with all due respect…"

He was getting tired of hearing those words. "I may not be a sworn officer any more, Deputy Cahill. But *with all due respect*, I suspect I was in law enforcement when you were still home watching *Barney the Dinosaur* or whatever." He held up the gun. "I still know how to use this. And if things have really gone into the crapper here, you and your partner are going to need all the help you can get. Am I right?" He noticed her quick grin. It seemed out of place in this situation. "What's so funny?" he demanded.

"Nothing," she said. "You just remind me of someone." The grin faded. "Okay. But I've got some uniforms checking the house out. The DEA says they're sending someone, but they didn't sound too keen. None of them know you, and in the neighborhood where we're headed, civilians people don't know carrying guns make everyone nervous. Let me do the talking."

"Sure. Makes sense. It's your town."

They had entered an area lined with older houses and run-down one- and two-story buildings housing various businesses, mostly closed now. A few bars and small stores were lit up like beacons. People stood about on the concrete outside, drinking from red cups and watching the shiny new car go by with wary eyes. Wyatt stared back.

"Not what you expected when you came to New Orleans, is it?" Cahill said.

"I didn't know what to expect," he admitted.

"Good. Hang on to that feeling. And follow my lead. Think you can do that with a girl?"

He looked from the window back at her. "I can follow the lead of a fellow officer who knows the area. Will that do?"

She nodded. That grin was back. "Yes, Sheriff McGee," she said, "that'll do just fine."

CHAPTER THIRTY-SIX

Lanny Knight had been looking forward to the end of the shift, a beer or five in the Old Arabi Bar, then an early bedtime back at his house in the Lower Ninth Ward, with how early being determined by what kind of strange he came across in the Old Arabi. So when the call came for him to check out the place on Esteban Street, he grunted with irritation. But he acknowledged the call and took the turn that would take him to the narrow, potholed back street. "One more broke-dick street in this broke-dick neighborhood," he muttered to himself. His cell phone went off, and he glanced down to see who was calling. *Delphine.* He smiled. Maybe this night was looking up. He opened the line. "Hey, girl," he answered in the gravelly baritone he knew made cocktail waitresses and bored housewives want to drop their panties. "You decided to take me up on my offer?"

"Not tonight, Lanny," she said, "shut up and listen, okay?"

Normally, he'd have some biting retort for being told to shut up, but there was something in her voice that got his attention. "What's up?"

"You need to be on your toes for this home check. You know Chance Cahill, right? Working a liaison with the feds?"

"Cahill…" Lanny thought for a minute. "Little bitty girl. Curly hair. Maybe a dyke."

"Oh, for the love of…just because she won't fall into your bed…" Delphine broke off and recovered her composure. "Try to stop thinking with your dick for five goddamn minutes. You think you can do that, *Deputy*?"

Lanny knew better than to push his luck. Cormier may have been a hot little number, and he thought she'd given him some promising looks around the station and in an after-hours gathering or two, but she still could be a ball-breaker, and those sergeant stripes she wore gave her the hammer and tongs with which to do it. "Yes, Sergeant," he said with as much contrition as he could muster.

"Good. Now listen up. The fed she was working with, a guy name of Winslow, was set up across the street on the house. He went dark a few minutes ago. Cahill can't raise him."

Lanny was beginning to get a bad feeling. "You think he got got? By whoever he was watching?"

"The guy in the house is a little shit-heel named Angus Charlebois. You know him?"

Lanny thought for a moment. "Seen him around," he said. "Didn't look like much. Hangs out with a pretty little redhead."

"You're right. He ain't much. But he and his girlfriend are mixed up with some heavy shit. So be careful."

"Shit, Delphine," Lanny said, "you think maybe I should wait for some backup?"

"I'm arranging it. Cahill's on the way. And the DEA. Maybe. What we need first is eyes on the situation. So just look it over. Don't even go to the door unless it looks okay. But keep the place under surveillance. And get back to me. Okay, shug?"

The endearment made him think that maybe there might still be a chance there. "You got it, darlin.'"

"One more thing. The girlfriend, Savannah Jakes, is a CI for the feds, too. But she's in the wind, probably headed there. She's driving a stolen truck. So pick her up. Hold her and get her back here."

"Got it. Anything else?"

"Yeah. Just to make things extra interestin', her two sons are headed into town to meet her there. They got warrants in North Carolina. So hold them there if they show up."

"Damn," Lanny said, "that's a lot of people to hold."

"I got help on the way. In the meantime, you be careful, okay?"

"I'm always careful, darlin.' Except where you're concerned. You make a man wanna be reckless."

"Easy, cowboy," she said. "Business before pleasure."

"Does that mean there's gonna be pleasure later?"

"You just keep a lookout, okay?"

"10-4," he said, undaunted. "By the way, who are these lowlifes mixed up with?"

"Well, it's supposed to be confidential. But…"

"But right now, it's me hanging my ass out."

"Fair enough. These people are getting ready to roll on Wallace Luther."

Lanny whistled. "Luther. Holy shit."

"So that's why you need to be careful."

"No worries, baby. I know better than to fuck around with the likes of Wallace Luther." He'd reached the house. He pulled another half block down the narrow street. "Okay. I'm here. I'll get back to you." He didn't wait for her to respond. He killed the engine and sat in the car, looking at the house over his shoulder. He got out, sliding his police baton into the ring on his belt. He walked slowly down the cracked and uneven sidewalk, listening to the cicadas singing in the tall grass in the vacant lot next to the house he was approaching. The shades were drawn, but he could see light through them. Someone was home. He stopped at the small front stoop and looked the place over. There was a flicker of movement behind one of the front curtains as someone pulled it aside to look, then dropped it back into place. Lanny stopped. In another moment, the curtain was twitched aside again and another face looked out, one he could see more clearly. One he recognized. As he mounted the steps he heard footsteps behind him and the unmistakable ratcheting sound of a shotgun slide being pumped. He didn't turn around. "Tell Mr. Luther," he said slowly and clearly, "that Lanny Knight is here. And I got somethin' he needs to hear."

Charleyboy couldn't believe they were inviting another cop into the house. But this was someone Luther seemed to know. "Lanny," the old man said. "Good to see you. How's the family?"

"Fine, sir," the cop said. He was a soft-looking man of medium height, with curly black hair and a dark complexion, dressed in the uniform of the St. Bernard Parish Sheriff's Department. He had an obsequious smile pasted on his face that only slipped a little bit when Zag reached out and took his gun out of the holster on his hip. "I'm glad it was me they called out. I mean, what are the odds, eh?"

"Better than average," Luther said curtly. "You ain't the only St. Bernard cop on the payroll."

"Right, right." The cop looked over to where Winslow lay in the doorway to the bedroom, where Zig had dropped him. "Is that guy the fed they're lookin' for?"

Luther's voice sharpened. "What makes you think he is?"

The cop flinched at the tone. "Because that's what I'm supposed to check out. The feds had this place under surveillance. Someone was talking to that guy," he motioned toward Winslow, "and he got cut off. There's backup on the way."

"Shit," Zag said. "We got to go."

Luther just nodded, unperturbed. "Zig, go get the van. Zag, Angus, get Sleeping Beauty over there. We'll take him out to the farm where we can wake his ass up and find out what we need to know." He turned to the cop. "Good work," he said. "You'll be gettin' a little somethin' extra this week."

"Thank you, sir," the cop said. "But…" He looked troubled.

"What is it, boy?" Luther said.

"A fed? That's…that's gonna bring down a lot of trouble."

"Don't you worry," Luther said. "I got it handled. Of course, if you're thinkin' that you might want to change sides, maybe give us up to save yourself…"

"Oh, no, sir," the cop said. "Nothin' like that. I know better."

"Good. Now I need you to stay here. Call off any backup. Tell 'em you knocked and there weren't nobody here. Think you can handle that?"

"Yes, sir," the cop said.

"Fine." He looked at Charleyboy. "What are you waitin' for, Angus? Get a move on."

Charleyboy moved towards Winslow, who was beginning to stir and moan. He had to do something to shut the DEA man up. If he started talking—and Charleyboy had no doubt that they could make him talk—his plan to betray Luther to Gutierrez was going to come out. And then he'd be meat for the dogs as well.

CHAPTER
THIRTY-SEVEN

Lanny watched the black van pull away from the curb with a twisted feeling in his guts. He'd done well the past few years out of his relationship with Mr. Luther. The money that went into the safe sunk into the concrete floor of his garage was going to provide him with a nicer retirement than anything he was going to get from the parish or the state. The cocaine and weed Luther's boys occasionally dropped off for him was always the best quality, and every now and then, after he'd slipped a particularly valuable tip about an upcoming drug raid, some hot little hooker would slip up beside him at the bar and whisper, "Mr. Luther sent me." He'd been well taken care of, and Mr. Luther had always seemed to respect the one rule he'd laid out when he first began working for him. "I ain't doin' nothing that's going to put another officer in danger," he'd said, and Luther had nodded approvingly. "'Course not," he'd said. Now, it seemed, the deal had changed. And the officer in question was a fed, no less. He didn't know what they meant to do with the poor bastard they'd carried to the van, but it couldn't be anything good. That meant real trouble, and real scrutiny, the likes of which Lanny wasn't sure any of them could bear. He didn't know what to do. If he told, he'd be putting his own nuts in the vise. He also remembered what Luther had said inside the house: *You ain't the only one on the payroll.* If he rolled over, Luther would probably know within the hour. People who crossed Wallace Luther tended to disappear. He sighed and walked to his car. He was going to have to keep playing the game. He only had three years left until he could retire, but they stretched out in front of him like centuries.

As he was getting into his own vehicle, he saw a car coming up the deserted street, moving at high speed. It slid to a halt in front of the house. Chance Cahill leaped out of the driver's side. An older man Lanny didn't recognize got out of the other, more slowly.

"Knight," Cahill called out as she recognized him. "You see anything?"

"Hey, Cahill," he said, walking toward them. "Nope. No one. No one's home at either place."

Cahill slammed the door. "*Fuck!*" She strode to the door of the house and quickly up the steps. "*Charleyboy!*" she hollered, pounding on the door. "*Open this goddamn door!*"

Lanny looked at the older guy and noticed the shoulder holster. The man noticed Lanny's attention and stuck out a hand. "Wyatt McGee."

Lanny didn't take the hand. "Uh-huh. And what's your interest here, Mr. McGee?"

"Personal."

Lanny wasn't buying it. The guy had cop written all over him. But he was in plainclothes, with no badge, but with a firearm in a shoulder rig. The whole thing seemed off-kilter. As they stared at each other, Cahill came charging back. She looked mad enough to eat nails and spit rust. "I already knocked, Cahill," Lanny said. "I told you, no one's home."

Cahill was smacking her hand against the top of the car in agitation, staring at the house. "Where the hell did he go?" she muttered. "Where…" She began walking across the street, to an abandoned house. Lanny assumed it was the place Delphine had mentioned, where the fed had been set up doing surveillance.

"So," he called out, "I'm gonna just move along, okay?"

"No," Cahill called back over her shoulder. "Stay there. Keep an eye out." She stopped and turned back. "Give me your flashlight." Reluctantly, Lanny pulled his Maglite from his belt and handed it over.

"Thanks." She headed back to the house. The older guy, McGee, was following her.

"Fuck this," Lanny muttered, but he stood by the car anyway. He didn't know what else to do.

Chance pushed her way through the overgrown alley beside the house, headed for the back door. It opened up into a tiny backyard, also choked with knee-high weeds. The tiny sputtering flares of lightning bugs provided the only illumination until Cahill snapped on the flashlight. The back door was standing open.

"Wait," McGee said as she drew her pistol and started inside.

She turned back, brow furrowed in irritation. She hoped he wasn't going to pull any shit about going in first. "What?"

He was holding up a black cable. The silvered ends of the plugs gleamed in the light. "This was in the grass."

She looked back into the darkness of the house. "That's from the surveillance gear." She paused for a moment, wondering. Then she headed inside; light held off and way from her body, pistol held out before her.

The house was empty and silent. Chance played the light across the walls and floor as she walked to the front room. The desk where they'd set up the recorders was empty. The place had been cleaned out, as if the operation had never occurred. She quickly checked the other rooms, knowing she wouldn't find anything, but needing to make sure. She went to the front room again and stood there, trying to think, her frustration almost boiling over. She knew something had happened to Winslow, that it was almost certainly bad, and that it had something to do with Luther. She went back out.

McGee was at the back of the lot, examining the trampled vegetation. "Someone's been through here," he said. "Let me see the light."

She shone the light on the space where a low, vine-covered metal fence marked the back of the lot. There was a metal gate in the fence, also nearly covered with vines. "That's how we get in," Chance said. "To avoid being seen from the road. There's a vacant lot in back."

McGee opened the gate. "Come on." She followed, trying to hold the light high enough to shine it over his shoulder. She couldn't reach. He looked back at her and chuckled. "Maybe you should go first."

"Good idea." She took the lead and he followed her through the short tunnel of long-untended shrubbery that led to the back lot. The grass here was also trampled down, as if a large vehicle had been parked there. She frowned. "We don't leave a vehicle here. We get dropped off so as not to draw any more attention than we have to."

"Well, someone's been parked here. And recently. Who knows about this place? And how it leads to the house?"

"Well, Winslow and me, of course. Whoever's in charge of this at the DEA. And...anyone who lives in the neighborhood."

"Like this guy Charleyboy?"

"Yeah."

"Does he, maybe, know a back way to his own house? Some way where you couldn't see someone coming in?"

"I don't know. But probably. That...that fucking *lowlife!*" She spat the last word. "He set Winslow up."

"That fits the evidence." McGee's voice was calm.

Chance realized that her anger and outrage weren't going to solve anything. She took a deep breath. "He's alive," she said, wishing it could be with more conviction. "Until we know for sure otherwise, he's alive."

"Yep," Wyatt said. "That's the only way to play this."

She sighed. "And we have to let the DEA know."

"Yeah. Not going to be a comfortable conversation. But hey, if this was easy, we wouldn't be pulling down the big bucks, right?"

She laughed and shook her head. "That's exactly the kind of thing my dad always says."

Wyatt smiled. "He in law enforcement?"

She nodded. "State police."

"Retired?"

"Disabled. Injured in the line. He got shot."

He grimaced. "That's hard. But it sounds like he raised you to take over the family business."

"Something like that." She started for the front of the house. "Come on." As she did, the flat bang of gunshots from the front of the house split the night.

"Shit," Chance said. She broke into a run.

CHAPTER THIRTY-EIGHT

"Turn left here," Lana said. She was slumped down in the passenger seat, holding her phone up in front of her face. The shotgun they'd taken from the country store was propped up next to her. The harsh light of the screen accentuated the dark circles under her eyes and the light sheen of sweat on her brow. Tyler could tell she needed her "medicine."

"Are you sure this is the right place?" Mick demanded.

Tyler looked out the window at the darkened streets. This area looked extremely sketchy to him. But then, where else would he expect to find his birth mother? The thought made him immediately ashamed. Then the shame made him angry. Why the hell should he even be here, looking for the woman who'd left him to be raised by others? The people who'd brought him up were his parents. He owed Savannah nothing.

Then he saw her.

They were stopped at a four-way intersection, with Lana and Mick squabbling over whether they were even in the right neighborhood and whether they should keep trusting Google Maps to guide them to the address Savannah had provided. A green pickup truck pulled up to the cross street and waited for them to go. When they didn't, the person behind the wheel looked over at them impatiently, leaning forward slightly to get a better look. The sight of her face behind the glass hit Tyler like an electric shock.

"Mick," he said.

"I'm telling you," Mick was telling Lana, "the hurricane messed up all the maps—"

"*Mick!*" Tyler blurted out. "That's her."

"It's Google, Mick," Lana argued back. "They done these maps since the—"

"*Shut up!*" Tyler screamed. The driver of the truck, apparently giving up on waiting for them to go, accelerated through the intersection.

"What the fuck is wrong with you?" Lana said.

Tyler ignored her. "Mick. That was her. In that green pickup. That was…that was Savannah."

Mick blinked at him. "What? No way."

"I'm telling you! She looked out the window. I saw her! That was her! From the pictures!"

"Told you we were in the right neighborhood," Lana said smugly.

"Shut up," Mick said. He put the car in gear and turned to follow the pickup. Tyler could see the tail lights a couple of blocks ahead, then a turn signal. Mick stomped on the gas and the big car leaped down the narrow streets, engine roaring. Tyler grabbed onto the door, white-knuckled. Mick ran the stop sign where the truck had turned and headed down another narrow street. Tyler saw the green pickup stopped in the middle of the road. Savannah was out of it, the driver's side door standing open. Someone was approaching the vehicle from the front. Tyler couldn't say who it was.

"Shit," Mick said. "That's a cop." He reached down into the gap between the driver's seat and the center console and pulled out his pistol. Lana reached for the shotgun.

No, Tyler thought, but he couldn't speak.

Lanny Knight had worked his way up from uncertain to fuming. What authority did this Cahill bitch have to take his Maglite and order him around? She wasn't in his chain of command. She wasn't even on duty from the looks of things. He was about ready to just pull up stakes, call it end of shift, and go clock out. He'd get his flashlight back from Cahill later. Then he saw the green pickup. It was moving swiftly at first, but as it got closer, he saw it slow to a creep, as if the driver was checking out what was going on. He saw a vaguely familiar face behind the wheel, caught a glimpse of red hair. It was Charleyboy's girlfriend, the one Delphine had said was a CI for the feds. Driving a stolen truck, Delphine said. Lanny raised a hand and advanced toward the car. The pickup pulled to a stop. The driver's side door opened. He could see the driver's face more clearly in the car's interior light. Definitely the girlfriend.

"Stay in the car, ma'am!" he called out. He reached down and unsnapped the safety strap on his holster. Slowly, she eased back into the cab of the truck. He stepped up to the driver's side. "License and—" Before he could get to "registration," he heard the sound of a big engine and looked up. A low-slung black Firebird was shooting toward them like a torpedo. Lanny stepped back and put his hand on his weapon.

The driver of the Firebird leaped out. "*Hey!*" the driver yelled. "Get away from her!"

"Get back in your car, sir!" Lanny yelled back, his pistol clearing his holster a half second too late as he registered the gun already in the driver's hand. He saw the muzzle flash, heard the report, and his first shot was spoiled as he flinched away. He never got a second one. The driver's second and third shots caught him in the upper chest and knocked him back, stumbling and finally crashing to his ass on the pavement. *Well, this fucking sucks*, was the last thought he had before he fell over backward and lay on his back, looking up at a sky he couldn't see for the overhanging trees and the glow of the city lights. The light slowly faded and went completely black.

Chance burst out of the alley into the tiny front yard of the abandoned house in time to see the dark-haired young man standing outside of the car, firing. Training took over and she crouched down, assumed firing position, and aimed for center mass. Just before the trigger broke under her tightening finger, something hit her arm and knocked her aim sideways. The shot went off, somewhere into the night. She saw McGee charging forward past her, shouting something. The sounds of the shots were ringing in her ears as she tried to bring the gun to bear again, so she couldn't make out what he was yelling. Then he was in her line of fire. A flash of light came from inside the dark car, and McGee went down. As soon as he did, Chance had a clear shot, but a second blast from inside the car made her drop to the ground. She resisted the impulse to fire back wildly. When she looked up, the black car was pulling away. She got off one shot at it, then crawled to where McGee lay motionless, half on the narrow strip of grass and half on the broken sidewalk.

"McGee," she said.

He rolled onto his back, groaning with pain. "I'm okay," he gasped. "I think. Shotgun pellet in my side. Maybe two. Jesus, it hurts, though." He raised his head. "Check on your deputy."

Chance stood up and ran past her car to where Lanny Knight lay on his back. He was breathing, but not well. Each inhalation was a wet, rattling wheeze that signaled blood in the airway. "Come on,

Knight," she muttered, and smacked him on the face, lightly, then harder. "Stay with me, buddy. Come on." He didn't respond. Chance got up, looked around for further threats, and found none. She bolted to Knight's patrol car and yanked the radio mike off its stand. "St. Bernard, all units," she said. "Officers down." She gave the address. "Multiple shots fired. Repeat, officers down. Need assistance." From far away, she heard the distant whoop of sirens as every unit responded to the call. "Help's on the way, Lanny. Come on. You're gonna make it."

She only hoped that it was true.

Savannah curled up in the narrow backseat of the car and pulled her knees up to her chest, folding herself as small as she could around her fear. She was still in shock from what had just happened. Pulling up to the house to find a cop sitting there, then a scream of engines and a burst of gunfire. Then the dark-haired young man, who looked so much like her Mick, screaming at her to get in the car, they were leaving. And…she looked over at the young man in the passenger seat next to her. Could that be her Keith? This wasn't how she'd envisioned this meeting at all. He seemed as shell shocked as she was. She reached out for his hand. "Keith?"

He looked at her for a moment and blinked like someone waking up from a trance. Then he reached out and took her hand in his. "Yeah, Mama. It's Keith."

Her eyes filled with tears. "Oh. My god. My baby." She pulled his hand to draw him to her. They embraced in the cramped backseat as best they could. "Keith," she murmured. "My sweet little boy. I've missed you so much."

The girl in the front seat, the one who'd wielded the shotgun, looked around and stuck out her hand. "Hey," she said. "I'm Lana."

Savannah reluctantly took the hand. "Hey. And, um. You are?"

The girl smiled. "I'm Mick's fiancée. So I guess I should start calling you Mama, too."

"Yeah," Savannah said without enthusiasm. "I guess."

"Mick," Keith said. "Where are we going?"

"I'm open to suggestions, bro," Mick said. "I was kind of hoping to get some catching up time with Mama at her house. I guess that's not happening now."

"Because you shot a goddamn police officer, Mick!" Keith's voice was shaking with fear. Savannah reached out and put a hand on his arm. He didn't seem to notice. "Why the hell did you do that?"

"He drew on me first," Mick said sullenly. "And he was tryin' to take Mama in."

Keith flung himself back into the seat. "Jesus. I cannot believe you." He turned to her. "I don't know what we do now, Mama. I'm sorry. I just don't know."

Savannah felt as if she should know. She was the mother. It was her job to protect her boys. She'd held fast to that for the last ten years. She'd told herself when she got them back, she'd be wise and forgiving and give them the guidance they needed. Now, with the sound of gunfire still consuming her senses, she was as confused and at sea as the day she'd first brought Mick home. All that experience behind her, all those lessons she'd thought of passing down, and she still felt as if she hadn't learned a damn thing.

"Don't worry," Mick said from the driver's seat. "I got it all planned out."

That didn't make Savannah feel any better.

CHAPTER THIRTY-NINE

"You know, Charleyboy," Winslow said, "I'm not a brave man."

He was handcuffed to a metal pipe running across the ceiling inside a shed on Luther's farm. They'd taken him there, shackled him, and left him there with Zig and Charleyboy as guards. The farm was a bustle of activity, men and vehicles coming and going. Something big was going down, and Winslow had an idea what it was. After a couple of hours, Zig had wandered off to take a leak. Winslow took the opportunity to talk to Charleyboy. "You know when they start in on me, I'll talk. Hell, I don't see why I should hold out very long. Because when I start talking, the first thing I'm going to do is give up your plan to sell Luther out to Gutierrez."

Charleyboy wiped sweat off his upper lip. "He won't believe you."

"Won't he? He just barely trusts you now. Once I start spilling what I know, all of the suspicions Luther has about you are going to come right to the front of that lizard brain of his."

"Shut up," Charleyboy said.

"Well, you could shut me up. You could put a bullet in me right now. It'd keep me from talking. But then, Mr. Luther would wonder what you're hiding." Winslow shook his head as if he was the one who felt sorry for Charleyboy. "Yeah, you've really painted yourself into a corner on this one, Angus. It must really suck to be you right now."

"I said shut *up!*" Charleyboy crossed the dirty concrete floor of the shed in a few strides, hand raised as if to strike. Winslow didn't flinch, and Charleyboy stopped. He let his hand drop to his side.

Winslow nodded in approval. "We both know there's only one way you get out of this alive and uneaten. Go back to Plan A. Get me out of here, get us both to the DEA, and start telling us everything you know. I can talk to the Marshal's Service. Get you into WitSec."

"How the hell am I supposed to get us out?" Charleyboy demanded. "I don't even have a gun."

"My weapon's in the van. In the glove box. I saw one of those redneck bastards stuff it in there. You can get it out."

Charleyboy shook his head. "I never shot anybody. Not in my life."

"I know. It won't be easy. But if you don't…well, just look at everything they do to me and know that they'll be doing the same thing to you. If not worse."

Charleyboy ran his hands over his face. "I don't know."

"Yes, you do. You know what I'm saying is true. There's only one choice, Charleyboy. It's a hard one. But your choices have been getting narrower and narrower since you started dealing with Wallace Luther."

At that moment, Zig came back in. A cigarette hung from one corner of his mouth and his shotgun was cradled negligently in one arm. He gave Winslow a nasty grin. "Hey, Mr. Fed. It's almost showtime. Mr. Luther's gettin' the dogs all worked up. Giving 'em shots of go-juice to make 'em good and crazy. You may want to start thinkin' about what you want to tell us."

"I've got to take a whiz," Charleyboy said. "I'll be right back."

"Yeah," Zig said. "You do that." As he left, Zig flicked the end of the cigarette contemptuously at his back. "Surprised he ain't pissed hisself already." He turned back to Winslow. He leaned the shotgun against the wooden wall of the shed, then straightened up, cracking his knuckles loudly. "Now, Mr. Luther's got some things he wants to know. Like how much you know about his business. But me an' my brother has some personal interests. Like where we can find that lil' redheaded gal Charleyboy's been takin' up with. Me and ol' Zag, we got a little tag team routine we like to do, an' she'd be perfect for it."

"Yeah," Winslow said. "Sorry, I can't help you. We had her under wraps but she bolted. She's in the wind."

Zig shook his head. "Wrong answer." He delivered a short, vicious jab into Winslow's unprotected ribcage. The pain exploded through his body and his breath left him. He thrashed back and forth as if trying to get away, but his arms were held fast above him. "Hurts, don't it?" Zig said, and hit him again, harder this time. Winslow's vision went dark at the edges as he fought for breath and his knees went weak. The handcuffs bit into his wrists as he sagged. Zig stepped behind Winslow and wrapped his arms around him, lifting him up off the ground. His breath was hot in Winslow's ear. "You think this is bad? It's gonna get a lot worse." He let Winslow go and he cried out in agony as his wrists took the full weight of the drop.

"Hey," Winslow heard. "Cut that out." He looked over. Charleyboy was standing in the doorway, Winslow's pistol in his hand.

Zig turned to him and put his hands on his hips. "Now just what the fuck do you think you're doin', Angus?"

"We're getting out of here," Charleyboy said.

"We? As in you and Mr. Fed here? Guess what Mr. Luther was wonderin' about you is all true." Zig shook his head. "You're gonna be a long time dyin', Charleyboy. A long, hard, sad time."

Shoot him, Winslow wanted to say. *He's not safe to leave alive.* But he was still struggling for breath.

"Give me the keys to the handcuffs," Charleyboy said.

Zig shook his head. "No. I don't think I will. See, Angus, I don't think you have the balls to pull that trigger." He walked toward where the shotgun leaned against the wall. The report of the pistol sounded like a thunderclap in the small space. Zig staggered backward, his hand going to his chest. He pulled it away and stared in amazement at the blood there. He looked back at Charleyboy and his face contorted in an animal snarl as he went straight for his assailant, ignoring the shotgun on the wall, hands extended like claws ready to slash or choke the life out of the man who'd just shot him. The second shot caught Zig in the center of the forehead and snapped his head back. He stumbled and fell face down with a thud that felt heavy enough to shake the earth across the whole farm.

"Well," Charleyboy said, and his voice caught in a muffled sob, "look how wrong you can be."

"Quick," Winslow said, his voice a tortured wheeze, "get the key. Get me down. We've got to move."

Charleyboy didn't respond. He stood looking with fascination at the body of the man he'd just shot as the body went into its final twitches and shudders.

"*Charleyboy!*" Winslow barked.

Charleyboy looked up, blinking like a man just awakened from a bad dream into a worse one.

"Come on," Winslow snapped. "Someone probably heard those shots. Get me down, and let's get the fuck out of here."

Charleyboy looked at the body again, then began moving with a maddening slowness, still dazed.

"Come on," Winslow said through gritted teeth. "Come on…" Finally, Charleyboy fumbled in Zig's pocket and came up with the handcuff key. A moment later, Winslow was rubbing his wrists to restore the circulation. "Are the keys in the van?"

Charleyboy looked as if he didn't understand at first, then he nodded. "Oh. Yeah. I think."

Winslow briefly entertained the idea of picking up the shotgun and shooting Charleyboy himself. But duty and responsibility won out. He picked up the weapon, but turned and said, "Follow me."

Charleyboy followed, Winslow's pistol dangling limply from his hand.

CHAPTER FORTY

The van they'd arrived in sat just outside of the shed, parked at the verge of a white sand road under a spreading live oak. Winslow yanked the driver's side door open and climbed in, laying the shotgun down behind the seats. He popped the glove box open and located the keys just as Charleyboy got in the other side. As he cranked the ignition, he saw headlights coming down the road, moving quickly. Someone must have heard the shots up at the main house and was coming to investigate. "Shit. Shit." He turned to Charleyboy. "Which way's the gate?"

Charleyboy motioned vaguely in the opposite direction from which the van was facing. "That way." He looked down at the gun in his hand and pushed it into the center console between the front seats.

Winslow stomped on the gas and backed the van up, whipping it around in a spray of sand. Without turning on the headlights, he jammed the accelerator to the floor and looked in the side mirror. The headlights behind slowed, then stopped. Winslow squinted into the darkness ahead of them, trying to see the road in the dim moonlight, praying there were no sudden hairpin turns. The iron gate came up so fast he had no time to stop and open it. The van crashed through with a horrific grinding and rending noise, followed by banging and thudding like rifle fire as they dragged a remnant of the gate along the pavement. A shower of orange and white sparks lit up the night as metal dragged on asphalt. Finally, with a tortured shriek, the last of the gate tore loose and the van leaped ahead. Winslow pounded the dash and whooped in triumph. "Yeah!" He fumbled for the headlight switch and turned it on, the bright lights illuminating the way ahead.

"They're behind us," Charleyboy said in a dead, hopeless voice.

Winslow checked the side mirror and swore under his breath. There was a pair of headlights coming up fast behind them. As he watched, he saw a flash of white light from one side and the back door of the van resounded as if it had been hit by a hammer. A second flash, and the right back window blew out. "Charleyboy," Winslow said, "get back there with the shotgun and see if you can discourage those bastards a little, will you?"

For once, Charleyboy didn't hesitate. He picked up the shotgun and awkwardly clambered over the center console to the back of the van. Before he could reach a shooting position, there was another flash, a loud bang, and the van began shaking as if it was coming apart.

"Shit. They got a tire," Winslow said. The shaking was becoming intolerable. They'd surely crash if he kept trying to drive on the ruined tire. Winslow cursed and began pulling over to the side. He fumbled for the gun Charleyboy had left in the center console. If nothing else, he'd take some of the bastards down with him before he died. It was a better prospect than returning to what Luther and Zig's brother had in store for him after they'd seen what he'd done. Winslow had told Charleyboy he wasn't a brave man, and that was true. But sometimes a man terrified of an agonizing death can be indistinguishable from a brave one.

"There's someone else coming," Charleyboy said.

Winslow's heart leaped with sudden hope. Had the DEA figured things out and mounted a rescue so quickly? It seemed incredible, but then... He looked in the rearview and saw a flare of headlights rushing up beside the car that was tailing them. It was a big vehicle, probably another SUV, but he couldn't tell behind the hard, bright glare of new halogen bulbs. The SUV slowed to one side, knocking the car pursuing them sideways. It left the road, throwing up a rooster tail of black earth before coming to a stop. Winslow finally steered the van to a shuddering halt as well, about a hundred yards down the road. He put his head on the steering wheel for a second, nearly sobbing with relief. The *pop-pop-pop* of gunfire made him sit up straight again. If there was a fight, he needed to be in it. He picked up his weapon out of the center console. As he opened the driver's side door of the van, it was nearly torn off by the black SUV that screamed by him inches away, then slid to a stop, tires squealing on pavement. It looked enough like a generic government vehicle to make Winslow breathe a little easier. *Looks like the cavalry's here.* But his brow furrowed at the look of the man who got out. Instead of the usual tactical gear or government windbreaker, the man was dressed in a light grey suit that fit him so perfectly it had to have been tailored. His haircut looked as expensive as the suit. He was carrying a pistol in one hand, held down by his side. Winslow realized too late that he wasn't one of the good guys and started to raise his own weapon. There was the rattling sound of multiple weapons being cocked behind him. Winslow froze.

"Drop the weapon, Señor Winslow," the man approaching him said. "Or the men behind you will fire." He spoke with a pronounced Latino accent. As he approached, Winslow saw that he was grinning, his teeth very white in his dark face. The bastard was enjoying himself.

"We don't mean you any harm," the man said.

"I wish I could believe that," Winslow answered.

"Truly," the man said. "Put the gun down. Caspar Gutierrez would like a word with you, and with Mr. Charlebois."

"God*damn* it," Winslow said. He let the gun fall.

"**M**exico," Savannah said.

"Yeah." Mick was looking smug as he laid out his plan.

The four of them were sitting in a booth in a diner just off of I-10 in Metairie. Mick reached into his shirt pocket and pulled out a folded piece of paper. As he unfolded it, Keith could see it was a printout of one of the pictures Mick had shown him back at the trailer in North Carolina. "It's called San Pancho," he said as he pushed the paper across the table at Savannah. "It's like paradise."

She looked at it for a moment and shook her head. "I suppose we're going to drive there."

Mick looked puzzled at her attitude. "Well, yeah."

She sighed and pushed it back at him. "Mick. Sweetheart. You know that I love you. But, baby, you just shot a cop." She turned to Lana, who seemed absorbed by her phone. "And don't know who that guy was you shot, but I'm thinking he had to be a cop, too. Maybe DEA. They'd been set up on the house." Lana didn't answer. "Every law enforcement officer in Louisiana is going to be looking for us. And if they don't catch us, it's going to be every cop in Louisiana, Texas, Arkansas…you get what I'm saying?"

Mick's jaw tightened. "We can make it."

The waitress was just walking by. "You folks ready to order yet?" It was the third time she'd asked.

Savannah held up her nearly empty cup. "Just the coffee, please."

The last thing Keith's stomach could take at that moment was food, and he didn't drink coffee. "Water for me, please, ma'am."

"I'll have a burger, medium," Mick said. "And onion rings." He looked around, noticed how Savannah and Keith were looking at him. "What?"

"Western Omelet for me," Lana spoke up, and smiled at Savannah. "Got a long drive ahead. Got to keep our strength up."

Keith saw the look his mother shot across the table. There was going to be trouble there.

CHAPTER FORTY-ONE

"Cahill," her lieutenant said in a deceptively mild voice, "you really fucked this one up, wouldn't you agree?"

She was standing at attention in front of his desk inside his small office. She hadn't been offered a chair. Her back was ramrod straight and she was looking at a spot just over the lieutenant's bald head. "I couldn't say, sir."

His voice sharpened and his dark brown eyes narrowed. "Oh, no? Well, let's review." He raised a single finger. "Number one, we've got a deputy in the trauma unit at University Medical Center in critical condition from a gunshot wound. I'm hearing that if he lives, which is by no means a sure thing, he probably won't walk again." He raised another finger. "Two, we've also got a civilian wounded in the same incident, a civilian who, for some reason completely unknown to me, was armed and apparently acting in the capacity of a law enforcement officer in my goddamn jurisdiction."

"Sir," Chance said, "Mr. McGee is a retired sheriff—"

"The operative word there, Deputy, being 'retired.' Now shut the hell up." He raised a third finger and counted it off. "Three, the federal witness you were supposed to be watching not only got away from you, she stole your personal vehicle. And just to make things even more embarrassing for you, she seems to have done so with the express purpose of meeting up with the people who shot Deputy Knight."

She felt her face getting red. "That one was my fault, sir."

He lost his veneer of composure and slammed his hand down on the desk. She didn't flinch. "You're goddamn right it was your fault!"

"Yes, sir. May I ask about Agent Winslow, sir?"

"The DEA's on that one. I don't think they'll want any more of your help."

That one stung worse than anything else he'd said. "Yes, sir," was all she said.

He shook his head. "I knew your dad, Cahill. Worked with him several times. He was a damn fine officer. I can't imagine—"

That was too much. "Lieutenant Carver," she interrupted, eyes blazing. "My father has nothing to do with this. I'd appreciate you not bringing his name into it. Sir." She saw his eyes widen with shock, then narrow with anger. She figured she was finished anyway, so she plowed ahead. "And by the way, sir, my father's still alive, so there's no need to refer to him in past tense. But I will convey your regards, sir. I'm sure he'll be glad to hear from you, since I don't believe he's heard from you since his injury."

Carver's hands were clenched on the edge of the desk, as if he was trying to restrain himself from throttling her. "You know the drill," he said in a low voice. "You're suspended pending an investigation by the state police. An investigation which I believe and hope will cost you your badge. So turn in that badge and your weapon. And go home."

She blinked back tears. "Yes, sir." She turned on her heel and left.

Wyatt saw Cahill coming out of the lieutenant's office and knew that whatever had gone on in there, it wasn't good.

She almost didn't notice him as she walked past. Then she spotted him and stopped dead. "What are you doing here?" She looked down at his side. "You're out of the hospital?"

"They dug a pellet out of me, taped up the wound where another one grazed me, gave me some antibiotics, and sent me on my way. Guess my North Carolina insurance doesn't buy me much down her in Louisiana. Lucky that little girl in the car was a lousy shot."

"Girl? I didn't see her."

"Neither did I, till she shot me."

"So what are you doing here?"

He shrugged. "Thought you might need some backup. Sorry if I was too late."

She looked back at the door. He could see the anger in her eyes and the set of her jaw. She relaxed and looked back at him, her expression softening a little. "Thanks. Don't know if it'd do any good. Looks like we're both civilians now."

"For the moment," he said. "Can you hang around a bit? There's another thing I need to talk to your boss about."

"Mick and Keith Jakes?"

"Mick Jakes," he corrected her. "Tyler Welch."

She looked dubious. "I don't know if he's in a listening mood."

McGee smiled. "I can be right persuasive. And afterward, I'd like us to talk about what we do next."

"Next?" she shook her head. "McGee, there is no next. I'm suspended and you're a civilian."

"So we'll have coffee and talk about Saints football."

"Uh-huh. Why do I have the feeling I'm going to regret this?"

"I don't know, why?" He turned and knocked on the lieutenant's door. He entered without waiting for an answer.

The man behind the desk was holding a phone receiver in one hand, the fingers of the other poised to press the buttons. He was a dark-skinned black man with a shaved head and the kind of face that gave Wyatt the impression that irritation was a more or less permanent condition. "Lieutenant…" Wyatt checked the nameplate on the desk, "…Carver?"

"Yes?" Carver put the phone down.

Wyatt advanced on the desk and stuck out his hand. "Wyatt McGee," he said. The expression on Carver's face turned from annoyed to wary.

He stood up and extended his own hand as if he expected Wyatt to try and bite it off. "Mr. McGee," he said, "I'm glad you're okay. You are okay, aren't you?"

Wyatt figured the man was trying to get some sort of admission in case of a civil suit. "This?" he gestured at his side, where his shirt covered the bandages they'd put in at the hospital. "Been hurt worse breaking up a bar fight back home." He took Carver's hand and shook it firmly, enjoying the look of bafflement on the lieutenant's face.

"Good. I mean…" Carver withdrew his hand and sat down. "What can I do for you, Mr. McGee?"

"Well, the main thing I'm here for is to fill you in on Mick Jakes and Tyler Welch."

"Those the two young men who shot my deputy and wounded you?"

Wyatt shook his head. "The one who wounded me was a girl. I don't know her. She popped out of the backseat with a shotgun. I guess I'm lucky she was too excited to aim."

"With respect, Mr. McGee, it would have been luckier all around if you hadn't involved yourself in police business."

Wyatt fought down his irritation. He'd probably already been elected sheriff for the first time when this paper-pusher had been a rookie. "Well, I felt it was my business to let someone here know about these two boys. I think one of them—"

"Mr. McGee," Carver broke in. "I don't really care about the history of any of these people, or how they came from broken homes, or how no one gave them enough warm fuzzies when they were little. They shot one of my officers. That officer may die, or be crippled for life, because of those *boys*." The last word came out bitter. "And we're going after them for it. Hard. New Orleans hard. If they give themselves up, they'll survive. Probably. If not, well…" He spread his hands in feigned helplessness, as if the implied result was as inevitable as it was fatal. "You were a sheriff back in North Carolina, I hear. I'm surprised you don't understand that we can't let this kind of thing go unpunished."

"I'm not asking that they go unpunished. I'm trying to…" He stopped. He wasn't sure anymore what he was trying to do. He'd wanted to help his friend's son and assuage some of his guilt over Mick. But Carver had a point. If someone had shot one of his deputies, he'd have gone after them with everything he had. He'd have taken pleasure in gunning that person down himself. And he would have been applauded for it. Suddenly, he felt very tired. He felt old.

Carver shook his head in pity. "Go home, Sheriff McGee. Let us do our jobs."

Wyatt nodded. "Thanks for your time, Lieutenant." He turned as if to walk out, then turned back. "Oh, one more thing."

Carver sighed. "Yes?"

"Cahill. She's a good cop. She made a mistake, but no need to let it ruin her career."

"Goodbye, Mr. McGee." The loss of the honorific wasn't lost on Wyatt. His face burning, he turned and left the office.

Cahill was waiting for him in the lobby. "That bad, huh?" she said when she saw his face.

"Yeah. That bad."

"So what do we do now?"

"We get that cup of coffee," he said. "Then I go home."

CHAPTER FORTY-TWO

Mick and Lana lingered over their meals until Savannah wanted to reach across the table and smack them both. Keith nervously tapped the bottom of his empty water glass on the table until she gently reached out and put a hand on his wrist to stop him. "Sorry," he muttered. She gave the wrist a squeeze to let him know it was all right. She studied his face. He'd grown into such a handsome young man. He'd lost the baby fat, leaving cheekbones like a male model's. *He must be a real heartbreaker*, she thought to herself. She turned her attention to Mick. There was something about him that bothered her. He looked different from the picture on Facebook, but that wasn't it. Most people looked at least a little different than their Facebook profile. Maybe it was the way he acted. He'd always been so fierce. The fierceness was still there, but there was an ugly edge to it now. He also looked older than twenty. She felt an almost physical pain in her heart as she thought of what he must have gone through. It had changed him in ways she couldn't even imagine. She wanted to know. She wanted to comfort him. But she didn't know how that was going to happen now. After all this time, her dream of being reunified with her sons had turned into a nightmare of being on the run. Mick had shot a cop. Maybe even killed him. And this cockeyed plan he had of driving all the way to Mexico…

"Oh, shit," Keith said. He was looking at the TV behind the diner's long counter. She followed his gaze and gasped in shock. The sound was turned down, but the picture on the screen was her own face, the portrait she'd put on her Facebook profile. It was taken in soft focus, ten years ago, but it was unmistakably her. The lettering under the picture blazed out at her: *Mother, Two Sons Sought in Police Officer Shooting.*

She looked around. No one was looking at her. Mick noticed her look. He hadn't seen the TV. "What?" he asked.

"We made the news," Savannah said. She stole another look at the TV. Her picture was gone, replaced by a concerned-looking Asian anchorwoman. She'd seen enough similar stories to know what was being said without hearing: "If you see these people, do not approach, extremely dangerous," and so on.

"We need to go," she said. "Before someone recognizes us."

"We're fine, Mama," Mick said.

"No." Lana's tone was so emphatic that even Mick sat up straight and looked at her. She was looking up at the TV screen as well. "We need to go, baby. Now." She slid out of the booth.

Mick's cocky grin was gone. Lana's concern had affected him where Savannah's apparently hadn't. *Before this is over,* Savannah thought, *that girl and I are going to butt heads.*

"Okay," Mick said. He pulled out a wad of bills and tossed them on the counter. The waitress was approaching, check in hand. "That ought to cover it," Mick said with a bright smile.

The waitress was staring at the pile of bills. "Um. Okay. Can you wait just a minute while I figure this up?"

"No," Mick said. "It's fine. Keep the change."

Damn it, Savannah thought. *Way to be inconspicuous.* She had to jog to catch up with Mick and Lana as they strode out the door. Keith was right behind her.

"What's happening?" he asked. "Where are we going?"

"I don't know, Keith," she said as they walked to the parking lot in front of the diner. Ahead of them and forty feet overhead, the traffic on I-10 sighed by on the overpass. The night was lit with the hard orange glow of streetlamps. Savannah racked her brain, mentally going through the contact list on one of the phones in her purse, her regular phone. She didn't want to think about the other one, the one Winslow had given her that she'd stashed in her roller bag as she left the house, then transferred to the depths of her purse when she'd gotten to Cahill's trailer. Calling those two again wasn't even Plan B. If anything, it was Plan Z.

Suddenly, a name jumped out from her memory. It wasn't the name of someone she'd normally call on for anything. But it was the name of someone who had a place for them to hide, and access to vehicles, if the price was right.

She got to the car as Mick was firing up the engine. "Baby," she said to Keith, "get in the back." She saw with a flash of irritation that Lana had taken the front seat. "Lana," she said, smiling in a way she hoped conveyed not a degree of warmth, "can you take the back, too? I need to talk to Mick."

The girl looked up at Savannah, her emotions flickering across her face like distant summer lightning. Jealousy, uncertainty, insecurity. *This girl had better not ever play poker. Everything that goes through her mind shows up on her face.* She'd have felt sorry for the younger woman if the little bitch hadn't been standing in her way. She kept the smile pasted on her face until Lana broke eye contact and slid out of the bucket seat. "Thanks, sweetie." The dismissal couldn't have been more blatant if Savannah had given Lana the back of her hand.

As soon as she'd closed her door, Mick stepped on the gas. Tires squealed on pavement as they accelerated out of the parking lot. "Mick," Savannah said, "slow down."

He looked at her and she could see the uncertainty in his eyes as well. Now was the time for her to take control of this situation, now that she had some idea what to do. "We can't keep attracting attention to ourselves," she said. "That means not driving like a maniac." He tapped an irritated rhythm on the steering wheel, but he let off the gas pedal. She breathed a little easier. "Okay. Now. We can't head straight out of town. They're watching for this car on the interstates and all the ways out of town. Baby, we need to get rid of it."

He looked at her as if she'd suggested cutting off a leg. "No. It's my car."

"And it's beautiful, Mick." Actually, she'd never liked this model, which she privately called the "redneck racer." But she knew how boys liked it, and she'd become an expert over the years at knowing how to use what boys liked. "It's a beautiful car," she repeated. "A classic. Which is why every cop in a hundred miles is going to have eyes out for it."

He'd reached the on-ramp. "I guess you can get us a new one. Like magic."

"Actually," she said, "I think I can." She reached into her bag and fumbled around for her phone. Her fingers closed around a hard plastic object. She pulled it out. *Wrong one.* She stuffed it back in her bag and pulled out her own phone. "Head back into the city. I need to make a phone call."

He didn't answer, but pulled out onto the highway following the signs for Baton Rouge. She watched him for a moment, willing him to listen to her. Without speaking, he took an exit onto a side street, then followed the signs for the ramps that would lead them back to I-10, going back into the heart of the city.

She breathed a sigh of relief and dialed the number she'd dredged up out of her phone contacts. She might have to make a bargain with the man on the other side of that number. That bargain might include herself. She fought the tears back. No one here was going to see her cry. A mother couldn't afford that. Not if she and her boys were going to survive. She thought about the burner phone in her purse, the one she'd taken from the house, the lifeline she'd had to Winslow and Cahill. That was another bridge burned, she guessed. *Only way to go now is forward*, she thought.

N one of this was going the way he'd planned.

The idea had taken root for the first time the day he'd found out about Mick's death. He'd been Mick's roommate at the time, continuing the friendship they'd struck up in prison. They'd hung out, drunk beer together, chased women. And all the time, Mick had talked about the family he was going to see as soon as he got his shit straight and made some money. How nice it was going to be when they were all together. How beautiful his Mama was, and how she loved Mick and his brother.

Kevin DeWalt's family had been a horror show from the day he was born. At least that's what he'd been told. Most of his memory of the time was a void, a blank space where he couldn't remember anything at all. The therapist at the hospital where he'd spent most of his teenage years said that was a common reaction. The mind's way of defending itself. But Kevin hated that blank space. It made him feel as if he wasn't even real. Not an actual human being at all. He envied Mick for having his memories. Even the bad ones. He'd found himself wishing that those memories were his. Then he'd gotten the news that Mick had been killed. He'd been surprised when he discovered that Mick had put him down as his contact at the jail, but he guessed it made sense.

When he'd shown up to ID the body, the morgue attendant had

done a double take. "Were you guys twins?" he'd asked. Kevin had just nodded. It was easier that way. When the man had pulled aside the concealing sheet and he'd looked down into the face of the dead man, he'd seen himself lying there. At that moment, he'd come up with his plan. How he could have a family. A home. Memories that were his. When he picked up his roommate's personal effects, he'd flipped the wallet open and looked at the driver's license. It was his face looking back at him. He'd found pictures of Savannah and Keith. With his only close friend dead, he'd felt completely alone in the world. Until that moment. At that moment, he felt real. He felt like someone with memories. With a family. He'd vowed to himself on that day that they'd be together. He took Mick's computer and picked up the trail he'd been following online to search for his mother and brother. The cipher that had once been Kevin DeWalt felt like a real person for the first time.

But it hadn't worked out that way. Now Mama was mad at him. His brother was scared to death. And every cop in the state was looking to gun them down. Mick clenched his teeth. He wasn't going to let that happen. This was his family now, and he was going to protect them. Whatever it took.

CHAPTER FORTY-THREE

They had blindfolded Winslow before guiding him into the back of the SUV. Before that, his new captors made sure he saw the bodies in the car that had been chasing him. He couldn't tell if one of them was Zag. All he could see was blood and grayish-white streaks that may have been bone or brain matter on the car windows. After that, the black bag had gone over his head and he'd been hustled into the back of a vehicle. He tried to count the turns as they took him further and further from the farm, even though he knew it was useless. Eventually, he gave up.

Finally, the SUV stopped. He heard the door open. A hand on his shoulder led him out of the vehicle. All he could hear at first was his own heavy breathing. Then, the sounds of nature began to penetrate the fabric and he could pick out the deep calls of bullfrogs and the steady drone of cicadas. Eventually, he was guided inside a building and the insect sounds grew softer. The hand on his shoulder sat him down in a chair that wobbled alarmingly as he collapsed into it. The hood was jerked from his head so roughly it made him gasp. He looked around, trying to get his bearings.

He was in a large interior space with corrugated metal walls. There was no floor beneath his feet, only dirt. Some kind of barn, then, which made the man seated at the rough wooden table in front of him look even more out of place.

He was a man of medium height, his perfectly trimmed jet-black hair streaked with gray. His beard, as immaculately cut as his hair, was also shot through with patches of gray. He was reading something inside a file folder in the harsh white light of a pair of propane lanterns set at either end of the table. The perfectly tailored cream-colored suit he wore gave him the air of perfect assurance, like a general being briefed at a battlefield command post. The man dressed in army fatigue pants and a black t-shirt who stood off to one side, an AK-47 rifle slung on his shoulder, completed the impression. Winslow was aware of other presences in the room behind him. He assumed they, too, were armed and kept his eyes resolutely ahead. "You'd be Caspar Gutierrez," he said.

The man behind the table held up an index finger to indicate he'd be with Winslow in a moment. He spoke in a low voice to the man with the AK-47 and closed the file folder. The man in the black T-shirt nodded, took the folder, and left without another word. Only then did the man behind the table turn his attention to Winslow.

"Yes," he said, "I am Caspar Gutierrez. I'm pleased to make your acquaintance, Agent Winslow."

"I doubt that's true." Winslow looked around. "So where is Angus Charlebois?"

Gutierrez leaned back, his eyes bright with interest. "And why would you like to know? Is he perhaps someone you want to protect? Perhaps a source of information?"

Winslow knew he was treading dangerous ground. If Gutierrez thought he was lying, he'd torture Winslow until he was satisfied that what the DEA man told him contained the truth. But the truth could subject Charleyboy to the same unimaginable agony. He decided on a version of the truth. "He hasn't told us anything. We were going to take him in and sweat him and see what he gave up."

Gutierrez nodded. "Ah. And what was it that made you think he might have something to give up?" Winslow didn't answer. Gutierrez smiled. "Perhaps it was something his girlfriend spilled to you? In exchange for federal help to find out something she wanted?"

Winslow felt a shock run through him. There was only one way Gutierrez could know that. Before he could speak up, Gutierrez looked over Winslow's shoulder. "Bring in Charleyboy."

In a few moments, a pair of men, dressed in the same fatigue pants and black t-shirts, came in holding the stumbling figure of Charleyboy propped up between them. His face was chalk-white, and he clutched a blood-soaked handkerchief to his right hand with his left. One of the guards slammed a wooden chair down next to Winslow's while the other shoved Charleyboy into it. Charleyboy stared at Gutierrez with all the terror of a rabbit seeing a snake peering into its warren.

"Charleyboy," Gutierrez said, "I believe it's time we were honest with one another."

"I'm not lying," Charleyboy whimpered. "I swear it."

One of the guards made a sudden lunge toward him and he flinched away with a moan of terror. Both guards laughed. "Let us take another finger, *jefe*," the one who'd feinted towards Charleyboy said to Gutierrez. "He'll be singing like a little bird after that. I promise."

Gutierrez shook his head. "Not now, my friend." He smiled at Winslow. "We are, after all, civilized men, no?"

"It you're asking me," Winslow said, "you may not want to hear the answer."

"Hah." Gutierrez sat back and clapped his hands in approval. "I admire cleverness." He turned to Charleyboy. "But not too much cleverness. Now. Let me sum up what I think has happened." The smile vanished and he leaned forward, dark eyes focused on Charleyboy's face. "You were in debt to Wallace Luther. You learned I was hoping to establish my business interests in Louisiana, so you came to me, hoping to betray Luther and gain my favor. You would make Luther think you were setting me up, but I would be there first, and ready to take out Luther." He sat back and sighed. "But your girlfriend, the beautiful Savannah, had other desires. She hoped to find her long lost sons. And to do that, she was willing to make a deal. And shop all of us to the DEA. Now…" He leaned forward again. "Tell me the truth, before I let my boys here start cutting more pieces off of you. Am I right or am I wrong?"

Winslow thought at first that Charleyboy had passed out. He sat slumped in the other chair, head down. Finally, he raised his head up. His face was streaked with tears. "No," he said, "you're wrong. It was all me."

"Really?" Gutierrez inclined his head skeptically. "You expect me to believe that?"

"I don't give a fuck if you believe it or not, you greaser spic bastard," Charleyboy said. "It wasn't her. It was me. I sold you out. And you know why? Because I hate you fucking Mexicans. You're a goddamn cancer on our country."

The guard who'd spoken up before stepped forward and clouted Charleyboy on the back of the head. Gutierrez raised a hand. "Stop." The man pulled back the hand he'd raised to hit Charleyboy again and stepped back. Gutierrez shook his head. "Charleyboy," he said, and his voice was so sorrowful Winslow was tempted to believe it was sincere. "You almost convinced me. But then you had to go and lay it on too thick." He sighed. "I know why you're saying what you're saying. To tell you the truth, it appeals to the romantic in me that you hope to save your lover, even though she has betrayed you. But you may find out that dying for love is not so sweet a thing as you have convinced yourself it is. In the end, dying is…just dying. It is messy and undignified. And, I assure you, very, very painful." He gestured to the guard who'd hit Charleyboy. "Take him away. I'll decide what to do with him later." The man walked over and yanked Charleyboy to his feet. Winslow watched as he was led away.

"Now, Agent Winslow," Gutierrez said. "You, I'm going to let go." He saw the look on Winslow's face and smiled. "You don't believe me. But I tell you, sincerely, I don't want the blood of a DEA agent on my hands. I don't need that kind of heat coming down on me." He shrugged, that sorrowful look on his face again. "I am forced to admit it. I have failed. Louisiana has not, how shall I say it, worked out for me. So, I'm returning to Mexico. Perhaps we will meet again. But not soon."

"Uh-huh," Winslow said. "And I suppose we won't see Charleyboy anymore because…let's see, he's going to live on a farm upstate."

For the first time, Gutierrez looked confused. "Sorry," Winslow said. "Guess you didn't get the reference."

"I suppose not." Gutierrez's smile was back. He gestured to the other guard. "Take him and release him in the French Quarter. Let him make his way back to his agency."

Winslow didn't believe for a moment he was going to be released, but he stood up anyway. "You know, this reminds me of something I said to someone else not too long ago."

Gutierrez had already dismissed Winslow from his mind, and having his attention drawn back to the man standing in front of him was clearly irritating him. "Yes?" he said.

"Guys like you," Winslow said, "you'll always be assholes. We may not get you today. But someday, probably soon, you'll fuck up some other way and we'll get you then. We're the U.S. Government." He forced himself to smile, even though he knew it probably looked like lockjaw. "We've got all the time in the world."

Gutierrez shook his head. "I understand why Charleyboy

insulted me. He risks his own death as a ploy to try and distract me from his woman's betrayal. But you, I don't understand. What was the point of that?"

Winslow shrugged. "I'm just a simple civil servant. I don't do ploys. I'm not smart enough. I just wanted you to know how things are."

"Ah. And now that you've told me, do you feel better?"

Winslow considered for a moment. "Actually, yeah." He smiled. "I do."

"How nice." Gutierrez nodded to the guard and Winslow was led away.

CHAPTER FORTY-FOUR

Since coming to New Orleans, Savannah had seen a lot of ads for tours of the antebellum mansions of the area. This place just outside the city was never going to make it onto that circuit. The thick columns that held up the two-story roof over the broad front porch were cracked, the paint peeling in the humidity. One of the tall front windows had been broken and replaced with plywood. The others were too grimy to see through. Off to their right of the driveway sat a greenhouse with many of the glass panes shattered. The aggressive tropical vegetation of southern Louisiana was swarming over everything that stood upright, taking full advantage of years of neglect.

The man standing at the cast-iron gate in the stone wall surrounding the mansion was painfully skinny, with long, lank black hair and skin so pale Savannah always thought of vampires. He swung the gate back and Mick eased the Firebird down the long dirt driveway. The pale man walked behind them.

"Mama," Keith asked. "Who is that guy? Why are we here?"

"He's a friend. Sort of. A friend of a friend, I guess," Savannah answered. "Anyway, he can help us. I hope. He's got…resources."

The pale man was motioning them off to one side. A long, low structure was hidden from the view of people coming up the drive by a high, wildly overgrown hedge. The building was an old carriage house, judging from the size and number of doors in the front. The pale man motioned them to where one of those doors gaped open like a cave mouth. Mick hesitated a moment, then eased the car in. The door slammed shut behind them with a shriek of rusty hinges and a bang that made Lana squeak with alarm.

"Just let me handle him," Savannah said as she got out of the car. There were no lights in the carriage house. The only illumination was provided by their headlights reflecting off the back wall. She took a deep breath and plastered a smile on her face. "Cully. Hey." She held out her arms to the pale man. After a moment's hesitation, he let her hug him. He felt awkward in her grasp, as if he didn't know how to react. She hugged him harder. This had to work.

Keith could see Savannah embracing the pale man who had let them in.

"Who the fuck is that freak?" Lana spoke up.

Mick didn't answer. He stared at the two people embracing for a moment before he killed the engine and got out, leaving the headlights on. He sidled through the narrow space between the front bumper and the pale green wall of the garage. Keith hesitated, then pushed the front driver's seat forward and got out. There was space for multiple vehicles, but the only other one he could see was a nondescript white van. Mick had walked over to where Savannah and the pale man were and thrust out his hand, an aggressively friendly smile on his face. "Hey," he said. "I'm Savannah's son. I'm Mick."

The pale man looked at the outstretched hand as if it were a poisonous snake. "I'm Cully. Sorry, but I don't shake hands."

Mick blinked. The smile slipped, and Keith was afraid for a moment that he'd start throwing fists or worse. The moment passed, and Mick dropped the hand, cranking his smile back up to full intensity. "Sure. Can't be too careful. Germs, right?"

Cully looked at him blankly for a moment, then turned back to Savannah. "You can come inside. But guns stay in the car. And cell phones."

"Whoa, just a minute," Mick began, but Savannah interrupted.

"That's fine." She laughed nervously. "Your house, your rules, right?" She opened the door of the car and reached into her purse, coming out with a slim black cell phone. She handed it to Cully. "There you go."

Cully shook his head. "No. Leave it in the car." He looked at Keith, still standing on the side of the car opposite him. "How about you?"

Keith held up his hands. "I'm good. No phone, no guns."

Cully turned his attention back to Mick. "How about you, cowboy? Okay to leave your popgun in the car?" When Mick hesitated, Cully went on. "Or you could just back this redneck piece of shit out of here and go off on your own." Keith saw Mick's face go slack, then tense with rage. Cully never lost his blank expression.

"Stop it, you two," Savannah broke in. She turned to Mick. "It's okay, baby. We're all friends here."

"He doesn't seem all that friendly to me," Mick said.

"I'm not," Cully said. "I'm what you might call the opposite of friendly. Savannah, you can stay." He looked at Keith, then bent down to regard Lana who was still seated in the vehicle. "These two. Okay." He glared at Mick. "This one, no. Sorry."

"I'm sorry, too, Cully," Savannah said with an ingratiating smile. "But we're kind of a package deal. These are my sons. I'm not picking one over the other."

Cully's lack of affect was sending warning shivers up and down Keith's spine. The pale man looked around the cavernous space, his eyes not coming to rest on any of them. "Fine," he said at last. "All of you. But no guns in my house. And no phones."

Savannah spoke up before Mick could. "Okay." She turned to the three of them. "All guns in the car. And all phones. Trust me. It's the only way."

Keith thought for a moment that Mick might rebel, but their mother's influence won out in the end. He nodded sullenly.

"Follow me," she said. She opened a door leading out of the garage. They followed, Mick falling in behind her, Lana climbing out of the backseat and flashing a smile at Cully, which was completely ignored, then Keith, who slid his way around the hood in the narrow confines of the garage and fell in behind them.

The door out of the garage led to a flagstone walkway that wound its way to the main house. All the windows of the house were dark, save the one at the end of the walk. Keith stole a glance back to where Cully was locking the door to the carriage house. They were cut off from weapons and communication, totally dependent on a man who gave Keith the creeps. He wanted more than anything in the world for this nightmare to end, to be back in North Carolina with the people who had raised him.

He wanted to be Tyler again. Being Keith was terrifying.

The black bag they'd pulled back over his head did strange things to Winslow's sense of time. He couldn't tell how long they'd been driving. They hadn't bothered to bind his hands or feet as he sat in the front passenger seat, but he could hear that there were at least two men in the seats behind him, presumably armed. There was no way to fight them and live. He had no doubt they were taking him somewhere to kill him, somewhere away from Gutierrez where his body could be dumped. One of the men in back murmured something to the driver and the SUV slowed, shuddering and bumping as they drove over the rough shoulder. When the car stopped, someone reached from the back and pulled the hood from his head. A voice came from behind him. "Get out."

This is it, he thought. He considered threatening them, reminding them of the shit-storm that would come down on them for murdering a federal agent. He considered bargaining. He considered pleading. All of those alternatives raced through his mind as he got out. In the instant that he thought of each one, he knew it would be futile.

The night was deep black and starless. There were no lighted houses or streetlights nearby. The only illumination was the cone of hard white light thrown off by the high beams of the SUV. He could smell the water before he saw it, the low, razor-straight banks of a canal at his feet. He nearly stumbled into it before he stopped. Someone was getting out of the back, the door blocking his view. He moved before the plan was even fully formed in his mind, lunging forward toward the black water. One of the men behind him yelled as he ran into water up to his knees. Winslow raised his arms, took a deep breath and dove, as flat and as far as he could. He heard the report of a gunshot, then another. Something burning blazed a trail along his back and he ducked under, swimming in blind animal panic as hard as he could for the bottom. He heard the *zip-zip* of bullets hitting the water. He couldn't seem to make his right arm obey him. Using his left arm and his legs, he pushed through the water. His waterlogged suit pants were dragging him down. The air in his lungs was getting stale and he fought the urge to breathe until it became unbearable and he pulled frantically for the surface. Breaking the surface with a gasp, he took a deep breath and dove again. He realized that he'd been struggling against a strong current, one that would carry him downstream and away from the gunmen if he let it. He changed direction and let the water do the work. The adrenaline was wearing off, leaving him feeling weak and shaky. This time, when he surfaced, he did it slowly. He paused, gently treading water with arms and legs that were turning increasingly heavy. He saw the headlights of the SUV. The car was far behind him, but he could hear the shouting of the gunmen coming up the bank as they searched for him. The beam of a powerful flashlight played across the water, but came nowhere near. Then he saw the dark shape moving toward him through the water.

Alligator, his mind blared. He nearly cried out in panic, but instead inhaled a gulp of foul tasting water. He choked and spewed it out, gagging and coughing. The dark shape was moving closer and closer. It seemed to grow huge as it approached. He kicked out blindly at it, expecting at any time to feel the agony of serrated knifelike teeth in his flesh. His foot struck something hard and unyielding and the evil black shape veered away slightly before resuming its course toward him. He kicked at it again. It swung away, then back toward him. With a quickly stifled laugh of hysterical relief, he realized he was kicking a floating log. He glanced back down the river and saw with alarm that the SUV was now moving slowly down the road parallel to the canal, the flashlight probing the darkness on the surface. Reaching out with his left arm, he snagged a protruding branch and got the log between him and the car, ducking his head behind it. He tried to reach up again with his right, but it was still numb and useless. *I've been hit,* he thought. The weakness and light-headedness he was feeling was more than exhaustion. He was losing blood, and fast. He could hear the SUV slowing, and suddenly the flashlight beam shone over the top of the log. Winslow held his breath and dove.

CHAPTER FORTY-FIVE

The living room of the old house was enormous, with dusty and frayed furniture forming au-shaped conversation space around a large fireplace with cobwebs in it. It looked as though it hadn't seen a flame in decades. The only illumination was a Tiffany lamp that Cully switched on as they entered. The old and dusty lamp cast a dim light and left the rest of the room in darkness. "Wait here," Cully said, and disappeared through a swinging door.

"Mama," Keith said as he took a seat on the ragged sofa, "who is that guy? How do you know him?"

She picked up a pile of old magazines sitting in one of the east chairs and put it down on the floor before taking a seat. "He's someone I met through Charleyboy. He's from old New Orleans money. Some kind of trust-fund baby. He's supposed to be a genius. He was first in his class at Tulane. Then his parents died and left him this place. He's been living alone here ever since."

"What the hell's the matter with him?" Lana demanded.

Savannah glared at her. "Just because someone's a little different doesn't mean something's the matter with them, honey."

"My name's Lana, not 'honey,'" the younger woman snapped back. "And I don't think something's the matter with him because he's a little different. I think something's the matter with him because he's fucking creepy."

"Cut it out, Lana," Mick said. He turned to Savannah. "Why are we here?"

Keith noticed that Savannah had trouble meeting his eyes. "Like I said. Cully's got more than money. He knows people. He can get things."

"Like what?" Keith asked.

Savannah's voice took on an edge and she glanced at Mick. "Like a car that every cop in three states isn't looking for, for one thing."

"I ain't givin' up my car," Mick said.

"You should have thought of that before you shot a police officer," Savannah said. "You go out of here in that car, they'll catch you. They'll probably kill you, because that's what cops do to people who shoot other cops. My god, son, what the hell were you *thinking*?" her voice had risen to a shout.

Mick slammed his hand down on the arm of the couch. "He drew on me first!" he shouted back.

"Please," Keith begged, "stop fighting."

Cully entered the room. "Okay. Security system's armed. Nobody can get in. Let's talk."

"We need a car, Cully," Savannah said, "and we need a way out of town, fast."

"I know. I saw the news. Your idiot son over there shot a cop."

Mick sprang to his feet. "I don't have to take this shit."

Cully didn't raise his voice. "You want my help, cowboy, you'll take any shit I give you, and you'll thank me for it while you ask for more."

"Cully, please," Savannah begged. "Mick, calm down."

"Like hell." Mick grabbed a rusty poker from a rack next to the fireplace. Cully reached behind him, into the waistband of his slacks. His hand came back holding a black semi-automatic pistol.

Savannah leaped up and interposed herself between them. "Stop it!" Cully's gun never wavered. Savannah turned back to Mick. "Put that down," she ordered. "And apologize."

Mick's eyes widened in amazement. "Apologize?"

"Yes. Apologize. We're guests here." She stared into his eyes for a moment, her own gaze locked with his. After a moment, Keith saw Mick's face crumple and his eyes fill with tears. "Why are you doin' me like this, Mama? After all I've done to bring us together?"

Her voice was soft. "Because I'll do anything in this world to protect you." She looked at Keith. "Anything." She turned to Cully. "I can get some money. And I know they have some. But please, Cully, help us. I know you and Charleyboy are friends. And I hope we are."

Cully looked at her with that unnerving stare, then put the gun back. "I need to make some phone calls," he said. "I'll see what I can do. And then I'll tell you the price."

"Thank you," she said.

He nodded. "In the meantime, bedrooms are upstairs. I'll show you the guest rooms."

Lana spoke up from the other easy chair. "Hey. You think you can get me somethin' for pain? I got a bad back." Apparently, she was willing to put aside her earlier distaste. At least if it meant access to her "medicine."

For the first time, the ghost of a smile played across Cully's lips. "Bad back, eh? What do you need? I got oxycodone, hydrocodone, codeine, fentanyl…"

Lana's eyes were bright. "Cully, I think we may end up being friends after all."

Savannah didn't like the look that passed between them. This was not the refuge she'd hoped for.

The sun wasn't up yet when Lionel Hebert pulled up outside his cousin Remy's house, but the lights were on inside. He picked up the brown paper bag from the passenger seat of his Ford pickup and walked to the door. Remy opened it as he approached. "I got ham biscuits," Lionel said, holding out the bag. "Want one?"

Remy shook his head. "Let's get on the way first. You got the beers?"

Lionel nodded toward the rear of the truck. "In the cooler."

"Aiight." Remy was never talkative, and even less so in the morning. It was one of the things that made him Lionel's favorite fishing companion. With the efficiency of long practice, they hooked Remy's bass boat to the back of the truck and headed out into the dark.

"I figured we'd try Lake Lery today." Lionel took a bite of his biscuit. Remy nodded and took a bite of his, washing it down with a swallow of Abita from the cooler.

A few miles down the highway, they found a place to put in. It took a couple of tries to get Remy's temperamental outboard motor started, but after a few minutes, they were heading up the channel towards the lake. Remy sat in the front of the boat and cracked open another beer as Lionel steered. He was humming to himself. It was supposed to be a beautiful morning. *Fishing poles, a cooler full of beer, and good company. What more can a fellow ask for*, he thought. Suddenly, Remy sat up straighter.

"What?" Lionel said. Remy pointed. The sun was barely a sliver on the horizon, but Lionel could make out something white on the bank. "Is that…" He trailed off. Remy shrugged. With an anxious feeling creeping up his spine, Lionel brought the boat nearer. "Oh shit," he said. It was definitely a body. As they reached shallow water, Remy jumped out and waded to it. "He dead?" Lionel called out.

Remy was kneeling by the man. He shook his head. "Still breathin'. He been shot, though."

"Goddamn it," Lionel muttered. "And this is my only day off, too."

"So that's it?" Chance said. "You're going to just give up and go home?"

They were seated at a booth in a diner in the Quarter. The place was mostly empty except for the two of them and a quartet of bleary-eyed frat boys dressed in stained Loyola t-shirts, necks festooned with beads. They looked tired but perfectly willing to carry last night's debauchery into the light of another day.

Wyatt stared into his coffee cup. "I don't know what else to do. Your lieutenant pretty well shut me down." He drained the last dregs of the cup and sighed. He'd never been so tired in his life.

The waitress arrived with their plates, pancakes and sausages for Wyatt, eggs, bacon, and toast for Chance. Now that he'd gotten his food, Wyatt found he'd lost his appetite. "So what are you going to do?"

She shrugged and picked up her fork. "Not sure. Maybe contact DEA, see if I can help them find Winslow."

"You think they'll listen to you?"

"I don't know. But I need to do something."

Wyatt was momentarily distracted by a ragged whoop of joy that went up from the table of frat boys. The waitress had brought a tray of beers. A man in a dress shirt and tie, probably the manager, followed behind with another tray with shots of amber liquid. Each of the boys seized a bottle and they all clinked them together in the middle of the table.

Chance shook her head. "Got to admire their stamina." She saw the look on Wyatt's face and frowned. "You want a drink?"

He licked his lips. "Yeah." He rubbed his hand down his face and tore his eyes away. "But I'm not twenty years old anymore."

She was looking at him appraisingly. "You want one, don't let me stop you."

"No. No, I'm good."

She nodded and went back to her breakfast. The waitress came back and refilled Wyatt's coffee. She looked at the untouched food. "Somethin' wrong with your breakfast, hon?"

"No." He said. "It's fine." He picked up his fork and took a bite of sausage. He blinked in surprise. It had a slightly spicy but full and complex flavor that was like nothing he'd had before.

The waitress smiled. "You never had andouille, have ya?"

"Is that what this is? It's great."

"Yeah, it is. Enjoy." She walked away.

Chance was smiling. "Long as you're down here, you ought to stay for a while. Try some more of the food. You just about can't get a bad meal in New Orleans." Her phone buzzed and she fished it out of her purse. She looked at the screen, then pressed the button and put the phone to her ear. "Hey, Delphine." She listened for a moment as Wyatt continued to eat, his appetite restored. "Thanks, I appreciate it." The next thing she heard made her sit up straight, her eyes widening. Wyatt stopped eating and listened to her end of the conversation. "You sure? They know it's him? How bad? Okay. Where'd they take him? Thanks, girl. I owe you big time." She put down the phone. "Sorry to interrupt your meal. But two fishermen pulled Winslow out of a canal down near Delacroix this morning."

Wyatt got up and reached for his wallet to pay the check. "Dead?"

She shook her head. "Wounded. Half drowned. But alive. He's at the trauma unit at University Medical Center. I can get a cab if you want to get back to the hotel."

"Don't be ridiculous. I'm coming with you." He motioned for the check.

CHAPTER FORTY-SIX

Caspar Gutierrez looked down at the man tied to the chair, the bloody wreck that was all that remained of Angus Charlebois. He shook his head. "You must love her very much," he said.

Charleyboy's head lolled to one side and he looked at Gutierrez with his one remaining eye. He tried to say something, but all that came out was a bubbling wheeze. He'd given up all the information he had about Wallace Luther and his operations almost immediately, and Gutierrez had already taken action on that information. His men were fanning out across Southern Louisiana to hit the targets Charleyboy had identified. But he'd stubbornly clung to the story that it had been he, not Savannah, who'd gone to the DEA, he who'd arranged for the wire they'd found in the house.

Gutierrez squatted down beside the chair. "I don't understand you, Charleyboy. She betrayed you. She betrayed both of us. And yet you try to protect her." He stood up. "But you see, I know it was her. I have other sources." He grimaced with distaste as he saw that he'd gotten blood on his shoes. He really liked those shoes, and now they were ruined. Despite his irritation, he kept his voice even and reasonable. "So, while you may think that this is an interrogation, it's not. It ceased to be that a few hours ago. No, Charleyboy, this is punishment. Punishment for lying to me. And it will only stop when you tell the truth." He gestured to the man standing by a table covered with tools.

The man picked up a short-handled hammer in one hand and a wicked-looking iron spike in the other. Tied as he was, Charleyboy couldn't see him, but he could hear the slow tread of boots as the man advanced, slowly so as to increase the anticipation and terror. He whimpered like the terrified animal he'd become. "You think I'm bluffing, don't you? You think I'm only pretending to know more than I do to get you to confess. Well, that's unfortunate." He looked at the man with the hammer and spike and nodded. "Again."

The hospital staff wasn't inclined to cooperate with non-family members. Chance had to flash her badge and bully the woman at the desk to find out where Winslow was. As they got on the elevator, Wyatt said, "I thought you were supposed to turn that badge in."

She smiled sardonically. "You going to report me?"

He shook his head. "I wouldn't know which office to go to."

"Okay, then."

Winslow was sitting up in bed, his shoulder bandaged and an IV running into the other arm. He smiled weakly as they entered. "Hey, Cahill." He looked over at Wyatt. "Who's your friend?"

Wyatt stuck out his hand. "Wyatt McGee. From North Carolina."

Winslow nodded. "So you're the one that's been tracking Savannah Jakes's sons. Or maybe I should say son."

"No," McGee said. "There's two boys. One of them, Mick, shot a police officer at the house on Esteban Street. We were there looking for you."

"Thanks. But you'd better pull up a chair. I've got some stuff to tell you. Let's just say things have taken a turn for the weird."

Savannah awoke late in the morning, the sun streaming through the high windows of the upstairs bedroom. She'd slept well in the huge antique canopy bed that looked as if it had been made before the turn of the twentieth century. This room, at least, had been cleaned sometime in the last few weeks. She couldn't say the same for some of the other rooms she'd looked into as they passed down the long hallway. "The boys are going to get a decent place to sleep, right?" she'd asked, adding, "and Mick's girlfriend," as an afterthought.

He'd nodded. "It's the servant's quarters," he'd said, "but they're clean."

She'd refused Cully's offer of a t-shirt to sleep in. She was trying to inveigle the strange man into helping her and the boys while still keeping her distance, and wearing Cully's clothes felt too much as if it might encourage him to be more forward. The room had its own bathroom, and she took the opportunity to relieve herself before searching for the skirt and blouse she'd been wearing. As she put them back on, she wrinkled her nose. First order of business was a car, but a change of clothes wasn't far behind. She'd been in these for what seemed like a year. Her stomach was growling. *Wonder if there's any food in the house.*

When she went to the door, it was locked from the outside.

"Holy shit," Chance said. "That's...unexpected."

Wyatt shook his head. "I'm not sure I believe it. This DeWalt character stole Mick Jakes's identity? And Tyler Welch doesn't recognize that the guy he's with isn't his own brother?"

"It's been a lot of years," Winslow said. "And this guy's a dead ringer. I've seen his picture."

"But why?" Chance said. "I mean, stealing Mick's identity is one thing. But then going off on this crusade to help the woman who's not actually his mom? What's the point?"

Winslow nodded to acknowledge the point. "I've been thinking about that while I've been lying here." He pushed the button to raise the bed so he could see them better. "Say you're Kevin DeWalt. You end up in jail with Mick Jakes. Both of you can't help but notice the resemblance. You laugh about it. You get to be friends. People make jokes about how you could be brothers. And Mick opens up. He talks about his mom and his long-lost brother. How he was torn away from his family and everything's been shit since. And how if he could only get back to that family, life would be better. It'd be like starting over."

Chance frowned. "I still don't see—"

Winslow interrupted her. "Say you hear this and you have no family of your own. Or your family's the kind of nightmare that creates guys like you, guys with more loose screws than a thirty dollar bookcase from Walmart. Mick's fantasy starts becoming your own. You start thinking about them as your own family. Then you hear that Mick's dead. You see a message on Facebook that Mom's looking for you. That's your chance. A chance to have a better life. A chance to have the family you never had."

Wyatt rubbed his hand over his face, trying to process it all. "It's crazy. But it fits."

"If it's true," Chance said, "then Savannah's in more danger than ever. She's following some kind of goddamn psychopath."

Winslow shook his head. "I don't think DeWalt will hurt Savannah directly. Remember, in this fantasy, she's his long-lost mom. But he also sees himself as her white knight. He'll do anything to protect her. But his judgment isn't the best."

"That's putting it mildly," Chance said. "So we can't let him know we know. Or her. I mean, what happens when this fantasy of his comes crashing down around his ears? What happens when Savannah finds out the guy she thought was her son is an imposter and rejects him?"

"Good question. Let's not find out if we don't have to."

"Okay," Chance said. "So when are they going let you out of here?"

Winslow shrugged. "A couple of days. The bullet wound fucked up the nerves in my shoulder and arm and I'm going to be doing a lot of PT. But what they're mostly concerned about is infection. Apparently, South Louisiana water isn't the cleanest in the world. Maybe all the chemicals will give me superpowers."

She laughed. "You just get better, Winslow."

"That's the plan. So what are you doing next?"

She looked at Wyatt. "Well, he's going home. I'm going to try to talk to your agent in charge. See what he knows. Maybe he's chased down who this impostor is."

"But you're…" Wyatt stopped at her look.

"She's what?" Winslow spoke up.

"Up for way too long," Wyatt amended. "She needs some sleep."

Winslow didn't look convinced. "Look," he said, "there's something you should know." He took a deep breath. "Caspar Gutierrez told me things. Things about this operation. Things that only someone with a source in the DEA could know."

Chance whistled. "Fuck."

Winslow nodded. "Well put. And he's going to war with Luther. Going after Luther's assets. It's going to get nasty out there. So be careful, okay?"

"You too, Winslow. Will you be all right?"

"Yeah. I'm fine."

"Just get well, man." Chance took Wyatt by the arm to steer him out of the room. "Look," she said, "while I'm here, you mind if I see if I can track down Knight?"

"Who?"

"The deputy who got shot. The lieutenant said he was here, too. I want to drop in. Pay my respects."

Wyatt nodded. "Sure. No problem."

CHAPTER FORTY-SEVEN

Savannah fought back the urge to scream and pound on the door. She knocked as calmly as she could. "Cully?" she said. She couldn't stop her voice from shaking. "Cully?"

In a moment, she heard the rattle of a key. The lock clicked. "Step back from the door," Cully's voice came through the thick wood. "Stand against the back wall." Heart pounding, she complied. The door opened and Cully entered, holding a pistol in his right hand. She wondered if he'd been standing outside. Waiting. Listening for her to discover she was trapped. Maybe even savoring the moment. Savannah felt as if she was going to throw up.

"What's going on, Cully?"

He just stared at her with his dead eyes. "You didn't tell me the person you're running from is Mr. Luther."

"What?" She laughed, a high, tense laugh that would fool no one. "No. Mr. Luther, he's a friend."

"Don't lie, Savannah," he said. "It's all over the street. He's looking for you. And your boys."

"Cully. Please. Where are my boys?"

"I can't save them. But I can save you."

She couldn't hold back the tears. "Please," she sobbed. "I'm begging you. Charleyboy's your friend."

"Charleyboy's dead."

She felt the breath go out of her. "Dead."

"Caspar Gutierrez has him. If he's not dead, he's begging for death by now."

She felt her stomach leaping into her throat and barely made the bathroom before she was spewing into the antique porcelain toilet. The spasms racked her, over and over, combining with her convulsive sobs until she hung onto the toilet to keep from toppling over on her side. She could hear his voice behind her, that toneless, unaffected voice that made her skin crawl.

"I've talked to Luther," Cully said. "His people are on their way. They'll take you. And the boys. And that girl, although she's so out of it, they may not have much use for her. Maybe in one of their houses. You know the type I mean."

Shut up, she thought desperately. *Shut up.* She noticed the toilet paper stand next to the commode. It was sturdy, made of pitted brass, with a broad, heavy base. Cully's maddeningly calm voice went on. "But I can bargain with him. Tell them you're with me. I can cut a deal for you. All you have to do is—"

"Shut *up*!" She staggered to her feet, heedless of the snot running down her nose or the drool on her chin. She snatched up the stand with desperate strength and swung the base hard at him, stepping into the swing like Babe Ruth going for the fences. The brass rod holding the roll of paper came loose and clattered onto the bathroom floor. Cully stepped back out of the way as the base of the stand smashed into the door. His rapid retreat caused him to stumble and fall backward.

Sobbing with rage and terror, she jumped forward and swung again, overhand this time, her strength that of desperation and fury. The base connected with the lintel of the door, smashing plaster and splinters of wood down on her. Cully pushed on the floor with his heels, eyes wide with panic, scuttling away like a bug. She stepped forward, clearing the doorway as he raised the gun. His shot smacked into the plaster of the ceiling as she brought the stand down like an ax. The heavy brass base caught Cully across the bridge of his nose, the crunch of breaking bone vibrating all the way up the shaft to her shoulders. She groaned with the effort as she raised the stand, then brought it down again on his face. And again. And again, until there was nothing left of the front of Cully's skull but bloody meat with bone shards sticking out. She fell to her knees and let the stand drop, panting like a marathon runner. She looked at Cully's smashed face. One eye had been popped from its socket and stared up at her from the blood covered chin. "I have fucking *had it*," she whispered savagely to that eye, "with people fucking with my family."

After a moment, she staggered to her feet. Her stomach twisted again as she saw what she'd done, but there was nothing left for her to throw up. Her knees wobbled a bit as she walked out of the bedroom and down the hallway. There were a half-dozen doors before you got to the stairway, all closed. "Mick?" she called out. "Keith!" There was no answer. She remembered Cully had said they were in the servant's quarters. She roamed the darkened house until she came to a place where the hallways were narrower, with no decoration or artwork on the walls. "Mick! Keith!"

"Mama?" Keith's voice came from behind one of the doors. "Mama!"

She ran to it. "Keith?" She tried the knob. Locked. Cully had fixed all the doors on this floor to lock from the outside. Why he'd done that was something she didn't want to think about right now. "Keith, baby, have you seen Mick?"

From the door across the hall, she heard the pounding of a fist from inside. "Mama!" Mick yelled. "Are you okay?"

"I'm fine, Mick." *Stop shaking*, she ordered her legs. *Stop it.* "I need to go find a key. I'll be right back." She remembered the rattling of the key in her bedroom door and realized with a sick feeling she was going to have to go back in the room where Cully's body lay and search his corpse for the keys. *No*, something in her shrieked. *No. No. Run. Run as far and fast as you can.*

She spoke out loud. "I'm not leaving my boys." She had to force herself back down the hallway by a sheer effort of will, back to where Cully lay in a slowly spreading pool of blood on the hardwood floor. She gritted her teeth, knelt down, and felt inside one front pocket, then the other. "Where the hell are your keys, you son of a..." She bowed her head for a moment, dreading what she had to do next. She grabbed his body and rolled him over. The action caused the air still in his lungs to escape in a long, low shuddering moan. She screamed and leaped away. Then she gathered herself together, forced herself to crawl back to him, and found a keyring in his back pocket. She ran out of the room and down the hall. She let Keith out of his room, then Mick. The three of them embraced for a moment, Savannah fighting back tears, Keith not even trying. Mick broke the hug first and looked around. "Where's Lana?"

"I don't know, baby, but we have to go. Now. Cully said they were coming."

"Who?" Keith asked.

"Bad people. People who'll hurt us."

Mick shook his head. "I ain't leaving without Lana."

"Damn it, Mick, she's just a..." She stopped.

Mick's face darkened. "Just a what?"

Just a whore, Savannah had been thinking. What stopped her was the memory of how many times she'd heard that term applied to herself. Mothers of boys she'd had crushes on. Ex-girlfriends of boys she'd loved. She remembered the sting of Winslow's words. *What's the shelf life of an aging drug whore?* That bastard.

"Okay, Mick. Go find her." She handed him the keyring. "But hurry. We've got to go." He took the ring, nodded, and began going door to door.

The thought of Winslow made her remember the phone still buried deep in her purse. She'd thought that lifeline permanently severed when she'd stolen Cahill's car. But Cahill was a cop. And, Savannah admitted grudgingly to herself, a good one. If Savannah called for help, Cahill would come, and most likely bring the cavalry. She went back to the bedroom and fetched her bag, trying not to look at the body on the floor. *Self-defense*, she said. *I'll say it was self-defense.* She hesitated before picking up the gun that still lay on the floor. She stuck that in her bag and went back out in the hallway.

Keith was sitting there, on the floor, knees drawn up to his chest. He looked so forlorn, it broke Savannah's heart. She sat down on the floor next to him, so close that their shoulders and hips touched. "You okay, Keith?" He nodded, but his eyes were far away. Someplace he'd rather be. The thought strengthened her resolve. All her options were closed, save one. It wasn't good, but she had nowhere else to turn. She reached in her bag and pulled out the burner.

"What's that, Mama?" Keith's voice sounded like he'd been drugged.

"It's a phone a…a friend gave me," she said. "If I needed to call for help. And I think this is a good time, don't you?"

His response was to throw his arms around her and bury his head in her shoulder. She leaned back and wrapped her free arm around him and turned the burner phone on. When it had gone through its short boot-up process, she hit the speed dial button with one hand. *Anything for you. Anything.* The phone rang on the other end. Someone immediately picked up.

It was Cahill. "Savannah."

"Mama." The voice came from down the hall. She turned her head.

Mick was standing by the room where she'd killed Cully. He was carrying what looked like an AK-47. A pistol hung in a leather holster on his belt. Lana stood beside him. Savannah noticed with alarm that her face was bruised. There were other bruises on her skinny arms. But what mostly got her attention were the stubby black machine pistols she carried in each hand. "Come look what we found, Mama," Mick said, beaming as if he was a kid showing off a frog he'd caught or an interesting rock.

Lana smiled, and Savannah saw her lower lip was split and swollen. "You said that son of a bitch could get things." Her voice was slurred, but her eyes were bright and hard. "And damned if you ain't right."

"Savannah!" Cahill's voice was tinny and distant in the phone's tiny speaker.

Savannah killed the connection and stood up, bringing Keith up with her. "Show me what you found."

CHAPTER FORTY-EIGHT

They'd tracked Lanny Knight to the ICU, a collection of small rooms with sliding glass doors around a central nurse's station. The nurses there had been even fiercer about restricting access to their patient than the ones around Winslow. Even Chance's badge didn't seem to impress them, until a woman carrying a Styrofoam cup in one hand stepped up to where Chance was arguing with a dark-haired nurse who was built as solidly as an Omaha Beach pillbox and was about as easy to pass. "Excuse me," the woman said.

Chance turned on her, ready to snap a tart reply, but pulled back from it. "You're Lanny's wife, aren't you?"

The woman nodded. She was lovely, with light brown skin and hazel eyes. Her hair and nails looked like they would cost half a deputy's weekly paycheck. She held out one perfectly manicured hand to Chance. "I'm Latiesha Knight. You're from the sheriff's department, right?" She cast a doubtful eye on McGee, who was hanging back, apparently trying to be invisible.

Chance took the hand in both of hers. "Yes. I'm Chance Cahill. Latiesha, I'm so sorry for what happened to Lanny. We're going to get the people who did this. I promise."

Latiesha's lower lip quivered. "Thank you. This has been… really…." She took a deep, shuddering breath and squared her shoulders. "Thank you for coming." She turned to the scowling nurse. "If she wants to visit my husband, it's okay." She looked over at Wyatt McGee. "And him, too. I guess."

"That's okay," McGee said. "I'm just her ride."

"I'll have to ask the doctor," the nurse said, and stalked off, clearly unhappy with her authority being questioned.

"Thanks," Chance said. She didn't wait, but headed determinedly for one of the cubicles. A paper sign on the chart rack next to the door said, *Knight, L.*

Inside the tiny room, Lanny Knight lay, eyes closed, under a thin hospital blanket. Tubes and wires ran beneath the blanket from incomprehensible medical devices and monitors. A heart monitor beeped, slow and regular. A rhythmic *click-hissss* let Chance know he was still breathing. She sat down in a metal chair next to the bed and took Lanny's hand. The hand seemed so cold, it was as if he was already dead. "Hey, buddy," she said softly, "it's Chance Cahill."

He didn't respond at first. She squeezed his hand. "It's okay, Lanny. We're going to get the guy who shot you."

Lanny's eyes opened, only halfway, but they opened. "Cahill," he said in a raspy voice. He licked his dry lips with a tongue like sandpaper. "Water. Need water."

Chance looked around helplessly. "I don't know if you can have water yet. Maybe some ice chips. I'll ask. I promise."

Lanny made a choking sound, deep in his throat. Then, "Sorry."

"Sorry? For what? You got tagged by some lowlife. We'll—"

He squeezed her hand back, hard. "No." He wheezed for a moment, then caught his breath. "Sorry for…the fed. That guy. I…

shouldn't have..."

She leaned forward, her grip on his hand becoming harder. "What are you saying. Lanny? You know who took Winslow? The federal guy?"

"Let...it happen..."

"What do you mean, you let it happen? Are you saying you were there when they took Winslow? And you didn't stop it?"

Lanny's head lolled to one side. The beeping of his heart monitor sped up. Chance leaned forward and took Lanny's chin in one hand. "Lanny. Tell me the truth. Did you set Winslow up?" There was no answer. She shook his chin, as gently as she could considering her desperation. "*Answer* me!"

His eyes opened again. "No. There when I got there. I should have..." Lanny closed his eyes and a single tear ran down his cheek. "Should have...Luther...sorry..."

Chance released his chin and sat back in the chair, numb with shock. The heart monitor was going crazy. The dark-haired nurse stormed into the room. "What the *hell* are you doing to my patient?" she raged.

Chance stood up. "Sorry. I was just leaving."

The nurse was checking the monitors. "You're damn right you're leaving." She made an adjustment on the hanging IV bag. "I ought to call the cops on you."

I am a cop, Chance wanted to remind her, but that distinction didn't seem to matter as much to her as it once did. She got up and walked out, staring straight ahead. In the waiting room outside, McGee was sitting in a chair across from Latiesha. An infant carrier sat on the floor in front of him and he was dangling and shaking a set of oversized plastic keys over it. The baby reclining in the carrier was giggling with delight. The sight made Chance feel sick. "Come on. Let's go."

McGee looked up. When he saw the look on Chance's face, he

stood up. "Okay." The toy keys dangled uselessly from his hand.

Latiesha stood up and took them. "What's wrong? Is Lanny…" Her hand went to her mouth. "Is he…"

"He'll be okay." Chance looked at Latiesha. "I'm so sorry. Really."

Latiesha caught the edge in her voice. "Thank you," she said, all the former warmth gone. She picked up the baby carrier and walked off through the doors to the ICU without another word.

"What's happening?" McGee asked.

Chance collapsed into a chair. "I think Lanny was dirty. He was one of Luther's people. He…" She leaned forward and put her head between her knees for a moment, then straightened up. "He watched Luther's people take Winslow. And he did nothing."

"Christ." McGee walked over and sat in the chair beside her. "I'm sorry," he said. Chance saw him reach out, as if to take her hand, then pull back.

She reached over, found his hand, and squeezed it before letting go. "Thanks. I know." She leaned back. "So my department's compromised by Luther."

McGee nodded. "And DEA's compromised by Gutierrez."

She smiled, a little sadly. "Looks like the only people we can trust are each other."

He smiled back. "Except you're on suspension, and I'm…I guess I'm not really anything."

"Is it weird that I actually feel kind of good about that?"

Before McGee could answer, Chance felt a vibration in her pocket. She pulled out her phone and looked at the screen. What she saw there stunned her. She opened the line. "Savannah."

McGee leaped up. "Savannah?"

There was no answer on the line, just the sound of breathing. Chance could hear a voice in the background, a male one. "Come see what we found, Mama."

A female voice replied. Chance couldn't make out the words.

"Savannah!" she barked. The connection was broken. Chance stared at the phone for a moment, then turned back to him. "It was her. Savannah. And at least one of the boys was with her. I heard him call her mama."

"If one's there," McGee said, "chances are they both are. But she hung up."

Chance swiped a finger on the screen of her phone, looking for something. "The good news is…there."

"What?"

She looked up and smiled. "Savannah's using the burner we gave her to call for help if there was an emergency. And we put a GPS tracker in it. Winslow and I both have apps on our phones to track it. Now that she's turned her phone back on, I can get a fix on where she is. Give me just a minute." She looked down at the screen and the smile vanished. "Huh."

"Where is she?"

Chance shook her head. "Nowhere that makes sense."

"You're sure that thing works?"

She pushed the button and stuck the phone in her jeans pocket. "One way to find out."

"We calling for backup?" He knew the answer to the question as soon as it was out of his mouth.

"You got anyone you trust?" she asked.

"How about your friend Delphine?"

She grimaced. "I hope to hell Delphine isn't one of Luther's people. But if she isn't, she probably doesn't know who is."

"Which puts it all back to you and me."

She nodded. "So…"

"So let's go."

CHAPTER FORTY-NINE

"**G**ood lord," Savannah said as she surveyed the room. "What the hell is this?"

"It's a damn arsenal, is what it is," Mick said.

He wasn't wrong. What had once been a library, or possibly a billiard room, now held racks along both walls. The racks were filled with weapons, ranging from pistols small enough to fit in a pocket to what looked like some kind of rocket launcher.

"That ain't all," Lana said. "Check this shit out." She pulled a footlocker away from the wall and opened it. It was full of small round objects.

Savannah put a hand to her mouth. "Are those *grenades*?"

Mick's smile was like Christmas morning. "They sure are." He picked one up and bounced it in his hand.

"Put that down," Savannah said.

He shook his head. "We need these, Mama." He picked up another grenade.

She thought of Cully's words. *Luther's people are on their way. They'll take you.*

Lana's next words distracted her. "And now, for the main event." Lana said. She pulled another footlocker up and flipped open the top. It was full of cash. Savannah leaned over. It was all large-denomination bills. "How did you find this?"

For the first time, Lana's face lost its hard expression. "He...likes to show off." Savannah noticed her knees had begun to shake. "He brought me here before...before he..."

Mick had been distracted by the weapons all around, but he saw Lana and his face froze. "What did he do?" She started to sob. "What did that bastard *do*?" The shouting only made her cry harder.

Savannah put her arm around the weeping girl's thin shoulders. "It's okay," she murmured, although she knew in her heart that it wasn't okay, that it might not ever be okay. She didn't know what Cully had done to the girl after getting her wasted on whatever drugs she asked for, but she had an idea. She'd heard stories about Cully. *And I let her go with him*, she thought. It made her feel sick with shame. Then she looked over at Mick. Why hadn't he done anything? Maybe, however, she could make it right. Or at least better. She leaned over and whispered in the girl's ear. "Lana," she said. "Let me show you something."

She guided her out the door and through the hallways, back to the main wing. The boys followed.

When Lana saw Cully's body laid out on the floor of the bedroom, she gave a small cry and pulled away from Savannah. She stared at the body, then back. "You...you did this?"

"He didn't give me much choice," Savannah said.

When Lana looked back at her, there was something in her eyes that Savannah could swear was adoration. She sprang forward and threw her arms around Savannah, sobbing into her chest, but this time with relief. Savannah felt a rush of maternal feeling for the girl that surprised her.

She hugged Lana closer. "It's okay now," she whispered. "He can't hurt you. Ever again." She became aware that the boys were standing behind her, crowded together in the doorway. She heard one of them make a small sound, then heard his footsteps going away. *Keith*, she thought sadly. He was always the sweet one. But sweet wasn't what they needed now. She looked back. She was right. Mick, tough little Mick, the one she'd set to look after his baby brother, was still there, his face grim, a rifle slung over his shoulder. Grenades hung from a pair of web belts he'd found and crisscrossed over his chest. But, she realized with despair, it wasn't enough. The people coming for them were worse than anything he'd ever known. Mick, her sweet Keith, and this broken girl in her arms weren't going to be enough to stop them. There was only one thing to do.

"Mick," she said. "We need to run. There are people coming. Very bad people."

He grinned maniacally, shifting the rifle from his shoulder and holding it out before him like a prize. "We're bad people too, Mama. We can take them."

"No, honey," she said. "We can't. Get your brother. Load that money in the van."

His jaw set stubbornly. "We've got guns. We've got—"

"Mick," she snapped. "Do as I say."

Downstairs, she heard a crash, then the sound of shouting voices. *They're here*, she thought.

Keith stood at the top of the stairs, clutching the banister and trying desperately not to puke. The sight of that man, with his face smashed, the blood already congealing on the ruin of his face... *Strawberry jam*, he thought. He almost lost it at that point, even fell to his knees, but he was distracted by the rumble of big engines outside in the driveway, the slamming of car doors, the sound of yelling. He staggered to his feet, blinking in confusion, just as the first heavy blow came at the front door. He looked down at the pistol he'd left on the floor behind him, the one Mick had insisted he take from the room downstairs. As he bent to pick it up, the door crashed open. A large man in a leather jacket entered, a rifle held out in front of him, scanning for targets. He was big and bald, with a goatee braided tightly until it looked like a handle protruding from his chin. Keith must have made some sound, because the man turned and fired blindly up at him, the bullets splintering the woodwork and plaster over Keith's head. He screamed and fired back in raw panic, too frightened to aim. His shots, poorly aimed as they were, had some effect as the man swore and backpedaled out of the smashed door. He called out to someone behind him. Through his all-consuming fog of terror, Keith could swear that the man was shouting in Spanish.

"*Mick!*" he called out. "*Mama!*"

As if summoned by magic, Mick was beside him, aiming his rifle down at the entryway. "Who's down there, lil' bro?" he demanded.

Keith could hear the question, and some part of it could understand it, but terror stopped up his throat and kept him from answering. "I...I..."

"Come on, get it together, Keith. Tell me. Who's—oh shit..."

Keith looked down to see a square object that looked like a canvas backpack land in the entryway, just inside the door. He felt Mick's hand on his collar, pulling him backward, then the fabric of his shirt ripped. He tried to regain his balance, but Mick suddenly tackled him, bearing him to the floor, covering him like a blanket. Keith had landed hard enough to knock the wind out of him. As he struggled to draw breath, a sound louder than any he'd ever imagined possible shook the floor beneath him. It sounded like the crack of summer thunder heard from beneath a lightning-struck tree and rattled the house like an earthquake.

Mick groaned and rolled off him, staggering to his feet. "Come on, Keith," he gasped. "They're coming." He leaned down and picked up the pistol that was lying on the floor. He pulled the slide back, the round chambering with an audible metallic click, and handed it to Keith. "Please," he said, his voice breaking. "We need you to step up, bro."

Keith looked at the gun stupidly for a moment, then he heard the sound of Mick's rifle, a steady hammering right over his head. He turned. The man with the braided goatee had mounted the stairs after detonating his satchel charge, and he was aiming his rifle at Mick. He was smiling in a way that filled Keith with a rage he'd never felt in his short life. *My brother. He's trying to hurt my brother.* Without thinking, he rolled over and fired, again and again. One shot caught Goatee Man in the throat and knocked him backward. His eyes were wide and unbelieving until Mick put a rifle round between them and he staggered back against the wall, slamming into the plaster before toppling onto his face.

"Good shot, lil' bro," Mick rasped.

"You killed him," Keith whispered.

"Maybe," Mick said, "but you got his fucking attention."

Keith's reply was cut off by the sound of more feet pounding up the stairs and voices shouting in Spanish. Mick clawed one of the grenades off the belt on his chest, pulled the pin, and tossed it. It landed at the feet of a dark-haired man in a black wife-beater t-shirt who appeared at the top landing, pointing another military-looking rifle down the hallway. The man looked down and scuttled backward, an almost comical expression of panic on his face. Before the grenade could go off, Savannah appeared behind them, a pistol in each hand. It was hard to tell what killed the man in the t-shirt, the pistol shots or the grenade that detonated and sprayed shrapnel at his feet, but he collapsed at the top of the stairs, bleeding from a dozen or more mortal wounds. Angry and confused voices came from below.

"Come on," Savannah said, "Luther's people are here. We don't want to—"

"No," Keith said, "they're speaking Spanish. Listen."

Savannah halted for a moment and listened. As she did, another thunderous detonation shook the house. "Shit. Gutierrez. He's going after Luther's people."

"Who?" Keith said.

She shook her head. "Doesn't matter. Two big dogs just went to war, and we're in the middle of it. That's not a good place to be. Let's move."

"Where?" Mick said. The sound of feet on the stairs prompted another burst of fire from Mick's rifle.

Keith heard shouted orders, the sound of running footsteps, then silence. The acrid tang of smoke filled the air, then the crackling of flames below. "The house is on fire," he said.

"Yeah," Savannah answered. "But we found a way out. Down the servant's stairs. We can get out. I hope."

CHAPTER FIFTY

The servant's stairs were narrow and winding, a semi-secret passage at the back of the house where the lower classes that had once served the local lords of all creation could come and go about their duties without disturbing their masters. They wound their way down that passage, rough wood creaking under their feet and making them wince until they realized there was probably no one listening. The shouted Spanish voices had receded. Savannah figured they'd backed off, waiting for the fire to drive their quarry out and onto the guns. Or worse. She gritted her teeth. She wasn't going to burn. She wasn't going to get shot. She was going to get her family out of here.

They exited from the back stairs into a tiny vestibule meant to further shield the preparations of servants from the gaze of their masters. Savannah opened the door carefully and peered around it. It opened into a hallway just outside the billiard room-turned-arsenal they'd seen earlier. Lana had pulled the footlocker full of money out to the hallway, and now she sat on it, a black machine pistol in each hand. "About time y'all got here," she said. "You know the house is burning down, right?"

Savannah couldn't help but smile. "Yeah, hon, we figured that out." She looked around and pointed down the hallway. "Side door is that way, right?"

Lana nodded. "Straight shot to the garage. But what about those guys outside?"

There was a fresh eruption of gunfire outside, screams of pain, harshly shouted orders. Mick looked around, the whites of his eyes showing his fear and confusion. "What the fuck?"

Savannah cocked her head to listen. "Cully said Luther's people were coming. Coming to take us. I think they just ran into Gutierrez's soldiers."

"Take us where?" Keith piped up.

She looked over at him, saw the desolation in his eyes, and felt her heart shattering inside her chest. Her sweet boy, her innocent one, and he'd been dragged into killing. "Hell, baby," she said. "Where they want to take us is hell. But I'm not going to let that happen, okay? Just trust me. We're getting out of here. With," she smacked her hand down on the footlocker and forced a smile onto her face, "a fucking shit-ton of cash. Thanks to our girl here."

The smile Lana gave her might have melted her heart again, but she willed that heart to become steel. Steel was what they needed now. "Let's go," she said. "Mick, Keith, pick up that footlocker. Keep your eyes open." She looked at Lana. "Guns up, girl. Let's move."

"Got your back." Lana grinned. "Mama."

They made it out of the house, down the short path, and to the garage, the sounds of gunfire and shouting rising to a crescendo, then gradually trailing off. Someone was winning and someone was losing, but Savannah had no intention of sticking around to find out who was who. *The problem with playing both sides against each other,* she thought, *is that whoever wins, it probably isn't going to be u*s. She wished she'd figured that out earlier, before she'd put her boys in the middle.

Mick and Keith loaded the locker in the van. Savannah got behind the wheel, shoved the key they'd taken off of Cully into the ignition, and flipped on the headlights. "Keith. Get the door open. Then get in quick. We're going to have to—" She was interrupted by Keith's cry of pain as he crumpled to the ground. He'd only gotten the door halfway open before he fell, but it swung wide open as he collapsed. Savannah looked out over the steering wheel, through the van's pitted and scratched windshield. What she saw made her slump over the wheel, her forehead resting on the hard plastic.

A pair of big pickup trucks sat across their path. A half-dozen men stood in a line in front of the trucks. They held a variety of guns, all pointed at the van. In the middle of the line stood Mr. Luther. In the headlights, his smile made him look even more ghoulish than usual.

"Savannah!" he called out. "Come on out, gal. And bring those two boys with you. We need to have a talk." His grin widened. "A long talk."

"**W**here exactly are we going?" Wyatt asked.

"I'm not completely sure," Chance replied. She was staring down into the screen of her phone. "It looks like the middle of nowhere. Out in the country somewhere." She looked up and through the front windshield as if it would tell her something. "It's not anywhere Savannah ever told us about."

"But she's there. And she's in trouble."

Chance grimaced. "Maybe she's there. I don't know."

Wyatt didn't slow down. "Only lead we've got, right?"

"Right."

"So we're going anyway." He didn't look over at her.

"Right," she said.

"Okay, then."

"**C**ome on, gal," Luther called again. "It's just gonna get harder on you if you make me wait."

Savannah looked through the windshield, craning her neck to try and see what had happened to Keith. She couldn't see him.

"That one of your boys tryin' to open the door?" Luther said. "Looks like he's still breathin'. Right now. 'Course, you keep makin' me wait…" He nodded to the gunman immediately to his left, a short, rail-thin man in a Confederate flag T-shirt. The little man was wielding a rifle so long it made him look like a boy playing soldier. He grinned, showing a mouthful of missing teeth, and raised the gun. Luther said something to him that Savannah couldn't catch, then raised his voice so she could hear. "I can let Lester here shoot him to pieces, bit by bit, till you come out. If that's what you want."

"Mama," Mick's agonized voice came from the back of the van, "let me—"

"No," she said, marveling at how steady her voice was. "Put the gun down." She turned in the seat to look at him, fixing his eyes with hers. "I can talk to him. I'm the one he wants. I can get him to let you go." She looked back to where Lana was huddled next to Mick. "You, too. He doesn't care about you." Before there was any response, she leaned out of the van window. "Okay. I'm coming out." Her hands were shaking so badly, she could barely open the door, and when she stepped out, her knees almost buckled beneath her.

"Good girl," Luther said. It was the voice of one speaking to a pet, and Savannah saw in a flash the life that he had planned for her. That would be all right, she thought, if she could only get her sons out of this. And Lana. She was surprised at the sudden impulse she had to protect the girl. But why not? She was family, or would be soon. If they survived.

"Please," she said to Luther. "Let me look at my son."

The smile on his face never slipped. "Sure," he said. "Go to your boy."

She ran over to where Keith lay, next to the open carriage house door. He was breathing shallowly, each exhalation ending in a pitiful moan. There was a red stain on his shirt, just above the belt line.

"He's gut-shot," Luther said. "He'll be a long time dying if he don't get some help."

She looked up, the tears she couldn't hold back any more streaming hotly down her face. "Please. I'll do anything. Anything you want. Take me. Punish me. But let my boys go."

"But that's the thing, gal," Luther said. "Best way to punish you is to hurt your boys."

"*Please!*" she screamed.

"Tell you what," Luther said. "Just to show you I'm not an unreasonable man." He turned to the gunmen who flanked him on either side. "I'm not an unreasonable man, am I boys?" The men around him shook their heads, grinning, and murmured that no, sir, bossman, you're a real reasonable man. Luther nodded his satisfaction. "Plus, I got a war to fight. This ain't the only stash house of mine that Gutierrez has tried to hit. I'm kinda busy, is what I'm sayin'. So I tell you what I'll do. I'll only kill one of your boys. I was gonna give one of 'em to my dogs, but like I say, I got a lot on my plate right now. So we do it right here, and right now. You get to pick." He nodded at Keith, cradled in Savannah's arms. "I'd suggest that one. He looks like he's about played out anyway. I'll make it quick, I promise. Better than dyin' from a belly wound. But it's up to you."

"Just kill me," Savannah begged. "Let them go."

"Oh, no, gal," Luther said, and the false smile fell from his face. "You gonna live. You gonna live, and you gonna suffer. You gonna suffer as long and as hard as I want. Losin' a son, well, that's just the beginnin'. Now choose. Or I'll kill 'em both."

"No," a voice said. Savannah looked up. Mick had stepped out of the truck. "Take me. Shoot me."

CHAPTER FIFTY-ONE

They saw the first body as they pulled up to the iron gate. It was a man in jeans and a leather vest with no shirt. He was lying across the entrance.

"Jesus," Chance whispered. Wyatt could see other bodies lying in the drive. "What the hell happened here?"

"Winslow said Gutierrez was going to war with Luther. This is what that war would look like, I think."

"That guy's blocking the road," Chance said.

Wyatt sighed. "I know."

"And Savannah's call came from in there."

"I know." Wyatt got out, his pistol drawn and ready. He advanced on the body, noticing the SKS semi-automatic rifle lying a few feet away. He saw that someone else, possibly several someones, hadn't been so squeamish about driving over the body in the way. There were the marks of tires across the small of the back and the body seemed oddly compressed there. Wyatt considered for a moment whether to drag the body by the arms or the legs. He had a brief sickening image of the body separating and coming apart at the tread marks. He gritted his teeth and grabbed the legs. The body didn't come apart. *Thanks for small favors, God*, he thought. He picked up the rifle and stuck it behind the seat as he got back in the car.

"Bad?" Chance asked.

"Bad enough." He started up the driveway again.

"Wait," Chance said. "Stop here. Kill the lights."

"What?"

She didn't answer, just opened the door and got out.

"Where..." Wyatt started, but she was gone.

In a moment, she was back, carrying an AR-15. "Guy I took this from was Latino. Judging from the face and neck tattoos, some kind of gangbanger."

"Gutierrez's people," Wyatt said.

"Yeah. My guess is, Gutierrez tried to raid this place and ran into an ambush. Or they were in mid-raid when Luther's guys showed up."

"So why was Savannah in the middle of—" He was interrupted by the rattle and pop of gunfire, then the dull thud of an explosion. It sounded very close.

"Shit," Chance said.

Wyatt was already out of the car, pulling the SKS from behind the seat. Chance followed with the AR-15.

"**M**ick, no," Savannah moaned. "Please. No. Let me—"

Mick looked at her and smiled. "I love you, Mama. I always will." He bent and kissed Keith on the top of the head before he straightened up. "I've come too far. Done too much. It's not the way I thought it would be. We're not goin' out like this. Not this family." As he spoke, he was unbuttoning his top two shirt buttons. Still smiling, he looked Luther in the eye. "Let my mama and my brother go." He started walking forward, hands up.

"Ain't gonna work that way, boy," Luther said. "You just stop right there."

Mick kept walking. "Why? So you can shoot me down like a dog? I don't fucking think so."

Luther scowled. "I'm tellin' you, boy—"

"Or what? Tell me what?" His voice was rising, almost cracking with strain. The line of men on either side of Luther raised their weapons. When Mick reached into his shirt, they began firing. The first bullet struck Mick in the side and made him stagger. His right hand came from inside the shirt. Another bullet went through the palm of that hand, blood spraying in a crimson arc behind him. The impact dislodged the three grenade pins wrapped around his fingers. They landed in the dirt just as Mick, grinning, lunged forward and wrapped his arms around the frantically backpedaling Luther.

"Who's your *daddy*, motherfuck—" he screamed before the grenades blew them both apart.

"*Mick!*" Savannah screamed. The ragged bits of the two men collapsed to the ground, Luther and Mick falling apart like a single body divided in two. Their flesh had absorbed the force of the explosion and contained the shrapnel, but everything above the waists and below the necks of both men was shredded meat. The line of gunmen looked on, stunned into immobility for a moment. As the shock wore off, they raised their guns again, but the volley that would have killed Savannah and finished off Keith was interrupted by Lana, who came out of the van carrying the machine pistols, screaming and firing blindly with both hands. The sudden fusillade broke the line. They fled in a disorganized rout, two of them falling to Lana's guns and the rest bolting away around the sheltering hedge.

Directly into the guns of Chance Cahill and Wyatt McGee.

Chance and Wyatt were coming up the drive, rifles at the ready, when the remaining four gunmen of Luther's contingent came pelting around the corner. Later, they'd agree, in both their own private talks and in seemingly endless official inquiries, that had the men thrown down their guns, they might have lived. As it was, they startled two armed and nervous law enforcement officers. That meant they were cut down in seconds, the sound of the volley that killed them leaving a huge silence behind it. Into that sudden, stunned quiet came a raw, anguished wailing. Wyatt thought of a passage he'd heard in church, back in the days when he still went: *In Rama was there a voice heard, lamentation, and weeping, and great mourning, Rachel weeping for her children, and would not be comforted, because they are not.* The sound sent a shiver up his spine and he broke into a run, Chance a step behind him.

They came around the concealing hedge to a scene from a horror movie. Two ripped and bloody bodies lay a few feet apart in the dirt courtyard. A young girl knelt beside one of them, rocking back and forth, her face streaked with tears. Two more bodies lay a few feet away. Behind the girl and the ruined bodies, Wyatt could see the form of Savannah Jakes, holding yet another body in her arms.

She gave another heartbroken cry just as Chance barked out, "*Gun!*" Wyatt looked back and recognized the girl from the back of the car in Arabi, the one who'd shot at him. She held a black MAC-10 machine pistol in each hand. He raised his rifle.

Beside him, he heard Chance shout, "Police! Drop the weapon!"

Wyatt joined in, bellowing at the top of his lungs, "Drop it! *Now!* Put it down!"

Their combined shouts seemed to hit the girl like a physical blow. She flinched backward, nearly falling over, but she dropped the guns.

"Sheriff McGee," Chance said, her voice steady, "would you secure those weapons, please?"

Still holding his rifle in one hand, he walked over and picked up one of the ugly little machine pistols and shoved the other one out of the girl's reach with his foot. "Stand up," he ordered her.

She looked up at him uncomprehendingly. "He saved us," she said. "Mick saved us. He killed Luther."

Wyatt glanced over at the body she'd been kneeling beside. The bottom half of the face was mostly gone, but he could see the eyes. He could believe it was the face from the robbery video, the face of Kevin DeWalt. That would, he supposed, make the other body Wallace Luther. He turned back to the girl on the ground. "Stand up," he repeated. Slowly, she complied. "I don't suppose you brought cuffs with you?" Wyatt called back.

"Sorry."

Wyatt nodded. "Stand over there," he told the girl, motioning with his rifle to where Savannah was still weeping, her wails turned to convulsive sobbing. He recognized the body held in her arms as Tyler Welch. She was sitting down in the wide-open door of what looked like a carriage house, the boy's head in her lap. A white van loomed behind her in the garage. Another car sat off to the side. He reached them in a few long steps and crouched down. The boy was still breathing, but his eyes were closed, his face so pale it was like seeing the skull beneath. "Savannah," he said as gently as he could, "let me look at him."

She shook her head no, still sobbing, but didn't resist when he moved the arm she'd thrown across his chest. He sucked in his breath. The front of his shirt below the breastbone was soaked with blood. It looked like an abdominal wound, and it was bleeding badly. "He's shot, Cahill. Belly wound, and it looks bad. We need…" He realized she was already speaking into her phone.

"On it," she said to him before returning to her call.

"No!" Savannah screamed. "*No!* Don't take my Keith from me!" She tried to stand up, pulling Tyler with her.

His eyes opened and he let out an agonized whimper. "Mama. It hurts, Mama."

Wyatt held on tight. "Savannah. Listen to me. He's going to die if we don't get him to a hospital. And I mean right goddamn now."

She shook her head. "No. We need to get away. Mick sacrificed himself so we could get away. Give him to me. Give me my Keith."

Tyler grasped her arm, his grip as weak as a baby's. "Mama," he whispered. "That's…not…my name."

She let him slip from her arms. "Don't say that." She got to her feet, leaving Wyatt the only one holding him. "Don't you ever say that again!"

"I want…I want to go home, Mama. Please let me…go home…"

"You're my *son*!" she yelled. "Your home is with your *family*!"

Tyler didn't respond. He'd slipped back into unconsciousness.

"Savannah," Wyatt said. "You once said in court you'd do anything for your sons."

"I did. And I will. I will."

"Then let him go to the hospital. And then just let him go. If he comes with you, he's going to die."

She closed her eyes and shook her head violently, as if she was trying to make everything go away. Wyatt tried again. "Look, Savannah, we both have made some really shitty choices. And because of that, we hurt the people we love. This is your one shot—only shot—to save Keith. This is your one chance to be the mom you wanted to be. And the only way to do that is to get in the van and go. Get out of his life. Forever. It's the best thing for your son. You know it is."

"Um, McGee?" Chance said. "She's still—"

He interrupted her. "That's the deal, Savannah. Your freedom. His life. It's a good deal. Take it."

She opened her eyes and looked down at Tyler. "I love you, son. And I never brought you nothing but pain. I'm sorry. I'm so, so sorry." She looked back at McGee. Her weeping had stopped. "Okay. I'll go.

But one condition." She pointed at the girl who'd had the machine pistols. "She comes with me."

Chance spoke up. "Oh, now, wait just a damn minute."

Savannah didn't look at Chance. She kept her eyes on Wyatt's. "She's Micks' fiancée. She's the closest thing to family I got left."

"Okay," McGee said.

Chance was outraged. "McGee, she *shot* you!"

"Yeah, well, I'm real sorry about that," the girl said.

"No doubt," Wyatt said. "I can let it go, just this once. But don't let me see you again." He turned to Savannah. "Or you."

"Don't worry, hon," the girl said. "You won't."

"I'm really not okay with this," Chance said.

He turned to her. "Hey, I'm the one she shot. And this is what's best for him." He nodded at the bleeding boy on the ground, then pointed at the dead man across the courtyard. "And the guy who shot your deputy is there."

She gritted her teeth. Finally, however, she shook her head angrily. "Fine. Go."

"Come on," the girl said. She got in the driver's seat of the van. Savannah took one last look at Tyler on the ground. She didn't speak again or look at Wyatt or Chance as they pulled away.

Wyatt knelt beside Tyler. "Come on, buddy," he whispered. "Hang in there." He raised Tyler's shirt and exposed the wound in his belly.

Chance ran up and knelt next to him. She held out a blanket. "This was in the car over there. Can't really say how clean it is."

He nodded and took it. Once it was folded over, he put it under Tyler's head. He held his own hands against the wound, trying to slow the bleeding.

"Ambulance ETA is three minutes."

He nodded and looked at her. "It was the only way to get her out of his life for good. She won't come back if it could get her arrested."

She grimaced. "Yeah. I know. But you didn't tell her about Mick.

Or how that wasn't Mick."

"I know."

"Why?"

He sighed. "The real Mick Jakes died a stupid, sordid death in a Tennessee jail." He nodded towards the bodies. "That version of Mick Jakes died saving her life. Why not let her believe he was a hero?"

She shook her head. "You're a strange one, McGee."

"I guess that's true."

The sound of the sirens drew closer.

CHAPTER FIFTY-TWO

Chance handed a Styrofoam cup to McGee. "It's pretty bad, even for hospital cafeteria coffee."

McGee took the cup. "Thanks." He took a sip and shrugged. "I've had worse."

"You get hold of the family?"

He nodded. She couldn't help notice how tired he looked. "Tyler's father's going to catch the next plane down. Glenda's going over to sit with his mom."

Chance looked at the door of the waiting area, out into the hallway where doctors and nurses were bustling by. "Any word?"

McGee rubbed his eyes. "Too early to tell, the nurse said. He's lost a lot of blood. He may lose a few feet of intestine. He's in surgery."

"He's young, strong, looked to be in decent shape. He'll make it."

"I hope you're right." He turned to her. "Thanks."

"No problem." She took a sip of her coffee. It was truly terrible, bitter, tasting as if had been scorched. She wondered if it was a bad sign that she was getting used to it. *I am spending way too much time in this damn hospital*, she thought. There was a brief silence. "So... Glenda's your wife?"

"Yeah."

"What did she think of you coming down here on this mission?"

He grimaced. "She thought...well, she probably thinks I'm a damn fool. She's probably right. But she knew it was something I had to do."

"Sounds like a good woman."

He nodded. "That she is." He took a sip of coffee. "Sometimes I don't let her know that enough."

"Well, you can do that when you get home."

"Yeah." He turned to her. "How about you? You got anyone in your life?"

For a moment, the question nettled her, but then she thought of what they'd been through together. And it was pretty clear he wasn't asking the question as a prelude to a come-on. "No," she said. "It's kind of hard to maintain relationships in this job."

He laughed. "Boy, don't I know it."

She smiled. "From the way you say that, there's a story there."

"Yeah. It's a long one. Let's just say I screwed up one marriage, and nearly screwed up this one. For the job."

"Only nearly, though. Not completely."

He shook his head. "I hope not."

"Sounds like you have some work to do when you get home."

"I do." He looked at her. "Thanks again for being here. But if you need to get home, I can hold things down here."

"Nah, I'm good. You need to know, though, there are a couple of detectives coming. They're going to want to know what happened. Hell of a mess out there. They found another body inside. Bludgeoned to death. There are a lot of questions to answer."

He frowned. "You in trouble?"

She shrugged. "No more than I can handle."

"Well, you know I got your back."

She nodded. "I do. And I got yours. Partner."

He smiled and stuck out a hand. "It's been an honor to work with you, Deputy Cahill."

She took it. "Likewise, Sheriff McGee. But let's not ever do this again."

He laughed. "No problem. Next time I come down here, it'll be for the food."

"The music's pretty amazing, too. I'll take you and Glenda around to the good places. Look me up."

"Will do."

She finished her coffee and stood up. "Before the detectives get here, I'm going up to see Winslow. Let him know what happened. Want to come?"

"Sure." McGee polished off his own cup. "Lead the way."

Winslow was sitting up in bed, reading a paperback book. The IV was out of his arm and his color was much better. "Hey," he said.

"Hey yourself," Chance said. "You still lazing around?"

He grinned. "They're discharging me today." The smile slipped a bit. "Then back to work. That'll be interesting."

McGee spoke up. "You got wounded in the line of duty, Agent Winslow. You're a hero. They're going to have balloons and banners and shit when you get back."

Winslow shook his head. "I got shot after getting my ass captured and losing not one, but two informants. And we didn't get any closer to taking down Luther."

"You don't have to worry about that," Chance said. "Luther's dead." She ran down the story for him. When she got to the part about the mansion, Winslow broke in.

"Cullen Landry. He's been a supplier of Luther's, or so we and ATF have been thinking. But we could never put anything together."

Chance nodded. "Well, he may be off the board, too. He may be the one they found killed inside."

The DEA man whistled. "Man. That's going to create a vacuum for Gutierrez to fill."

"There's always another asshole, right?" McGee said.

"Yep. But that particular asshole has someone inside my agency."

"Any ideas who it might be?" Chance asked.

Winslow nodded. "Some."

"I hope you get him," Chance said.

"Seconded," Wyatt added.

"Thanks. Hey, Cahill, don't be a stranger, okay?"

She put out a hand. "Okay." He took it and looked at Wyatt. "And next time you come down here, Mr. McGee, I hope it's as a tourist."

McGee laughed. "We've already discussed that plan."

As they left, they met a man coming down the hallway, dressed in dark suit and narrow tie. He was looking at the room numbers, obviously searching for a particular one. As they reached the elevator, Wyatt said "Deputy Cahill, did you notice something peculiar about that man?"

"The one in the suit? As a matter of fact, I did. He was sweating like he'd just run a mile in that suit."

"And yet, they've got the air conditioning cranked down in this place."

"It's like a meat locker," she agreed. Both had turned and started back down the hall toward Winslow's room. As they rounded a corner, they saw the man in the dark suit going into the room. They broke into a run.

They entered the room to find the man in the dark suit standing at the foot of the bed. Winslow regarded them curiously. "Hey. You forget something?"

"Winslow," Chance said, "do you know this gentleman?"

The man in the dark suit was looking at them, wide-eyed.

"Sure," Winslow said. "This is Special Agent Kimball. He works for my boss." He regarded the man quizzically. "Sort of surprised to see you here though, Kimball."

Kimball smiled, a sickly smile that didn't reach his eyes. "Just, ah, bringing regards from everyone at the office."

"Agent Kimball," Wyatt said, "You look a little warm. Why don't you take that coat off?"

Winslow was frowning. "What's going on?"

"Yeah," Chance said. "You look like you're burning up." Her voice hardened. "Take the coat off."

Kimball looked around for a moment like a trapped rabbit, then bolted for the door. Wyatt caught him easily and spun him into the wall with an impact that knocked a cheerful picture of a flower vase onto the floor. "Let me go!" Kimball yelled.

"What the fuck, McGee?" Winslow shouted, jumping out of the bed in his hospital gown.

"Cahill," Wyatt grunted. "Check his coat pockets." He turned Kimball around so Chance could get to him. He kicked out at her, forcing her to jump backward. "What's in your pockets, Kimball?" Wyatt said. "What?"

"Fuck you!" Kimball spat and snapped his head back, trying to butt Wyatt in the nose. Wyatt bobbed his head and avoided the blow.

Winslow stood behind Chance, shifting nervously from foot to foot. "McGee. Cahill. Stop this. Right fucking now. He's a federal agent."

"I think he's your mole, Winslow," Chance said.

"That's insane," Kimball said. He relaxed slightly, and when he did, Wyatt changed his grip and ripped the jacket off of Kimball's shoulders. He tried to run again, and the sleeves turned inside out as Wyatt pulled it free of his body. Chance blocked Kimball's exit just as Wyatt dipped a hand into the inside pocket and came out with a syringe. The needle was capped with a small piece of cork. "And what is this, exactly?"

Winslow was staring at the syringe. "Yeah, Kimball. What is that?"

Cahill examined it carefully. "Whatever it is, I'm betting it's not good for you, Winslow. I'm betting he's supposed to come here and find out how much you learned about Gutierrez and especially how much you know about who'd penetrated the agency. Then, you were going to suffer a tragic relapse. Am I right, Kimball?"

Kimball stood in his shirtsleeves, panting with rage and fear. "I want a lawyer."

"Oh, you won't need a lawyer, Kimball," Chance said. "You can just walk out that door."

"What?" Wyatt and Winslow said simultaneously.

"Sure," Chance said. "You walk out of here. But Gutierrez will know soon that you're blown. And I bet there's a lot in your head that he doesn't want to come out. And the best way to make sure that it doesn't…" She left that hanging with a smile.

"So," Winslow said. "You ready to make a deal?"

Kimball's bravado collapsed like a birthday balloon on the day after. "Yeah."

An orderly had appeared in the door. What's going on in here?"

"Call security," Chance said.

"What?"

She fixed the orderly with a stare. "Did I mumble? Call security. We just stopped a murder here in your facility."

"And don't call the police," Winslow said. "Call the DEA." He rattled off the number. "Ask for Special Agent in Charge Hammond."

The orderly stared at him for a moment, then disappeared.

"Winslow?" Chance said. "I think you're going to need to be the one to make the arrest."

"In this?" Winslow gestured to his hospital robe.

"Well," Wyatt said, "strange as it may seem, you're the only one here who's actually still a cop on active duty."

Winslow thought about that for a second, then spoke to Kimball: "Agent Kimball, you're under arrest for attempted murder of a federal agent. You have the right to remain silent…"

EPILOGUE

NINE MONTHS LATER

The redhaired woman came in at 2 p.m. every day, sat at the same table on the terrace with a view of the beach, and ordered the same thing: bourbon, straight up, water back. She sat and sipped and watched the waves, sometimes for hours. She rarely spoke except to order and say "thank you" when the drink was delivered. From time to time, men would approach her and try to strike up a conversation. She was, after all, an attractive woman. All of them came away baffled. A few would ask Ignacio, the proprietor and owner of the beachfront restaurant, what her story was. He'd just smile and shrug. "She owns a house in town," he'd say. "She lives with her daughter. That's all I know." He kept to himself the rumors he'd heard: that she'd bought the house with cash, that she was the widow of some drug kingpin in America. Sometimes, Ignacio heard from his cousin Mariel, who worked as her housekeeper, she had red eyes in the morning, as if she'd been crying all night. *Or drinking*, Mariel snickered. And the girl, Mariel said, she has an entire _farmacia_ on her bedside table. Ignacio kept that to himself as well. A bartender was like a priest. He should keep his patrons' secrets to himself.

Today was different. Today, she left her seat on the terrace and came into the bar. It was still early, and the place was empty. She took a seat at the bar.

"_Buenas dias, señorita,_" he said. "The usual?"

She nodded. As he poured the whiskey, she looked at the clock on the wall. "Hey. Can you turn on the football game?"

He assumed she meant American football. He had no real love for the sport; it lacked the beauty and grace of _fútbol,_ and it stopped too often for commercials. But with the American tourists and expats who came in, he'd finally invested in a satellite TV system. "Which game, señorita?"

"UNC and LSU." As he turned on the set over the bar, she clarified. "The University of North Carolina. Playing Louisiana State."

"Ah." He scrolled through the channels until he found the correct one.

As he turned the sound up, she said, "Today is my son's birthday. My oldest."

"_Sí?_" Ignacio said. "Well, _feliz cumpleaños a él._" He lifted his own water bottle from behind the counter and offered it in a toast.

She clinked her own glass against it and drained it in one gulp. Ignacio frowned. She was usually a sipper. When she put the glass back down, she said. "He died. My son, I mean."

"Aiii...I am truly sorry," Ignacio said, and meant it. He had two sons of his own, and the thought of losing them was too much to bear. "No parent should outlive their child."

"No," she said, and motioned for another. He poured a double.

"You said your oldest. You have another son?"

"Yes. He...doesn't live with me."

"Ah." He saw the pain in her face and didn't inquire further. She watched the game in silence for a few minutes as he wiped down the bar. Suddenly, she leaned forward, her face seeming to light up. Ignacio glanced at the screen. The camera was focused on the bench, where a group of young men, helmets off, were standing and cheering a play on the field. The camera cut away, and she leaned back.

He could see the tears glistening in her eyes, and he understood. "Your younger son?"

She nodded, the tears spilling over. She picked up a napkin from the holder on the bar and wiped the tears away. After a moment, she spoke. "He could have been first string. But he got…hurt…his senior year. Still came back and made the team as a walk-on. But he'd spent so much time out…" Her eyes shone again as she polished off her drink. She held out the glass.

He paused for a moment, then poured. "He sounds like an extraordinary young man. Perhaps next year…"

She only nodded. He knew there was more to the story, but he didn't pry. "I hope your daughter is a comfort to you."

"She is," the woman said. "She's actually my daughter-in-law. Sort of. She and my son were engaged. The one who died, I mean."

"Still. She is family, yes? There is family you are born to, and family you choose."

"Yes." She took a sip.

"And there is nothing greater than family."

"No," she said. "No, there isn't." She raised her glass and tipped it toward him. "To family."

He touched his water bottle to her glass again. "To family."

THE END

ACKNOWLEDGEMENTS

This is one of the toughest books I've ever written. But then, they all are. Thanks to my editor and publisher, Jason Pinter, who I'm pretty sure really wanted another Keller book right away, but who always lets me write the book that wants to be written. Thanks as well to Toni McGee Causey and her husband, Carl, of New Orleans, Louisiana, who provided invaluable fact checking on that amazing city. Toni also went way above and beyond the call and provided other insights that helped make this book 100% better. Thanks, Toni.

And, as always, thanks to my wife, Lynn, for her love and unwavering support.

About the Author

Born and raised in North Carolina, J.D. Rhoades has worked as a radio news reporter, club DJ, television cameraman, ad salesman, waiter, attorney, and newspaper columnist. His weekly column in North Carolina's *The Pilot* was twice named best column of the year in its division. He is the author of five novels in his acclaimed Jack Keller series: *The Devil's Right Hand, Good Day in Hell, Safe and Sound, Devil and Dust, Hellhound On My Trail* as well as *Ice Chest, Breaking Cover*, and *Broken Shield*. He lives, writes, and practices law in Carthage, NC.